WHY I CAN'T HAVE NICE KINGS

MATTHEW HELBIG

Printed in the United States of America
First Printing, December 2017

ISBN 978-1-7201353-2-6
www.matthewhelbig.com

DON'T DRINK AND WRITE

I must have been in an exceptionally bad mood, as my assistant was only looking at me like I was a genius and not "the smartest person to write fantasy since Albert Einstein." Hat didn't read a lot, though, to be fair, my series was really the only thing anyone would ever need to read. Well, in book form, anyway. I'd appreciate it if everyone continued to read stop signs and articles about me, Harry Olson.

We were all alone at my two-story cabin, deep in the woods of Minnesota. Hat knew that the best way to get me back to normal was to leave me alone and keep me away from anything that could stick to the walls. Even though I had had a pretty spectacular day, nothing, so far, had worked. Not staying up all night so I could get the drop on my alarm clock before it went off. Not winning a three-hour argument with my favorite fictional character. (It was a tie. I called him "Dumbleworf.") Not finally outrunning my arch-nemeses, Troop 713, and then celebrating by eating all of their candy. Not being named the World's Greatest Fantasy Author on my website. Not even boobs. The word, not . . . well, not even actual boobs, either.

I stopped pacing in the middle of the spacious living room and put my hand on my chin to look extra-smart. "Come to think of it, there might be a reason for that last one. What did that critic call me, again?"

"A reason for what, sir?" Hat leaned forward on the couch and opened up the magazine on the end table. "She said your book was 'obviously written by an immature boob who doesn't understand women, politics, horses, relationships, gravity, or even how swords work.'"

Hat had been with me for three years. Great assistant. Always knew when to listen and when to shut up and leave me alone. He was so nice that I had secretly given him the rights to my series in my will. He didn't know, of course. I wouldn't want him thinking he could contribute to my books. Besides, it wasn't like I had anyone else to give them to.

Now, back to the hero of this story—me.

"That geriatric hack. The only things he likes are hairy kids with rings and girls who shoot arrows at planes. What would he know about writing novels, anyway? The longest thing he's ever written is an obituary for his protégé."

"That's kind of mean, sir. I mean, the protégé did die." Hat gave me his best sad puppy dog look. I should have felt bad, but I had to stay focused if I wanted a really spectacular tirade.

"I was alluding to the fact that he's really old, and his protégé has probably died of old age by now."

"Ahh. Very funny, sir. That's why you're the professional writer and not me."

"That's right, Hat." Hat just got me. Heck of a guy. "And what was with that personal attack, anyway? I don't smell funny, do I?"

"No, sir. I bathed you myself right before you met *her*. I think it had something to do with her being a woman. Women don't seem to like you much."

"That was a woman? I couldn't tell."

He gave me a confused puppy dog look. "Then, why did you keep staring at her butt?"

"Must have been a reflex. I really can't stop leering at women, can I? Even when I don't realize they're women."

"I guess the classes aren't working."

"Anyway, where was I? Oh, yeah. And what would those other authors know? They're just jealous because I outsell them. Always talking behind my back and laughing at me because their books have dragons. Ha! And I'm the one who's clichéd."

"I've heard those books are pretty good. The TV show does have great sex scenes."

"Whose side are you on, anyway? If your answer isn't 'the guy whose lawyer signs my paychecks,' then get out."

He didn't answer immediately, so I grabbed a book off the shelf and threw it at him. Not one of mine, of course. Hat could be a jerk sometimes.

"I think I'll go into town for the night, sir. Give you some time alone to write without my interruptions."

The mark of a good assistant is knowing when to assist and when to leave you alone to be creative. And the mark of a spectacular assistant is knowing when to bring you powdered donuts and a juice box right before he leaves. Hat even remembered to put the straw in. He gently opened the door and left.

I decided to go up to my room to start my next book, *Screams of Garandia*. When I sat down, I went through my usual routine: I took off my shoes and put on the ring my grandpa had given me when I announced I was going to be a writer. My grandpa was also a professional writer, though he wrote about Norse history and myths—in between the occasional *Harry and the Hendersons* fan fiction.

As I sat there writing for over three hours without much to show for it besides creative descriptions of my critics, I decided I needed some stronger liquid inspiration. "Liquid inspiration."

See, I could be creative. Those critics didn't know what they were talking about.

After a few drinks of peppermint Schnapps, I decided the queen would secretly be from a race of flying people. And after a few more, that the Atlian advisor was a fantastic tap dancer, a skill not looked upon kindly by his people. After a few more feats of inspiration (feats that more often than not would be gibberish in the morning), I decided to rest a bit. Staring at a computer screen for several hours tired my eyes, and my glasses magnified the problem.

See, I can be funny, too. That is if you think puns are funny. You can blame my grandpa for that. Is there something about being a grandpa that makes you love puns?

A FAN AT KNIGHT

A slight breeze tickled my skin annoyingly. I reached over to turn off the fan, only to find some distinctly plant-like things where the button should have been. I opened my eyes and saw nothing but grass all around me. Funny, I didn't remember replacing my bed with a field.

The birds were chirping incessantly. Why do birds seem to chirp more and louder after you've been drinking? Oddly, my head didn't ache at all, and peppermint Schnapps always gave me a bad hangover. Well, really, any alcohol did, since I didn't drink that often. It's hard to write when you're drunk, though you do end up with some pretty creative stuff, assuming you can decipher it the next day. Had I really made the queen an angel last night? The advisor being a tap dancer was pretty good. I hadn't really explored the art of the dance in my world.

I looked around at my surroundings and gave the birds my best dirty glare. They seemed fairly intimidated and flew away.

The field didn't look familiar. The forest was in a full range of autumn colors: browns, reds, and fading greens abounded. Certainly odd in December. It was even stranger that there wasn't any snow on the ground. It was December in Minnesota, after all.

And why were there so many noisy birds about? They should have all flown south by now.

To the left, a dirt road wound through the forest. The word "ominous" sprang to mind. I soon heard the clopping of hoof-beats. Not that odd in the country. His armor and medieval weaponry were, however. Huh? There must have been a Renaissance fair nearby.

The rider slowed as he approached and gave me a dirty look. The word "onerous" sprang to mind. As he got closer, I could see he wasn't dressed quite like the traditional medieval knight one sees at most Renaissance fairs. At least, not the ones I'd been to. His armor was scaled like a fish, his helmet was conical, and his shield had several six-inch spikes protruding from it.

Wait a minute! That was how I'd described the Garandians in my first book, *The Garandian Empire*. His tabard was even accurate, indicating that he was pretending to be a royal guard, too.

My stomach churned with dread and a bit of that bad fish I'd eaten the day before. This was probably one of my crazy fans. I hoped he didn't ask me stupid, obscure questions, like why the gardener at the end of book 2 had a different name in the beginning of book 3. Hat always had good answers for those questions, but he wasn't here. Well, at least a fan would probably help me get back to town or lend me a cell phone.

Hat must have played a trick on me again, trying to teach me not to drink. He knew that drinking slowed down my process, and he was as anxious as anyone to read the next book. A relentless taskmaster, that one.

"Hail, good Garandian. Does thou have a cell phone with which I might call mine assistant?"

"What are you talking about, sir? And why are you talking in that idiotic fashion?"

I swear his helmet bent up in confusion.

"My apologies. My name is Harry Olson, and I seem to be stranded. I need to call my assistant to pick me up."

"Then, why don't you call him?"

I sighed. "Never mind. Can you give me a ride into town?"

The knight-wit appraised me. "Given your fancy glasses, odd dress, and rather fat stature, I would guess you are a merchant, or at least a man of wealth. What do you have to pay for passage?"

I pulled out my wallet. "I have this," I said, holding up a ten-dollar bill.

"What would I do with that paper?"

God, I hated overactors, especially when they were my supposed fans. I sighed again and pulled out a silver dollar. "How about this shiny coin?"

The knight took the coin and rolled it over in his hand. He even tried to take a bite out of it. That couldn't be very sanitary. Was he expecting chocolate inside? "Climb on. Town is only a few miles away."

After I made several failed attempts to get on the horse, the knight climbed off and pushed me onto his steed.

Hey, give me a break. I'm required to write about riding, not actually ride horses.

"You might want to try exercising and lay off the mutton, fatty."

"Thanks, Sir Richard of Simmons."

"My name is Sir Maillib of Garan, sir. I do not know of this Richard of Simmons."

"Never mind. Take me to town, and let's get this over with."

THIS RENAISSANCE ISN'T FAIR

After a few miles of cursing as I jostled about, we arrived at the Renaissance fair. Riding horses is not a pleasant experience for the uninitiated, by the way. I've heard it gets more comfortable as you do it, but at the time, the insides of my thighs burned terribly. Why couldn't they build saddles like they did seats in luxury cars?

Sir Maillib came to a halt in the middle of the town square. "I have delivered you as promised. Now, if you'll please debark, I shall be on my way."

I attempted to climb down but caught my foot in something and fell off. After I'd stood up and wiped my glasses off, I noticed he had already trotted off.

The Renaissance fair was different than any I'd seen before. A few yards away, several peasants were digging and shoveling mud, the purpose of their task lost on me. I was all for staying in character at a Renaissance fair, but it seemed a bit much.

The blacksmith shop was humming with activity as a woman hammered furiously on the anvil while her assistant displayed their wares to several men-at-arms. I had always wanted to see a working smithy. It would probably help my writing to have some firsthand experience with one instead of using random articles on the internet. I made a mental note to visit it after I had contacted Hat.

Two tall, scraggly barbarians were laughing furiously as a dark-skinned man in immaculate, two-toned purple robes motioned in exaggerated gestures toward a practicing infantry square. The infantry was moving in unison, shield to shield, against an imagined opponent. Their shields were overly large, square-shaped, and bowed back toward the body.

As I looked a bit harder, I realized this particular type of shield was also from my books, just like Sir Maillib's costume. The sigil on their shields even matched the one for the Garandian Empire. I was definitely at a fan convention.

I decided to head over to the barbarians and the Atlian. "Excuse me, good sirs. Do you happen to have a cell phone I could borrow?"

"I am well-versed in nearly all of the Continent's languages," the Atlian said with his head inclined, as if he was looking over me, "and I do not know what a cell phone is, sir." He sure did have the whole Atlian arrogance thing down.

The barbarians snickered.

Great. More fans stuck in character. I probably wasn't going to get anywhere with this lot. "Fine. Could you point me to the help booth, or perhaps to an employee?"

"The reeve is over there," he said, pointing behind me.

"Thank you."

The barbarians laughed hard at my back. I normally would have given them a piece of my mind, but they were huge and looked kind of smelly. It just isn't right to make fun of the creator of your favorite world.

As I turned around, I saw why they were laughing. The reeve was lying flat on his back in the smithy. Apparently, he had been trying to break up a fight, and it hadn't gone so well. I sighed.

Maybe the shoveling peasants could help. They had to be employees. No one would pay money to shovel for fun.

"Excuse me, good sirs . . ."

"I am not a sir, I'm a woman!" the shorter one shouted shrilly.

"My apologies, madam. It is hard to tell with all of the mud on you, and you're not wearing any makeup." She was also flat-chested, but I thought that would be rude to mention.

"Do I look like I can afford makeup, tubby?" she said as she continued to shovel.

"My apologies. So, why exactly are you shoveling all of this mud into the cart?"

"It's not mud. It's muck." She didn't even look up as she talked.

"Okay, why are you shoveling all of this muck into the cart?"

"That's our job."

"But, why?"

"That's what a muck removal engineer does. We shovel muck into a cart."

"And where does the muck go?"

She finally looked up. "I don't know. You'd have to ask the muck distribution specialist."

"Never mind." I shook my head in bewilderment. "Look, I've had a long day, and my assistant abandoned me in the woods. I just need to call him to come pick me up."

"Then, call him. This is a small village. I'm sure he can hear you."

Did everyone at this fair have to be in character? I really wished I had written science fiction, so phones would exist. "Look, ma'am, I'm the creator of Vyenra, the world this fair is representing. I'd be happy to sign anything you want if you could just give me a phone."

"Did he say he's the Creator, Giry?"

Giry appraised me. "He does have the right beard for it, but he's a bit too heavy. In all of the paintings I've seen, the Creator was much skinnier, with exceptional abs."

"But he didn't have a beard in the earlier works, those prior to the fifth century."

No, they weren't talking about Christianity. The religion of my world was called The One. Yes, I know it sounds like he was talking about Jesus, but he wasn't. You try creating a religion from scratch. It was really time-consuming, so I had decided to focus my time on more important things, like character and plot.

The woman nodded. "That's true. You don't really look like the Creator."

I stood, mouth hanging open, for what felt like several minutes. Great—they were completely in character and art history majors, too. I guess it made sense for an art history major to be shoveling mud. There's not a whole lot you can do with that degree but shovel mud . . . or write fantasy novels. That's right: I was an art history major before I changed to the much more useful philosophy.

I slowly edged away from the muck removal engineers, who were too absorbed in the higher-quality source of muck they had just discovered to notice me leaving.

Fortunately, the fight in the smithy seemed to have broken up, and the reeve was standing alone in the center of the square. He appeared a tad dazed, but otherwise fine. Good. Maybe in that condition, he wouldn't be as likely to stay in character.

"Excuse me, Mr. Reeve, could you perhaps help me out?"

"What's the problem, oddly bespectacled one?"

"I need some help getting out of here. Someone abandoned me in the woods. I need to call my assistant to get me out of here."

"That is quite the predicament. The only way we can communicate outside the village is by messenger. And since we are so near enemy lines, all of our messengers are being held back for military communications."

I breathed in a little. "Listen, I'm the creator of the world this town is based on. If you don't help me, I'll have my lawyer sue the lot of you." I didn't know if I could actually sue for anything that had happened so far, but I had found that when you really needed to get someone to do something they didn't want to, it was best to be intimidating.

The reeve paused and looked me over for a good minute. His face then turned bright red. "Blasphemer!" he said as he slapped me in a way that no man should ever slap another man. Is there a way a man should slap another man? Okay, granted, the Three Stooges get that to work, and I do love the Stooges, but outside of them, is there ever a situation where a man should slap another man?

That, of course, made me angry. So, I slapped him back. (OK, I guess there is a time to slap another man.) Normally, I'm not the kind of person to resort to violence, being that it often ends terribly for me, but I figured I could take this skinny old man.

He slapped me again.

I slapped him with my right hand and then my left hand in quick succession.

He slapped me on top of my head, then below the chin.

I tried to poke him in the eyes, but he blocked it with his hand. (Great. He was a Stooges fan too.) "Ha!"

I pushed him down on the ground and slapped him mercilessly.

"Guards! This lunatic is attacking me. Helllllllp!"

I decided I had won the exchange, but given that all of the actors seemed to be stuck in character, they would probably put me in the stocks (or whatever the equivalent of Renaissance fair jail was). If they stuck me in the stocks, I'd probably get pestered endlessly by fans about what color the horse was in chapter 2 of book 3 and what type of shoes the Atlians wore. I'd rather they threw rotten fruit at me.

I got up off the reeve and ran around the nearest corner. Even if those guards were actors, they did not look friendly. Now, I might have been a little out of shape, but I had run cross-country in college a decade ago. I could still run pretty fast, even if it was for only about twenty yards.

As I rounded the corner, I looked about frantically. I didn't want to be the author who was famous for being arrested by his fans in costume. I had heard that "No publicity is bad publicity," but being on YouTube in the stocks, pestered endlessly by fans, was not what I wanted to be known for. I could just picture the other authors snickering endlessly at me at every convention . . . forever. Not that I could blame anyone for laughing. It would be pretty funny if it happened to someone else.

Fortunately—and I use this term very loosely—the muck wagon was heading out of town. So I did what I had to and dove into the pile of muck. If you've never dived into a pile of mud, I can tell you that it's actually refreshing at first. That is, until you realize you're in a pile of mud.

As I sat in the pile, an idea came to me. Maybe this wasn't a Renaissance fair. I'd seen a reality show set in a fantasy world once. Were they doing a season set in my world? In my naiveté, I hadn't read the clauses at the end of my first contract and had given my publisher the media rights to my series. I'd thought they had to at least run any TV show ideas by me first, but perhaps not. Or maybe this was an elaborate hidden camera show, which would be very entertaining if it involved someone else. Either of those things would explain why everyone was so stuck on staying in character.

You might be thinking I was inside a dream. If you've been thinking that, you've also probably been screaming at me for the last few pages, calling me an idiot and such. Oh, yeah? You're the one screaming at a book. The book can't hear you, and neither can I, the character in said book. Now, who's the idiot?

Anyway, as you'll recall, I had fallen off a horse, which hurt. I'd also been slapped repeatedly, which also hurt. Perhaps you've heard that if you can feel pain, then you're not in a dream. Well, I did, and a lot of it. Case closed.

As I sat in the cart, immersed in mud, I wondered why pigs enjoyed rolling around in it so much. It was kind of refreshing at first, but it got cold pretty quickly. Granted, it did appear to be autumn, which is pretty cool, temperature-wise, but it was also around noon, with the sun fully overhead and the sky cloudless.

I decided to get out of the cart pretty soon, or I was likely to catch a cold; that, and I really had to pee. I have a pretty weak bladder when I get cold. Fortunately, a few minutes later, the cart came to a stop when a pair of riders passed in front of it on a crossroads.

It was now or never. I crawled out of the mud and rolled to the ground, making an odd combination of a squishing sound and a thud, the kind of sound you might hear when you throw pudding against the wall. It's a fun sound to hear, sure, still I don't recommend it. I mean, for one thing, you'll probably have to clean it up, and another, that's wasted pudding. Pudding is delicious, even butterscotch.

At least now that I was out of that damn town, I could find some regular non-actors who might be able to help. As I dusted myself off (no idea why; I mean, when you're covered with mud, a little dust is the least of your concerns), I checked, and the driver hadn't noticed the man-shaped pile of mud behind him. Apparently, I was safe for the time being. Now, I just had to find a lake or something to clean myself off in.

The cart turned at the intersection and headed off in the opposite direction from the riders; north, I think it was. I thought I saw a lake straight ahead. I only thought so because, well, mud is hard to keep out of your eyes, especially when your hands are covered in yet more mud. A rainbow appeared above the lake. I took it as a sign that the worst had to be over and started toward it.

"Look, a monster!"

I turned to see that both riders had wheeled about. Great. They thought I was a mud monster. If you think about it, a monster made of mud isn't really the scariest thing out there; I mean, unless you clean houses for a living. Cleaning up after a mud monster has to be pretty scary, but seeing as we weren't near any white sheets or recently cleaned floors, as disconcerting as I must look, I wasn't really all that threatening. Pathetic, maybe.

The riders charged at me, swords drawn, with violence in their eyes. They were either really good actors, or they hadn't liked my last book.

I cowered and yelled something like, "I'm not a monster. I'm a human being!" or "Please, no. I'm too pretty to die!" I won't comment on whether I peed myself or not.

The riders stopped. "I'm not so sure that's a monster."

"If it is, it may accost us on approach. We cannot hazard that."

The one on the right lowered his sword. "What if we ask it a few questions? Surely, a mud person would be baffled by a difficult question."

"How do you know that? Have you ever chanced upon a mud person before?"

The one on the left shook his head. "No, but I cannot imagine a person made of mud would be terribly intelligent."

"True, but he did just converse with us."

"How do you know it's a 'he'?"

"I think I saw it urinate upward."

"I'm pretty sure it was to the right, but point taken."

Reasonably sure that they weren't going to run me through, I stood up. "Hello, good sirs. I am an author, stranded in the woods . . ."

"He is a rather polite mud monster, but what is an 'author'?"

"Probably a mud monster chieftain of some sort."

The actors were really getting on my nerves, and I was still covered in mud. Tired. Hungry. Muddy. Frustrated. I decided I'd had enough of them and took off toward the lake. Surely, two actors wouldn't attack a famous author.

"He must be seeking reinforcements!"

The sound of hoofbeats drew steadily closer, but before the danger could register, the world went dark.

ATTACK OF THE THESAURUS

I awoke on a small rug inside a massive tent to an argument between the knights and another, better-dressed knight with long blond hair. I assumed I was the topic of discussion due to the over-enthusiastic gesturing and pointing in my direction. In my experience, when someone keeps pointing at you, it's almost never a good thing. It usually ends with food being tossed at places that aren't my mouth or the forced removal of clothing from embarrassing places. My head reminded me why I should always wear a helmet, and my ears decided it was time for a test of the emergency broadcast system.

If you're still convinced this was all a dream, I'd like to point out that I had just been knocked out. Have you ever heard of that happening in a dream? Didn't think so. And if you're still convinced this was a dream, please stop yelling at me for not realizing this was a dream. This is a book. I can't hear you.

Now, you're probably saying, "But, Harry, what if you're not in a movie or a TV show? What if you're really in the actual world of Vyenra?" I think I've already established that this wasn't a dream. I had pinched myself hard. It had hurt. Not a dream!

"But what if Vyenra is real, and you were transported there by a magic bottle of peppermint Schnapps?" you might ask. I had already written five books in this damn world. I would have remembered being able to see it somehow. It wasn't like some strange man had handed me an outline for this world in a dark alley or something. I always run screaming whenever strange men try to hand me anything in dark alleys. If you don't have a rule like that, you really should. And also, what kind of hackneyed, uncreative writer would create a plot like that?

The action in front of me seemed to be reaching its apex. Judging by the way the newcomer was yelling at the others, he was probably their superior, and not very happy that they'd brought me to him. I couldn't imagine why, as I was always the life of the party. How did he know he wouldn't like me? He hadn't even talked to me.

After a few minutes, their argument seemed to reach a conclusion, and the third knight approached me, carefully maneuvering around all of the trophies sprinkled around the tent. He opened his mouth, but the only thing I could hear were the words "cotton candy."

"My ears are still ringing, good knight. Give me a minute. It's starting to clear."

". . . fragrant . . . prison . . . unicorns . . . duct tape . . . waffles."

"I'm sorry, I only heard part of that. Could you repeat?"

He gave me a disgusted look, reached down, and smacked me on the back of my head. Mud squirted out of both ears, and a little splattered on the bottom of his immaculate tunic. He glanced at one of the many mirrors in the tent and shook his head in disgust. For some reason, he seemed angrier.

"Why is this muddy man ruining my best tunic?"

"My lord, it's a mud monster."

"What, exactly, is a mud monster?"

"A monster made of mud."

"And what, exactly, is threatening about that? I mean, besides more work for the servants."

That was what I'd thought! Their leader was just like me.

"But it's still a monster, even if it does speak rather politely, my lord," the first knight said.

The leader and I slapped our palms against our foreheads simultaneously. However, this caused more mud to splatter onto his previously pristine tunic. He didn't appear to care for that. You'd think my display of solidarity would have endeared me to him.

"What kind of monster speaks politely, Axin?" the leader said, managing to glare at all three of us simultaneously. "What kind of monster speaks at all? And how many monsters have you even seen?"

"Well, none, my lord, however I have heard of the dreaded butler vampires of Avringia. It is said that they serve you tea and give you a comfy chair before they suck your blood."

"There are no vampires, simpleton, and there is no Avringia, for that matter. Those are all folk tales meant to frighten children."

"The coopers will be glad to hear that, master," the second knight said. "Coopers are always frightened of vampires. I think it's because vampires always steal their arrows."

"Arrows?" the leader said. "Why would a cooper have arrows, Weel?"

"Coopers produce arrows, sir. It is the purpose of their profession."

"That's a fletcher, nitwit. Coopers make barrels."

Weel nodded like a dog. "You are correct, as always, master."

"As usual, you two are distracting me from my point. There is no such thing as monsters of any kind. This is only a man who happens to be covered in mud."

I wished he would hurry up, because I really had to go to the bathroom again. That mud was really cold. I raised my hand.

The leader glared at me, and I thought I heard the fabric behind me start to catch fire. "Yes? What is it?"

"I have to pee."

"Can't you see I'm yelling at my lackeys, here? You can wait." He turned back to his stooges. "I thought I had seen some moronic things from you two, but this, by far, is the worst."

"Even worse than when we attacked our own army?"

"Yes, much worse." He somehow managed to glare even harder. I was afraid his eyes might actually pop. I hoped he was going to see an anger management consultant after this was over.

"Worse than when we ransacked the nunnery and the orphanage?" Weel said.

Their master's skin immediately changed back from thermometer red to its normal pale state. "That one was actually pretty good. You got some good candy, and you know I have a sweet tooth."

"They had lots of jelly beans," Axin said.

"I hate jelly beans! And to think you almost had me in a good mood again."

Axin and Weel proceeded to cower like nerds cornered by a football team. I wasn't used to viewing that scene from the other side, so I let out a little giggle.

The leader's glare returned to me, and my bladder dutifully responded. Don't laugh, reader, I have a condition. He was about to punch me, but he must have realized just how muddy I was and decided against getting even dirtier. He stared at me for a good minute, trying to decide how to punish me without getting anything more on his fine clothes. His eyes stopped and focused on my surprisingly clean right hand. I was sure he would twist my fingers back painfully, like the local kids when I try to take their candy. I wanted to pull the hand back but found my limbs frozen.

He grabbed my ring finger, but, shockingly, did not pull my finger back. Instead, he did something much more painful: he took my grandfather's ring.

That ring was the sole reminder I had of the man who had raised me. My grandfather meant everything to me. He was the reason I had become a writer. How dare that actor take it from me? He was in my world, after all! I shook off my malaise, stood up, and furiously stuck out my finger. . . and then landed face-first back on the rug.

"For wasting my time, you two idiots will take him out of here and get him cleaned off. Then, you can figure out what to do with him. I still can't remember why I put up with you two." Our audience at an end, he returned to the nearest mirror and began to adjust his flawless blond hair while pointedly avoiding any glances toward the mud splotches on his clothes.

Axin looked me over, clearly not sure what to do. Weel pointed, and they both grabbed an end of the rug under me and hauled me out of the tent. Knights were evidently pretty strong, even pretend ones. After we exited the tent, they headed toward a small pond. Before I could get my bearings and figure out whether it was the same pond as before, they tossed me in.

Great. I was wet and cold yet again, though at least I didn't have to pee anymore. The instant I was sure all of the mud was gone, I struggled to shore. While the pond wasn't very deep— around three feet—I didn't know how to swim.

"My word! It really was a man under all that mud."

"The master is very wise, indeed. Now what do we do with him, Weel?"

"I'm not sure. Who are you? And why were you covered in mud?"

"I'm Harry Olson, a writer who seems to have been abandoned in the woods by my assistant." I decided at this point to abandon the idea of trying to use a phone since all of these actors were obviously not going to give me one. Also, getting into another slap fight didn't seem to be a good idea. I imagined these knights hit harder than the old, skinny reeve.

"You're a scribe, then," Axin said. "You must be rather important to have an assistant. Which noble do you serve?"

I wasn't sure what time period from my books I was in. They could have set this show at any time. "What year is it, good sirs?"

"I must have clouted you too vigorously," Weel said. "It is the 2497th year of the Garandian calendar."

I should have known it was right after my last book. That made the most sense, but it also gave the writers of this show an easy time ruining what I had planned for future books.

I decided to pick a minor noble who had been murdered in my last book. "I was in service to the Count of Minestro, and I was covered in mud because I ran from the assassins who murdered his whole house. My assistant pushed me down in the mud and abandoned me to save himself."

"That's a terrible story, indeed." Weel handed me a towel.

Since they were being really nice to me, I thought I would give them a little advice so my fans wouldn't tear them apart at the next convention. "Those blue sashes you two have are the wrong shade. The color of the Garandian Empire is royal blue, and yours are more powder blue."

"My mother gave them to us," Axin said.

Weel smiled. "Do you need passage back home? We might be able to secure that after the next battle."

While being on a battlefield might be kind of neat, it was probably better to avoid that, as filming a battle had to be really expensive. If this was a TV show, it might be better to keep the cost down, as I might have a financial stake in it, after all. Also, I might get hurt in the middle of a battle. They were very chaotic, even when they involved trained stuntmen, and I wasn't part of the stunt coordination.

"Yes, that would be fantastic."

Axin laughed. "Well, it sucks to be you, then."

"The master will love it when we tell him of this," Weel said. "This imbecile actually believed me."

"I wouldn't tell him yet. He's in a pretty foul mood."

Weel turned toward me. "I hate scribes."

Axin put his hand on Weel's shoulder. "Not this again. It's not the fault of every scribe out there that you were fired from your last job."

"My writing was brilliant. How dare they fire me?"

"I read some of it, and it was not. You didn't even write what they told you to."

Weel grimaced. "They couldn't handle a little creativity."

"You were supposed to be writing history."

"Well, history is dull. I thought I would spice it up and add some flair."

Axin shook his head. "You can't teach children that King Numerious conquered Upper Tynton with his army of reindeers and barbers."

"It's very memorable."

"Yes, but there was no King Numerious, Upper Tynton, or an army of reindeers and barbers."

"But the Thousand-Year Peace was boring. No one died in battle," Weel said.

"That's still not as bad as when I gave you a Word of the Day calendar for your birthday."

Now I knew why some of my fans thought it was a bad idea to have the printing press invented hundreds of years too early.

"The calendar made me sound so much more intellectual."

Axin crossed his arms. "No, you use most of the words wrong."

"Imbecilic!"

"That's what I mean. You really need to learn the difference between adverbs, adjectives, and nouns."

"Philistine!"

"Yes, there are plenty of those around here," I said. "They're right behind the English and the Romans and all those other people who do *not* exist in Vyenra."

I guessed the gift of a large vocabulary didn't include an appreciation of sarcasm, because Weel hit me in the head with his gauntlet. My head was already very sore. I thought I might have a concussion.

"What shall we do with the scribe?" Weel said.

"We could put him with the other one."

"And what, pray tell, for?"

"So . . . they could write faster?"

Weel raised his hand. "Ohhh. Ohhh! I've just had a master-stroke of a sentiment."

"Why can't you just speak normally, Weel? You're trying too hard. Honestly."

"By virtue of my having vocabulary in the copious does not negate my sentiment."

"My mother taught grammar, and you've made her roll over in her grave."

"While I know my opinion doesn't matter much to you two, I'm with Axin on this one," I said. "I think you just gave a few dozen teachers a heart attack."

"You are quite factual in your perception that I do not cognate your theorem," Weel said.

"Anyway . . . Weel, what was your idea?"

"We shall have them engage in a melee betwixt themselves!"

Axin nodded. "Finally, a good idea. We could give them pens, too."

"No, no. They should fight, not write."

"They could fight *with* the pens."

"Don't you mean quills?" I said.

Axin rolled his eyes. "No, we're not into any kinky stuff. No one wants to see you two tickling each other. You can do that on your own time. We want blood, and pens would make the fight last longer."

"This is my most ingenious concept in eternity!" Weel exclaimed.

DYFANTUS THE BIG, DUMB STUPID-HEAD AND FRIENDS

They led me a short distance away to a nice tall oak. The tree had leaves at that perfect autumn red that's almost purple, with smooth, flawless bark, and . . . you know what? It was a tree. You don't really need me to describe a tree for you, unless you're one of those weirdos who gets off on trees, in which case, this really isn't the right book for you. The important thing about this tree was the other man leashed to it.

If I had to fight him, I felt pretty good about my chances. With his ghostly complexion, I figured the sun would likely fell him before I could. I might choose sunscreen as my weapon—that way, I could win the fight but still feel good about saving his life. Or, if that didn't work, I could always use my classic move and steal his glasses. He seemed too absorbed in taking notes on his imaginary pad to notice our arrival.

Axin tied me around the waist and leashed me to the tree like an expert. He had clearly gotten his knot-tying merit badge, so I gave him the secret Boy Scout hand signal. In response, he gave a me a dirty look and hit me in the stomach. As I doubled over, I pondered whether he had missed the signal or hadn't recognized it. Was the signal specific to my old troop? The last time I had given it to other scouts, I'd gotten hit in the stomach, too. Maybe it meant "please hit me in the stomach" in sign language.

"We'll let you two get acquainted while we tell the master of our idea," Axin said. "This might even make him forget about the whole mud monster fiasco."

"Expressly!" Weel said.

"When we get back, I'm burning that calendar."

"You must nullify that apprehension, my compatriot."

"Tying me to a tree is a really crappy way to keep me from leaving your stupid show," I said.

I thought they were out of earshot until Weel ran back and punched me in the gut. I really hoped Axin found both the calendar and a big sock to stuff in his mouth, but I kept the last part in my head and made sure not to yell it this time.

I stood up and brushed myself off. I was wet, and now both my head and my stomach hurt. No matter how hard I tried, I couldn't untie the knot Axin had put in my rope. On the bright side, my companion didn't seem to be much of a threat. A butterfly was furiously circling his head, and when he attempted to swat it away, he tripped over a big root. The butterfly flew a short distance away and seemed to dance in victory.

"Are you OK?" I asked.

"Do you have to gloat, you winged terror? Just because your species is called a monarch does not mean you need to act the part. You may have won this round, but I will win the next." He quickly stood up and renewed his assault, but the butterfly stayed out of reach. Either it felt it had nothing more to prove, or it was too absorbed in normal butterfly thoughts to care. I'm far from an expert on butterfly psychology, though if I ever decide to switch careers, that might be a great scam.

"Come back here, you tiny bully. I'm not finished with you." Forgetting he was tied to a tree, he ran forward a couple of feet after the fleeing butterfly and then landed hard on his back. As he stared up at his fleeing foe, he raised his right arm in victory. "Ha! I am the victor, you coward. That'll teach you to ruin the concentration of Geoff, the head scribe of the illustrious Lord Hartin."

I really liked my chances in our upcoming fight, especially if there were butterflies in attendance. As you may have guessed, fighting is not even remotely one of the skills in my toolbox; cowering and running away are, but still not nearly as great as my abilities in badminton and yogurt sculpting.

I couldn't decide if I should help him up or kick him while he was down. I had a furious internal battle between my chivalrous side and the side that wanted to not be killed with a pen. I wasn't sure what was worse, the irony of being killed that way or that they had pens here. The chivalrous side of me won out, mostly out of fear that, if he was too beaten up, they might pair me with someone more dangerous, like a pacifist or an infant.

I stood over him so he didn't think the butterfly was talking to him. "Hi, there. Can I help you up?"

"My word. Where did you come from?"

"Axin and Weel brought me here and tied me to the tree. My name's Harry, by the way." I grabbed his upraised arm and hauled him up. He must've weighed about 90 pounds, the limit of all the strength in my body.

"I am Mopansin Trantinviavax III, the legendary scribe in service to Lord Hartin, though most people call me Geoff. I'm sure you've heard of me."

I had created no such character. "Oh, yes. Of course."

"Well, it appears that we are both in the same situation here. They captured me as well, after an epic fight of course. I would have been victorious if the awful wind hadn't conspired against me and forced me to the ground with her mighty breath, bitch goddess that she is."

"You believe in the Old Gods, then?"

"Well, no. That can get a man strung up. I am a loyal believer in The One, I'll have you know. My ancestor Mopansin Trantinvi-avax the negative XII was the first person on the entire island of Garandia to switch to the faith of The One. My family have always been the most loyal believers on the island. Some say we're more loyal than any of our Lord's 13.7 apostles, too."

"Who are these 'some' that you refer to?"

"Master cartographers, Archons, and cheesemongers, mostly."

"Cheesemongers?"

"Cheesemongering has long been the most holy of professions for devoted followers of The One. Everyone knows that. Our Lord and Savior, in his earthly guise, was training to be a cheesemonger before he became afflicted with lactose intolerance and decided to go into the business of saving souls."

"That is not part of the religion of The One." If this moron kept ruining the religion from my books, I would throttle him right there. I had spent a lot of time thinking up those precepts, and they did not involve a savior who was allergic to dairy products.

When he saw the angry look on my face and the fact that I towered over him, Geoff backed away. "My apologies, my good man. Perhaps I was mistaken."

I glared at him in sullen silence for a few minutes before I eventually calmed down. He was obviously terrified of me, as his sheepish eyes never let me leave his sight. I was clearly not as even of a match as his previous foe. It felt good to be the bully for once, especially when confronting a future opponent to the fake death.

As it was unpracticed in that art, my face got tired of being intimidating rather quickly. I decided to at least get to know my opponent, while steering clear of any religious topics; there really wasn't anything else to do, after all. Axin had tied the knot really tight, and I had given up on untying it. They could have left us some books to read, or maybe a board game.

"So, what kind of scribing do you do?"

"I manage the finances and organize the tournaments of the most glorious and noble Lord Hartin. He had told me that no man living or dead could ever match my brilliance with pen and numbers. Why, the entire art of the knightly tournament would end were I not there to organize them, so ingenious is my organization and mathematical prowess. I once turned a mere fifty trakons into the greatest tournament the Continent has ever seen. Unbelievable, is it not?"

"Not really."

"Indeed, it is almost too much to believe. That tournament, which I shouldn't need to tell you was the tournament of Hake's Hall, had all of the greatest jousters from all of the lands: Qoon the Fearless, Cat of Lithia, Gilfan the Fair, Slightly Angry Havrug, Bland Gorg, Shutokan the Dyslexic, Bugger Charius, and, of course, our captor Dyfantus the Bold."

"That was Dyfantus?" I blurted. Dyfantus was by far the most famous and skilled of the Garandian knights and the main villain in my third book. He was also a major asshole, doubly so for taking my ring. He had once stabbed one of his own knights because he thought the knight would get credit for his victory in a sack race. He loved glory and himself and hated everything else. I should have recognized him, but give me a break; I had just recovered from a probable concussion and I really had had to tinkle. Also, their Dyfantus had his hair parted on the wrong side.

"Indeed. He was the victor of the joust at that very tournament. He unhorsed Slightly Angry Havrug and Gilfan the Fair in short order. The final match with Cat of Lithia lasted twelve tilts, the longest match in recent memory. The minstrels will be singing of it for generations to come. And it was all due to my unsurpassed ability!"

I seriously regretted my decision not to kick him while he was down. At the very least, I could have kicked some of the hot air out of him, though he likely had a never-ending supply of that substance. If I could steer the subject away from jousting, then he might be less obnoxious. "That is . . . fascinating. So, why did Dyfantus capture you, anyway? Didn't he recognize you?"

"Well, after his glorious victory at the greatest tournament in well over a century, organized by yours truly, he felt he deserved a much larger prize than what was offered. Through my brilliant financial maneuverings, I managed to gather a prize that was unheard of: 5,000 trakons. That is easily twice what has been offered at any tournament in the last few years, but for Dyfantus, it was not enough. When I presented him his prize, he got rather angry and demanded more from my master, the magnificent Lord Hartin. Dyfantus' two lieutenants kidnapped me the next night and are holding me for ransom until my master can come up with another 2,000 trakons."

"Why hasn't he been arrested? The king should surely intervene." King Berin the Great was, as his name implies, a fantastic king. He was very strict when it came to following the law. No one would ever get away with such a blatant disregard for the law under his watch, not even his favorite knight.

"The king is too busy building his latest shrine to care. But I am not worried. I am easily more valuable to my master than a trifling 2,000 trakons. He will no doubt pay shortly, and I will make the sum back for him in a fortnight. It is only a matter of time."

"Well, that's fantastic news. His two cronies were planning on having us fight each other to the death with pens. If you're so valuable, Dyfantus will never let them do that. He's already pretty angry with them. Maybe this suggestion will push him over the edge, and he'll have those two fight to the death instead."

"That would be fantastic, but I don't think he'd let them kill each other. It took him over three months of screening and interviewing candidates before he chose them."

"All that time, and he picked them?"

"Oh, yes. They're the only ones who could get the theme song quite right. They really knocked it out of the park on the singing portion of the interview."

Had he seriously used a baseball reference? As I'm sure you all know, the game of baseball and its terminology had not existed in the Middle Ages and did not exist on the fictional planet I had created based on that time period. I was beginning to feel that the writers of this show weren't really trying very hard on little things like accuracy and logic.

"Shouldn't competence and decision-making have been more important?"

"Oh, no. He has singing ability, nerd-bashing, agreeing with everything he says, and blind loyalty as his key attributes."

"That sounds like he was recruiting for a musical version of any 80s movie villain."

"Oh, I almost forgot the swimsuit competition at the end."

I got right in his face. I'm pretty sure he wet himself, which normally would have made my day (as I was usually the wetter and not the wettee), but I had had enough of the ridiculousness these actors kept vomiting out. "Swimsuit competition? I most certainly did not put swimsuits or related competitions in any of my books. This is a medieval-inspired world, and neither of those existed in that time period. Furthermore, you do not have baseball, pens, nerds, or Philistines."

He whimpered as he backed farther toward the tree. "My apologies, my good man, but all of those terms are from the Holy Book. Being such a devoted follower of The One, I learned all of them during my extensive studies when I was little, even if they all don't make sense to me."

For the record, the Holy Book was only supposed to be a placeholder name until I came up with something better, but I had forgotten to go back. My embarrassment caused me to back off from Geoff a little, even if my anger didn't lessen. "How would it make any more sense for an ancient holy person to use those terms than it would for you?"

"I don't know, though there are numerous theological treatises on that controversial subject. One book recently discovered in the ruins of a fortress in Bocango suggests the author of the Holy Book was not from Paruxia at all, as had been assumed for centuries, but was from somewhere called Earf. Another theory is that he had a very active imagination and liked to make things up. My personal theory is that he didn't hire an editor, and we have created meanings for those ancient mistakes to compensate."

Before I exploded into an expletive-laced tirade on the ridiculousness of pretty much everything this half-witted actor had said, Weel and Axin returned with idiotic grins on their faces. Those grins were definitely not a good sign for me or my companion, not that I really cared what happened to him after what he'd said.

"Well, well, Weel. It looks like our scribes have been bonding while we were away."

"Their plight will be all the more tragic when one abrogates his opposite."

"I'm guessing you didn't take the calendar away from him," I said.

Axin gave me a flustered look. "I destroyed it, but I think he has more of them somewhere."

"Ha! The preponderance of it is in my cranium at this nonce, and I have just obtained a thesaurus for my day of birthing as well. You can never discontinue erudition, savages."

"If you let me loose, I'll hold him down and you can take out his tongue," I said.

"Nice try, you towering nerd, but I was not chosen for this job by setting someone like you loose." He gave me a threatening look, and in case I wasn't sure of his intent, began to pound one of his fists into his other palm. Clearly, he and his partner had graduated from the Great Hollywood School of Movie Syco-phantry and Telemarketing or its rival, Television Toadies Tech.

What? You think it's easy being a villain's sidekick? That anyone can do that? No, my friends, that takes years of practice. Without proper training, you'd have flunkies being nice to the good guy, not holding the hero down while the main villain hits him, or worst of all, actually being smarter than their leader.

I thought I almost had him. Tricking someone like him should be easy, but apparently, I was no Bugs Bunny. I needed to change tactics. "Yes, I heard you were picked for your singing ability. You're one of the most famous singers in all of Garandia, equaled only by Weel."

I had never seen someone's face instantly change from menacing to bashful happiness before. "You've heard of me? I didn't know I was famous."

"This individual is excessively moronic, speculating that you are my equal in the proficient. I give his assessment no condensation."

"You're right, Weel. I'm *better* than you. And the word you're looking for is 'consideration!'" Axin gave Weel a shove, as fighting was obviously the only way for men to settle a dispute over singing ability.

Weel shoved him back, and soon they were both rolling on the ground. While they were absorbed in their dispute, I sidled closer to Geoff. "When they roll closer, we need to grab a knife or something sharp from one of them and cut ourselves loose."

"I knew you were a smart man when I saw your glasses. Why, that must be the most magnificent pair of spectacles I have ever encountered. They must be worth a fortune. Wherever did you acquire them?"

Why did I always have to be so nice? I regretted involving this pompous mouth-breather as soon as the words had left my mouth. Even if he didn't slow me down, he was going to be a very annoying companion. "I'll tell you later if you drop it for now. Focus, Geoff."

"Yes, of course. Do you think we should try for a dirk, a longsword, a throwing knife, a katana, a short sword, a machete, a hatchet, or a bastard sword?"

"Anything sharp will do. Besides, I doubt they have all of those. Just grab the first one you see."

"While a hatchet is probably the sharpest, it is not ideal for this type of work. A dirk would be easier to maneuver for such delicate cutting but not nearly as effective. A machete is the best of both worlds, unless they happen to have a katana, which I needn't tell you would be a rare find indeed in this part of the world."

"Just grab whatever you can," I groaned. "We don't have time to be picky."

"Now, if we could heat it, that would make our jobs so much easier, and we wouldn't fray the rope. A razor might be useful, as well. I know! We need to find a boat or rigging knife of some sort. Those are made for cutting rope, after all. Do you think they might have one of those, being that they are soldiers and not sailors?" After he had finally finished talking, something I would soon learn was a rare blessing, he turned toward me. I had just finished cutting through my rope and handed him the knife I had taken from Axin five minutes before. I immediately ran off into the forest.

While it would have been more honorable to help him cut through his ropes, or at least wait for him to join me, I felt I didn't have a lot of time to waste before the two singing knights finished their bout. I was also pretty sure I didn't want to travel with such an annoying man. I did feel kind of bad, because Geoff was likely to spend all of his time debating what type of cut to use to get himself free and would likely not free himself in time. He would, however, serve as a very effective distraction from pursuit.

AXIN GETS WEELY, WEELY UPSET

I ran as fast as my out-of-shape body would allow into the woods. I really needed to start laying off the late-night fast food runs. In college, I had outrun a horse. Sure, it was an old, partially lame horse, but it still counts as a horse.

After I made it about 300 yards, I could barely make out the knights' shouts over the pounding of my heart. I was so focused on my task that I wouldn't even let myself look back. I did not want to be seen on ads for this show fighting with a pen.

After another 200 yards, my lungs informed the rest of my body that I was going to stop. My mind screamed to push on, but my legs disagreed. I really regretted cancelling my gym membership the year before. Granted, I'd never used it in the three years I'd had it, but I still regretted getting rid of it. Even the thought of never-ending embarrassment couldn't keep me going. I barely managed to clear the bushes before I crashed face-first into the dirt.

It took me a few minutes to pull myself together enough to attempt to stand. Fortunately, I had managed to make it to one of the few clearings in that forest. I was overwhelmed with dread, sure that my pursuers must have caught up to me. I had run away in a very straight line, so they should have had an easy time finding me. I decided the next time I ran for my life, I would run in an unpredictable, zig-zagging fashion.

Before I pulled my head up, I heard the inevitable sound of hoofbeats. I took solace from the fact that my pursuers were on horseback. It really didn't matter what kind of shape I was in; I wasn't going to outrun a healthy horse. I knew they'd have an exceptionally annoying song cooked up to boast of my recapture.

"Are you all right, sir?" one of my pursuers said. He had a slightly nasally voice. One of the two must have taken a shot to the nose.

"Oh, I'm lovely. People are often in fantastic shape when they pull themselves out of the dirt. Can we dispense with the part where you pretend to be nice and then insult me? I'm completely exhausted. Just tie me up and take me back to the tree."

"Did any of that make sense to you, Verix?" a second voice said.

"I think he escaped from one of those Sculander sex rings we keep hearing about."

"That's probably what Dyfantus has been up to. He's been seen in the area, and I can see him being into something like that. He is a sick one."

My mood brightened as I pulled myself up. In spite of their similar armor, these fine fellows were not Axin and Weel. In fact, they sounded like they were enemies of Dyfantus' gang.

"Did you say Verix?" I asked.

"I most certainly did, good fellow." The smile on his face faded to a grimace. "Ewww. Smiling with all that dirt on your face does not suit you. Here—borrow my handkerchief and wipe yourself off."

"Thank you." I cleaned it off in short order.

Verix shook the dirt off his cloth and looked me in the eyes. "Ehh . . . Maybe you should put the dirt back on."

"I hear they have classes on smiling back at our camp," the second knight said.

I didn't know what they were talking about. I had always been told my smile was magnificent, the kind of smile that artists try to imitate but rarely succeed in capturing. I decided to let this one go, as they didn't seem to want to tie me to any trees, or worse yet, sing at me. "I thank you, sirs. I'm fleeing from Dyfantus, as you suspected, or more accurately, his two goons, Axin and Weel."

"Ahh," the second knight said. "Those two. While they've only been with him for a month, they're already getting on our nerves, always parroting whatever Dyfantus says and calling us mean names."

"They are awful, though I do think he picked the right lackeys," Verix said. "Weel really nailed the talent portion. His basket-weaving demonstration was mesmerizing."

"And Axin put himself over the rest in the swimsuit competition."

"The man does know how to wear a Speedo."

My smile evaporated. If those two hadn't just saved me, I would have gone into a tirade about how silly and completely out of place everything they said was. While I was no expert on the history of swimwear, I was positive that the Speedo had not been invented in the Middle Ages, and I knew I hadn't put it into any of my books.

"So, back on track. Since you are Verix, then may I presume you are Arik?"

"You are correct," the second knight said. "Do we know you?"

Arik and Verix were the closest of friends. Inseparable. The inspiration for buddy cop movies everywhere. The very definition of friendship. They were the main characters of most of my books.

Verix was the wit of the two, which the actor had evidently taken to mean having a near-permeant grin on. Most of his self-esteem issues were in the past, but he still followed Arik's lead in spite of his greater intelligence. He was the classic sidekick. His sister's marriage to Arik had cemented their bond from already strong to unbreakable. Being a bit of an underdog, he was also my favorite character. Since he was my favorite, I had also given him the same short haircut and dark brown hair as myself, though the similarities stopped there as I didn't want to make it too obvious and wanted to keep him separate in my mind so I could make him his own person.

Arik pulled off his helmet, and his long blond hair cascaded down his shoulders, covering his face. I held my breath as I looked to see if they'd gotten the right actor to play him and especially to see if they had gotten his Van Dyke just right. It always bothered me when in movies or TV shows based on books, they hadn't gotten the hair right. As he brushed his hair back to finally reveal his face, I found I wasn't as disappointed as I'd suspected I would be when he not only didn't have a Van Dyke, he didn't have any facial hair at all.

Arik was a woman.

Not that there was anything wrong with that, but I had distinctly written him as a man in my books. I didn't know why this didn't bother me, but after the pens and the jelly beans, this was hardly the worst thing they'd done.

"Why are you staring at me like that?" Arik asked. "You know, I've stabbed men for much less."

"You have not," Verix said. "But you should probably stop staring, friend."

"Sorry," I said. "You look like someone I knew once. We haven't met, but I am truly one of your greatest fans. I've written extensively about both of you."

They exchanged worried glances and slowly backed their

horses away from me. "Ah. Um," Verix said. "So, is that why you were involved in one of Dyfantus' crazy sex parties? Do you write erotic fiction about us?"

"I wasn't involved in any sex party! They only had us tied to a tree."

"I'd block it from my memory, too, if a bunch of evil knights had me tied to a tree and did unspeakable things to me," Verix said. "But we're not here to judge you."

"Quite right," Arik said. "Whatever happened is your own business."

"I swear to you, nothing happened to me. They had me tied to a tree, and they were going to have me fight a scribe named Geoff with a pen."

"With your penis?" Arik said.

Verix added, "That's a different type of 'sword fight' than I'm trained for."

"I said pen. Pen!"

"Oh. My apologies," Arik said. "We, of course, believe your story."

Verix snickered, then gave me the "sort of" sign with his hands. "Even if we've never heard of people dueling with pens before."

"We're both scribes!" I said. "They must have thought it was some sort of poetic justice. And how is it less believable than our dueling with our man parts? Who's ever heard of men dueling with those?"

"As I said, we believe you," Verix said.

Arik tried her hardest to suppress a laugh. "Whatever the case, you're safe from ever having to duel with anything again. We can take you to our camp nearby, then we'll come back with more men and arrest Dyfantus for his crimes. I still don't get why he doesn't like us."

"Well, you did beat him in the spelling bee," Verix pointed out.

"It wasn't my fault they picked 'Dyfantus' as the last word, and I still don't see why they put proper names in there."

"It's his thing. He always pays them off to use his name as the final word, though it's really more my fault for making faces at him so he'd misspell it first."

"Whatever you do," I said, "make sure you get my ring back. If he loses it, I'll sue."

There was a rustling noise from the bushes to their left as Weel and Axin emerged with poor Geoff tied to Weel's mount.

"Knights, bewaaaaaare!" Axin sang in a deep baritone. "The duo beyond compaaaaaare!"

"It's Axin and Weeeeeel!" Weel sang in a falsetto.

"Showing their steeeeel!"

"Oh, bravo," Arik said, clapping. "That was probably your finest performance yet."

"Very nice," Verix said, "though not quite as good as when you attacked the school full of sick children."

"You are both too kind," Axin said, "but I think I was a bit off. I didn't hold 'compare' quite as long as I would have liked."

"You are too demure, my companion. You held it splendidly."

"Thank you, Weel, but now on to business. You two have something I want."

"Self-respect?" Verix said.

"Morals?" Arik said.

"Literacy?" I said.

"Basic hygiene?" Geoff said.

"The capacity to grow chest hair?" Weel said.

Axin scowled. "Hey! Whose side are you on, Weel?"

"Sorry. I forgot. Hand over the scribe."

"You already have one," I said. "He's tied to your horse, and his name is Geoff."

"He's writing on your saddle right now, Weel," Verix said.

"Hey," Weel said. "We do have one. Why didn't you notice him, Axin?"

"My apologies, gentlemen. Everything seems to be in order. We'll just be going on our way now."

Weel smacked himself on the forehead. "How could we have neglected that? As greatly as I'd like assail you two nincompoops, we do have our priorities. We'll abscond from you dastards in this instance, but subsequently we shan't have a prisoner to surveil."

"Yeah, and next time . . ." Axin smacked his fist against the palm of his other hand. "Watch out."

They both left the way they'd come. After we were sure they were out of hearing range, we all let out a big laugh.

"I can't believe it worked," Arik said.

"You, my friend, are a genius," Verix said. "What is your name?"

"My name is Harrold, or Harry for short. I'm an author, or what you might call a scribe. I was named after a famous Viking king, Harrold Bluetooth."

"Well, your teeth don't appear very blue," Verix said. "They are actually the whitest teeth I've ever seen."

"He's a scribe," Arik said. "I'll bet his fingers are blue all the time. We should call him Harrold Bluefingers!"

"Was that an attempt at humor, Arik?" Verix gave her a patronizing smile. "You're getting there."

"I've been practicing for weeks." She motioned toward me. "Harry, climb on behind me."

I walked over and attempted to climb onto the back of her horse. I quickly slid off and landed on my butt. After five more unsuccessful attempts, I stared up in disbelief. It looked so easy in the movies. "Do you have a stepstool?"

"For the love of The One, Verix, climb off and push him up."

From the same bushes that Axin and Weel had left through,

there was another rustling. Dyfantus emerged with both followers held by the ear—a rather impressive feat for someone on horseback.

"We really need to put a lock on those bushes," Verix said.

"You may have fooled my assistants," Dyfantus said, "but you can't fool me."

"You tell 'em, boss," Axin said.

"You cannot fool the magnificent one!" Weel said.

"Quiet, half-wits."

"You know, Dyfantus, they can't kiss your butt as easily when you're holding on to their ears like that," Verix said.

Dyfantus let go of them and drew his sword. Arik and Verix followed suit. Geoff wielded a pen in the guard position.

"I'll take Dyfantus, Verix," Arik said.

He nodded. "And I'll see if I can pry the other two off his backside."

"As much as I do like to see you two fail," Dyfantus said, "this is hardly a fair fight. I'll take you both on. You'll find I'm much more difficult to slay than the sheep you killed last week."

"You know we didn't kill those sheep," Verix said. "Why did you tell the duke that?"

"I thought you should get credit for killing something. Besides, I still owe you for taking my sweet Syra from me."

Oh, lovely. They had made up a backstory that wasn't in my books. Now, I either had to create a new character or have some very confused readers. I guessed it could be worse; they could have made her a werewolf or some other creature that did not even exist in my world.

Verix and Arik attacked Dyfantus from opposite sides. Their swordsmanship was truly marvelous. At least these actors were highly trained. I had honestly expected them to attempt to stab each other with the wrong end of the sword. Dyfantus expertly managed to fend off both of my protectors and seemed bored with the effort.

While I do love a good sword fight, I decided that this didn't look like a sure thing, so I would sneak away while they were distracted. I figured that if I could run off the set, I might manage to ruin the show and end it early. I slowly inched to the right so I'd be as far out of everyone's line of sight as possible before I bolted. When I turned, I realized that direction led straight toward a field, so I made a quick right to get back to the cover of the forest.

That slight turn put me back into the peripheral vision of Weel.

"Axin! Our detainee is attempting a withdrawal."

"No, he's not, idiot. You still have him tied to your saddle." Axin pointed at Geoff.

"Not him. The other individual."

"What other one? We came here looking for our escaped scribe, and then Arik and Verix helpfully reminded us that we had had him tied to your saddle the whole time."

"We had two scriveners. Recall the mud monster?"

"That's right! And the fellow running away looks kind of like him."

"That *is* our mire fiend. Now, go obtain him. My equine cannot hasten with any alacrity while this other transcriber is affixed."

In a matter of seconds, Axin had chased me down and was circling in front of me. I was fearful of being hit in the head again, so I covered it and cowered in a ball. Don't think too poorly of me; I'm a writer, and my brain is my most useful asset. Some might argue my only useful asset, but they probably haven't seen me naked.

I could hear another horse closing in behind me, so I peeked between my fingers. It was Weel. He, surprisingly, had moved slowly enough to not drag Geoff on the ground. Perhaps he was not as despicable as he was advertised.

Weel said, "First, we have the duo over there, Axin, who are too valiant for their own prosperity, and then we have this invertebrate who cannot even impersonate a man for a millisecond."

"And I was so looking forward to smacking him around."

"You can nevertheless, companion."

"But there's no challenge when they get like that."

"Have you heard of polo? You could smack him with your hammer from horseback. It would be good practice."

"An excellent idea."

Axin charged his horse toward me, but I managed to roll to the side before he got to me. I was so upset that he had nearly hit me that I almost stood up and yelled at the idiot actor, but it dawned on me that he had probably missed on purpose. They couldn't afford to harm their star.

"Let me display how it is accomplished, compatriot. Observe this exhibition of excellence." Weel charged his horse as well, but it stumbled. "Something is unbalanced about this beast. Oh, yes: the scrivener. My recollection neglected him."

Fortunately, he had noticed Geoff after he had only dragged him a little way. I'd imagine it still hadn't been a pleasant experience, but Geoff only had a few scrapes and nothing worse. I was really hoping that Geoff's mouth might swell shut, but that was highly unlikely. Does thinking that make me a bad person?

"Let me cut him loose for you," Axin said. "I know you're right-handed, and that cut will be awkward for you." Axin moved his horse to the left of Weel's and a little behind him.

"I can get him myself, thank you. I am cognizant that you are merely attempting to disparage me in front of our master."

"I am not. He's not even looking at us. Just let me help."

As Axin attempted to cut the rope, Weel grabbed him, and they started to wrestle while still in their respective saddles.

Geoff, having learned his lesson from before, grabbed Weel's fallen sword and quickly cut himself loose.

A moment of bravery and inspiration hit me. I stood up from my crouch and waved my hands toward them. "Hey, dummies. Neither of you will get me if I run away."

I took off in the opposite direction from Weel.

Surprise and confusion registered on Axin's face. He immediately stopped fighting, and in his disorientation, assisted by Weel's jostling, attempted to turn his horse sharply in my direction. Unfortunately, Weel was also attempting to move forward, but not at quite the same angle. As I had planned, they ran their horses together.

I stopped to view the carnage, though I really should have continued running. It's really hard not to stop and stare at an accident. I was sure the horses would be all right, as they both stood up immediately after depositing their masters on the ground. They had to have been those specially trained stunt horses.

I begrudgingly waved Geoff toward me in my quest to run away. At the very least, he could provide a distraction from my eventual pursuers.

I SHALL CALL HIM MOPPY

With the sound of pursuit passed, we arrived at a beach that seemed to stretch into oblivion. The crystal-clear water appeared fairly calm, with the occasional wave limping in to the sand. No shore was visible across the way, so I assumed it must be Lake Superior or one of the larger lakes of Minnesota doubling as the Garandian Straits.

Finally, out of breath, we came to a much-needed stop. No cars or other indications of modern civilization were in sight, so my plan to escape this production had so far failed. The charade would have to go on a while longer. I was rather impressed that I hadn't seen a camera so far. They really did a good job of hiding them.

"Geoff, do you know of a safe place nearby?" I asked.

"Well, my best friend Geoffio is on a ship not too far from here. They've been hauling supplies and troops for my benefactor, the magnanimous Lord Hartin."

"Wait. Geoffio? Why don't they call him Geoff instead? Doesn't that get confusing?"

"No, we refer to him as Moppy."

"If your name is Mopansin, why don't they call you Moppy and him Geoff?"

"He likes to mop. He excels at it."

"Then, why do they call you Geoff?"

"Because Moppy was taken already, naturally."

"Couldn't you go by Pan, then? Oh, forget it. Lead the way to this ship."

Fortunately, Geoff had learned the art of moving and talking at the same time, and he began to move forward. "Moppy and I grew up together, you know. We were quite the rascals in our youth. The townsfolk in our home, Durnstil, called us the Three Wrapping Rapscallions of Repast. Care to guess why they called us that?"

"Not really." I was starting to learn my lesson with him. Unfortunately, he was only able to move and talk at the same time. Expecting him to listen as well was too much.

"Well, at our annual harvest feast once, the three of us snuck in early. We were all twelve at the time. Upon seeing the colossal feast before us, we, being the troublemakers that we were, decided to make a little mischief. Now, I know what you're thinking, but no, we were not the kind of rogues who would do something dastardly, like contaminate the food; we merely made up our minds to . . ." He had to stop for a good three minutes to contain his laughter, which gave me time to think over my life choices. "We . . . oh, my . . . we . . . took all of the food and replaced it with a very lifelike painting of the same food. Can you believe it?"

"Yes. Now, can we move on?"

"We then put the food back in the opposite order. Oh, our parents were so angry at us."

"That's great."

"The three of us were quite the trio. You know, I should tell you about the time we caught the reeve's three-year-old son. That one really got us our nom de prank, as it were."

You're probably wondering why he kept referring to himself and Moppy as three. Well, I, being thoroughly annoyed by the copious volume of uselessness projecting from his mouth, decided, in my infinite wisdom, not to ask, for fear of dying of old age waiting for him to get to the point.

"Fascinating. Now, the ship?"

We walked in surprising silence for the next ten minutes. His mouth must have finally gotten tired, as improbable as it seems, but I could think of no other explanation. I thought about running off into the trees, away from where this terrible show was taking me, but I could hear hoofbeats in the distance; clearly, they knew how to keep me here.

Geoff eventually led us into a pass between several large boulders, one that I would not have been able to see without his guidance. The path wound down to the sea, or the lake, or whatever it actually was.

We approached a small cargo ship that sat there like it was waiting for someone to wake it, or for a couple of actors to arrive. Its crew looked like a tattoo parlor had exploded onto a baldness convention. I hadn't seen that many shiny heads since I'd passed by a Vin Diesel lookalike contest. Clearly, this collection of baldness was not due to heredity, as the crew was probably the most ethnically diverse group I'd encountered outside of the It's a Small World ride at Disneyland.

"Does the captain only recruit bald men, or does he make them shave?" I asked.

"They are not all of the masculine persuasion."

Hmm . . . he was right. Some of them had breasts, and not man-boobs, as they were a rather fit group. Is it wrong that I was a little turned on? For some reason, most men find bald women very unattractive. Is it wrong that I've even asked, "Is it wrong that I was a little turned on"? I was, and still am, very confused.

"Why are they all bald?"

"The captain is of the opinion that their having glossy craniums will make his crew lighter and quicker."

"That can't make much of a difference."

"He's also self-conscious about his baldness."

"Is he going to make us shave?" God, I hoped not. Baldness is usually not a good look on a white guy, with a few notable exceptions like Patrick Stewart and . . . Patrick Stewart.

"He usually won't make passengers do it, unless he's in a really foul mood or it's his birthday."

"On his birthday?"

"He came into this world sans hair, so he thinks everyone else should be bald to celebrate that event."

"Do you perhaps have any other friends on boats nearby?"

"Well, there is Pan, but his captain makes everyone strip naked."

"Wouldn't everyone get sick in bad weather? What with being wet and naked, I mean."

"They do have a rather high mortality rate."

"Moppy's boat it is, then." I sprinted toward it to get this over with as soon as possible, and Geoff dutifully followed.

"Hail, good Moppy!" Geoff (Mopansin, not Geoffio) said to the boat of shiny-headed men and women.

A young, tanned man stuck his head over the side. ""Geoff! What brings you around?"

"I heard you were hauling supplies for my glorious patron, the Lord of Hartin. Are you perhaps going back to his beautiful and abundant territory soon?"

"We are under contract with Lord Hartin, but we're not going back to Forestin. Hammurabi Joudisz is aboard. We're heading to New Atlia City."

In my books, Hammurabi Joudisz was the New Atlian representative to Garandia. The semi-autonomous region of New Atlia was founded within Garandia by the survivors of Old Atlia after its fall about seventy-five years ago. The Atlians were the pillars of learning and intellect on this world. They were also the only practitioners of magic, outside of the Old Gods, who hadn't been heard from in a few hundred years. Most people assumed they had all retired.

"Do you want to travel there instead?" Geoff said to me.

"Anywhere is better than this."

"May we book passage, Moppy?"

Moppy disappeared from view, but I could hear him ask, "Captain, do we have room for two more passengers? I'll vouch for them."

The captain peeked over the side. "Can you pay?"

Geoff pulled out a few coins from his shoe, and I pulled out another silver dollar. I was so glad that my grandpa had taught me to always carry a few silver dollars with me. He had told me, "You never know when you'll need one," which, until this journey, had never been true. I mostly kept them on me as a way to remember him.

"Will this do, Captain?" I said.

"Get on, but hurry up about it. I don't have a lot of time."

A rope ladder rolled over the side.

"Do you think we'll have to shave our heads?" I whispered to Moppy.

"The captain wouldn't dare make a high-ranking official such as Hammurabi Joudisz shave, so you should be safe."

We both quickly climbed the ladder.

"We're about to shove off," the captain said. "All passengers need to be below while we prepare. And stay out of my way, if you know what's good for you."

I almost asked if we needed to also set our tray tables in the upright position and remain seated, but thought it best not to upset someone who had the power to shave me bald.

After paying the captain, we quickly went below deck to meet our fellow passenger. Geoff wanted desperately to catch up with Moppy, but his friend had told him to go below or else the captain wouldn't stop at just shaving his head.

In my books, Hammurabi was the highly intelligent, moral compass for the empire of Garandia. He didn't drink, smoke, gamble, swear, cheat on his taxes, jaywalk, or do anything else that's morally or legally wrong. He was like a less religious Jesus, but dark-skinned. (Unless you believe Jesus had dark skin; then he was exactly like Jesus.)

I grinned like an idiot as I approached Hammurabi. It's so cool to meet one of your characters in the flesh, even if he's being portrayed by an actor. (And, no, a fat white guy in a homemade costume at a convention doesn't count.) Hammurabi was dressed perfectly in the hooded multi-toned purple robes of the healer caste. He was sitting at a small table joking with a few crewmen.

As I got closer, he looked up. "What the &%$! are you looking at, you goofy #*^%?"

My jaw dropped. "Hammurabi Joudisz is supposed to be the pillar of moral virtue. Who do you think you are, taking such license with my character? Also, why are you speaking in symbols instead of using actual curse words?"

Hammurabi stood, towering over me. "I think I know who I am, you lily-white #$%^#$*. And who appointed you the moral police?" Then, he slapped me.

Evidently, my views on man-on-man slapping were not as widely held as I had thought. Being on camera during a slap fight with one of your best-known characters is probably not a good idea. Hilarious, sure, but probably not good for your reputation. I wondered if the director of this show was trying to get a good clip for advertisements, so I decided not to retaliate. Well, that and the fact that Hammurabi was about fifty pounds of muscle heavier than me.

"My apologies, sir," I said. "What exactly is there to do around here?"

The tension slowly drained from Hammurabi's face, and his left eyebrow rose slightly. "Do you have any money, gentlemen?"

"A little. Why?"

"Would you like to play a few hands of Garandian Slims? Buy-in is two trakons."

Did these writers even read my books? The next thing I knew, this character was going to bring in some prostitutes, down a keg of ale, and slap a few babies. Maybe they could follow that up with a remake of *Lord of the Rings* involving a seven-foot-tall Frodo and a female Gandalf?

Hmm . . . Shaq as Frodo and Betty White as Gandalf might not actually be too bad.

"I suppose," Geoff said. "There does not appear to be much else to do. I am a wizard at mathematics—no offense, sir wizard —so this should come easily to me."

"So, you two have never played before?" We both shook our heads no, which made Hammurabi grin widely. "Splendid! I think I've found some new friends."

I sighed and tossed in my last two silver dollars.

SHINY, HAPPY PIRATES

After a few hours under the exhausting gaze of Hammurabi, I managed to break even. I guess it helps when you've invented the rules of the game, though not as much as you'd think. Hammurabi was an expert of the game, unfortunately. He cleaned poor Geoff out of everything he had on him, minus (fortunately) the clothes on his back. Most of the sailors did little better than Geoff. One of them did literally lose the clothes off his back, and I do mean everything. It seemed the captain didn't stop at shaving his crewmen's heads; either that or this sailor had lost another game where he had somehow managed to gamble away every hair on his body.

"I think that's enough for me," I said.

"We still have at least an hour," Hammurabi said as he finished off his fifth beer. "What's wrong? Are your lady parts acting up?"

"Says the guy in the dress."

I know it's wrong to taunt a guy for wearing exactly what I wrote him in (and doubly so, since a robe isn't a dress), but it's not right for a guy to make fun of the creator of the world he's in.

He looked like he was going to reach across the table and do not-so-pleasant things to me, so I scampered out of his reach.

"My associate, here, is all out of money, and he really needs to talk to his childhood friend above. So, I think we'll be going."

"That's quite all right, Harrold," Geoff said. "This game is fascinating. I think I'm getting the hang of it. I don't suppose you could spare a little for a comrade in capture?"

"Harrold?" Hammurabi said. "Aren't you the guy that Axin and Weel had their way with?"

"How could you possibly know that?" I asked. "We only escaped from them a few hours ago."

"Hammurabi knows."

It really sucks, having one of your most famous sayings thrown back in your face. I gave him a dirty look, though not too dirty, as he still looked like he wanted to hit me.

"So, you *are* the guy, then?" Hammurabi said.

"No, and they only had me prisoner for under an hour."

"There's a lot you can do in under an hour. I do miss my single days. It's said that all of the prostitutes in Garandia wept for days when I got married."

I decided that enough was enough and that I had to get away from this highly inaccurate representation of my peerless character. Being that he was my only possible excuse to get away, I grabbed Geoff from his chair and dragged him along. Fortunately, Geoff weighed only as much as one of those large colonial dolls with the big frilly dresses—not that I'm an expert on those.

As we made our way to the stairs, Hammurabi locked me in his unnerving gaze. Already taller than I by several inches, he appeared to be getting even taller as he stood. His eyes seemed to search me for something hidden deep inside. When he appeared satisfied that there was neither anything deep nor hidden about me, he sat back down and waved me away. As I ascended the stairs, I glanced back and saw that he appeared to be mimicking what he thought had been done to me with his hands, to the uproarious laughter of the sailors. Normally, I would have offered a scathing rebuke, but I had more important things on my mind.

Once on deck, we could see land getting closer by the minute. As we had shoved off from Sculan a little over two hours before, this must have represented the northern coast of New Atlia. New Atlia City shouldn't have been too far away.

"How much longer do we have?" I said to the captain.

"About an hour," he replied without turning.

With nothing on land yet visible, I needed something else to occupy me. I wisely decided to stay distant from Geoff. Fortunately, my wait only lasted about ten minutes.

"Ship sighted to starboard!" a voice from the crow's nest said.

When I looked up, I was sure that his supposed spyglass was actually a small camera. Either they were getting sloppy, or I was seeing things. This show would have been so much better for them if I thought this was all real, but I was too clever.

When I turned around, the other ship was a lot closer than I had assumed, so close that I could see the faces of its crew. On its prow, the ship bore a rather fearsome dragon figurehead—not a good sign. I don't know of many friendly ships with dragons on the front, do you? Granted, modern ships don't have figureheads, but can you imagine any friendly ships in a fantasy world with dragons on them?

I didn't think so.

The captain gestured wildly. "All hands on deck! All hands on deck! Line up, men! Line to starboard!"

"Should I go get Hammurabi, Captain?" I asked.

"No, my men can handle this. Besides, what's he going to do? Heal them to death? Make all the plants grow *on a ship*? I can't risk the life of such an important person, anyway."

I considered suggesting that Hammurabi could just glare them into submission, but the captain was too far away.

From all about the ship, sailors scurried onto the deck. Some climbed down from the rigging. Others came charging from below. I think I even saw a few climb up the side of the ship. After about three minutes, the starboard side of the ship was full of sailors lined up perfectly in two rows, with the shortest in the front. Were they planning to combat the enemy with song?

"You all know the drill. In a couple of minutes, we'll show them that we are not to be trifled with."

I assumed they were preparing to be boarded, though I found it odd that so few of them seemed to be armed. Maybe they knew kung fu? They were all shaved like Shaolin monks, after all, and I had created a pirate crew that knew kung fu in my second book. I probably should have gone somewhere safer at this point, but I was too caught up in the spectacle.

"First line, kneel. Now, tilt!" All of the crewmen inclined the tops of their heads toward the approaching ship.

I had seen some strange things in my day, but this was probably the strangest. From the mass of bald heads, a glaring light shone onto the approaching ship. At the time, I couldn't believe that it actually worked, but I later found out that the captain had bought a "magic" wax and had made the crewmen wax their heads thoroughly before every meal.

On the other ship, the crewman on deck were cowering in their blindness, paralyzed by the power of bald. I couldn't believe how bright the light was. In my mind, the captain was no longer an eccentric with baldness inadequacies; the captain was a genius . . . who also happened to be an eccentric with baldness inadequacies.

After several minutes, I noticed a severe flaw in the captain's plan: the other ship was heading straight for us, and no one on board could see or move enough to steer. Now, I know what you're thinking, and yes, our captain had remembered to leave crewmen free to steer and navigate our ship. Unfortunately, the other ship had the wind and was coming fast.

As he settled from his glee-filled dance, our captain finally noticed this. "Prepare for boarding! To the weapons!"

As sailors frantically gathered weapons, the other ship crashed hard into our side. The power of the collision knocked me hard on my back, and I fell into a large pile of rope. While I grappled with my rope-ponent, I lost track of what was going on.

When I finally won my epic battle with the world's wiliest rope, fighting was going on all around me. To my dismay, none of the bald crewmen were using kung fu. At least there was some rather excellent swordplay going on. No, not the Hollywood swashbuckling kind. Actual men doing everything they could to try to kill each other, with lots of hacking, punching, spitting, elbowing, and eye gouging, without the least bit of slapping. Seeing this going on all around me, I did what any sensible person would: I cowered and rolled up into a ball. There are many great songs and stories about brave warriors in battle, but most people forget that most of them don't live to old age. I knew, deep down, that this was only a very well-choreographed act, but it all seemed so real.

As I looked up through the gaps between my fingers, I found the enemy captain. How did I know he was the enemy captain? Well, he had a majestic black beard, for one thing. Aren't all pirate captains well-bearded? He was also dressed much nicer than any of his men; his clothes screamed *pirate captain.*

"Kill the pirate scum, men!" the pirate captain said.

After what seemed like an hour, but was likely only a few minutes, the fighting finally died down. One crew being completely bald did make it very easy to see what side everyone was on. The pirates had killed several of our crew, but most of ours realized how outnumbered they were and surrendered.

"You, there, in the ball," the pirate captain said. "Come here."

I was greatly disappointed that my hiding spot right in front of the steps had been so easily uncovered. Realizing that I didn't really have a choice, I rose. I am proud to say that I did not wet myself in fear. I guess I was starting to get the hang of this whole peril thing.

"Who are you, and what part do you have in this crew?"

"I'm a writer and a passenger on this ship. Are you going to make me walk the plank?"

The pirate captain scratched his forehead. "Walk the what? Why would I do that?"

"You're a pirate, and pirates always make prisoners walk the plank."

"Why would anyone make people walk the plank? First, you have to carry a special extra-long plank around just for that. That's expensive. Then, you kill people unnecessarily. Why do that when you can ransom them? And really, dropping someone in the ocean is not a very effective way to kill them. They might swim away and live."

"You could shoot them after they fall in to make sure they die."

"Wouldn't it be more effective to shoot them on board? It's much easier to hit them, and then you don't need to bring a special plank."

He had really thought this out. That must be why he was the captain.

Why *do* pirates always make prisoners walk the plank? I wondered if Hollywood was being influenced by the powerful plank makers industry. Or was Hollywood secretly run by them? I would have to investigate this later.

"Why do you keep calling us pirates, anyway? Your ship attacked us."

"Well, you do have a dragon on your prow, and pirates always have fearsome or lewd figureheads."

"The dragon is the corporate symbol for Dragon Deliveries, LLC."

"Well, why was your ship charging us?"

"We weren't. We saw Lord Hartin's flag and thought we would ask your captain for news of the war."

"Oh. What will you do with the crew and this ship now?"

"If you're not pirates, as you allege, then we'll let you all go."

It was then that several members of the Dragon Deliveries crew brought the poorly acted and foul-mouthed Hammurabi Joudisz from below.

"Do you know who I am, you mermaid-sucking, fish-#%&* @%#&?"

The captain's eyes widened. "Unhand him, men. Of course we know who you are, Your Excellency."

"Damn right. And while I may be excellent, I am not a noble. You may address me as Representative Hammurabi, or you can kiss my $%^ some more for wasting my time. Now, what is the meaning of this?"

"Well, Representative, there appears to have been a misunderstanding. We thought that ship was a pirate ship, and their crew were evidently under the same impression of us." The dragon captain then motioned for his men to let Captain Bald loose.

Captain Bald brushed himself off and rubbed his head. "They appeared to be attacking."

Hammurabi stalked forward. "But they weren't, correct?"

Captain Bald's shoulders slumped. "I thought they were, Representative, but . . . perhaps they weren't? They appeared to be approaching in a threatening manner, I mean, sir. Their prow was definitely glaring at us."

Hammurabi scowled like I do when my computer forgets to save hours of quality writing, and let loose a blinding green bolt.

When my sight returned, the captain was weeping on the deck

in the fetal position—my signature move—though he appeared unharmed.

"For the sake of The One, man, get up. I was just angry at you. You know my magic can't hurt you."

"Yes, sir. Sorry, sir."

Hammurabi pulled the captain to his feet. "You should show a little more backbone, especially in front of your crew."

"You are correct, as always, sir."

Hammurabi caught the dragon captain out of the corner of his eye and beckoned him forward. "What is it?"

"My apologies, Representative, but, well—my boss has us on a very tight schedule, and seeing as how the crown of Garandia is one of our biggest shareholders, I was wondering if, maybe, we could, that is, ahh, leave?"

Hammurabi waved them away.

With a speed not seen since I outran those angry kindergarteners, the dragon captain and his crew scurried off and had their ship underway in the blink of an eye.

Hammurabi ground his teeth. "I guess I was a little hard on you, Captain, but I have a lot on my mind. I'll make it up to you by healing your wounded."

Without another word, he strode away, and the green glow of his magic soon covered the opposite side of the ship. The captain, now free from Hammurabi's overpowering aura, began barking orders like a mad dog.

It occurred to me that it had been quite some time since I had heard a peep out of Geoff. After searching for several minutes, I noticed a pile of rags moving on its own. At first, I thought it impossible that even such a thin, gangly man as Geoff could be hiding in a foot-high pile of rags, and I was amazed when his mop of eternally disheveled hair emerged.

"Are you double-jointed, or a contortionist?"

"Well, when I was younger," the pile of rags said, "I was

forever pursued by bullies. This was before I befriended Moppy and Pan, mind you. So, I became proficient at hiding in whatever was convenient: piles of laundry, packs of dogs, toy wagons, formations of lawn gnomes, tea sets . . ."

"How did you fit inside a tea set?"

A head popped out of the rags. "It was a giant tea set."

"Why would anyone make a giant tea set?"

"Giants need tea, too."

"Where have you ever seen a giant?" There were no giants in my world. None.

"Just because we haven't seen one doesn't mean we shouldn't be prepared."

"Shouldn't a tea set be pretty low on the list of things to make in case you meet a giant?"

"You don't know that giants dislike tea. They might favor tea a great deal, and if they do, they would really need a tea set."

I wept into my hands.

"If a giant were to arrive in our land and found we didn't have tea for him to consume, he might get very angry. And as we all know, angry giants do like to rampage. It's what they're known for, after all. So, in their infinite wisdom, the elders of my village, the cozy and underrated Durnstil, created a giant tea set to avoid just such a rampage."

It was at this moment that I decided there would never be giants in the world of Vyenra. I might not have really tall people, either. Six feet, three inches might be as tall as people would get in the series. I was also heavily in favor of not having tea.

Before I could attempt to slap the stupid out of Geoff, Hammurabi shambled over, hunching slightly due to the toll of his magic. In spite of his discomfort, he managed to maintain a nonchalant yet purposeful look on his face. "Greetings, gentlemen. My apologies for taking your money earlier, Geoff. I sometimes get caught up in the game and forget my manners." He handed Geoff a few coins. "So, where are you gentlemen heading in New Atlia?"

"I hope to get passage back to Lord Hartin's estate in the capital," Geoff said.

"I'm looking for a phone," I said. "I need to call my assistant."

"A phone . . . hmm. Do you mean the Phoine of Destiny, the ancient artifact that is kept in the Vault of Kings in the royal palace? It is reported to be the only thing that can reach the First World."

So, that was how they expected me to get out of there. The classic fantasy quest to find the all-powerful artifact. Did this mean I was Dorothy? I hoped so; I would really like some ruby slippers. Although, maybe not—shiny red things weren't super-manly and they wouldn't go with anything I had. Werewolf-hide boots? There weren't any werewolves in my world, but for some awesome boots, I could make an exception.

"I'm off to see the wizard, then!" I said.

"I *am* a wizard."

"Never mind. It's a metaphor. I guess I'm headed to the capital, too, then. Care for some company, Geoff?"

I really wasn't thinking at that point. I had a tendency to say things without thinking them through, though usually only around women.

"Your company would be most appreciated, Harrold."

"If you're headed that way, perhaps you can do me a favor," Hammurabi said. "It's probably best discussed over dinner. Would you care to accompany me back to my estate? I can give you lodgings for the night and should even be able to offer you an escort back to the capital."

Hammurabi's expression was eerily sincere as he spoke. Given that, and the fact that he hadn't cursed once through all of this, I had a very suspicious feeling.

"That sounds magnificent," Geoff said. "To be invited to the personal lodgings of one of the most illustrious individuals in all of the Garandian Empire? You honor us greatly, sir."

I raised my hand, and Hammurabi nodded reluctantly in response. "Why is the Phoine 'of Destiny'?"

"I'm not sure. All I know is that it's an all-powerful artifact. Only the king may grant access to it."

"Are there any other artifacts called 'Phoine,' like the Phoine of Power or the Phoine of Armpit Noises?"

"Well, no."

"It's always bothered me that they have to add a prepositional phrase to the names of powerful artifacts. Why can't it just be the Phoine?"

"Well," Hammurabi said, "that doesn't sound as impressive. I mean, 'of Destiny' says a lot more about it."

"What destiny does it fulfill?"

"No one knows. Perhaps its destiny is to tell us what its destiny is."

"I contend that it would sound more impressive and accurate if it was just called the Phoine, like 'Madonna' is better than Madonna Ciccone."

"You might be right, Harry. Perhaps you can take this matter up with the king."

The pit of my stomach dropped sharply. Me? Meet the king? But I was only an author, and too lowly to converse with a king, especially one as spectacular as Good King Berin.

Wait! What was I thinking? I had created this king, and he was only an actor. Of course I could meet this king, and he should bow to me! I was starting to get caught up in this whole show and believe it was real.

A BEAUTIFUL WOMAN MAKES ME DO SOMETHING STUPID

Captain Bald was all too happy to be rid of us and quickly chased us from the ship as soon as we hit the docks. I didn't mind the fact that he had treated the star of the show so rudely once I saw my beautiful city come to life. Thin white towers jutted in reckless abandon from all about the landscape, most of which was covered in a blinding white marble, the majesty of which could only be created through the use of the crafting line of Atlian magic, or an excessive amount of special effects. It's one thing to write about a fantastic city, but to see your creation displayed before you is a truly breathtaking experience. I'm not ashamed that I drooled a little.

The people bustling throughout the city bore the rainbow of colors that were the hallmark of Atlian society: the multi-hued purples of the healer caste, the browns and reds of the workers, the blacks and greens of the warrior caste, the yellows and whites of the artisans, the grays of the diplomats and politicians, and the blues of the naval and trade caste. Some might say the crowd looked like a crayon box had thrown up, but while the colorful crowd was a little jarring at first, I found myself transfixed in utter delight by the mesmerizing scene before me. My reaction may have been a bit biased, though. Sprinkled throughout the crowd were the occasional Garandians, visible both for their bland clothing and their pale skin.

I slapped myself to make sure I wasn't dreaming and found yet another time when it was alright for a man to slap a man. My theory on man-slapping was clearly failing miserably.

So transfixed was I by the sights that I barely observed where we were going as Hammurabi strong-armed me through the city. I finally became cognizant of my immediate surroundings when the light dimmed considerably as we entered Hammurabi's home. His house was actually a little bit of a letdown. It was possible my senses were skewed by the sight of the gorgeous city outside, however. The furnishings were of an exceptionally high quality, though I was struck by their scarcity. The only adornments in the main entranceway were two very bland chairs and a modest end table with a tiny painting behind it.

We exited the receiving area into the dining room. This room had an excessively long table made of a glimmering polished wood with a full complement of chairs—probably around thirty— as well as a few humble paintings. From such a large room, I expected more. Hammurabi was known as an extravagant host and a wealthy man, so this whole house was very out of place. You'd think they would have spent more money on furnishing the place, instead of on the city outside, since we were likely to spend more time inside than out.

Hammurabi gave me a wicked grin. "The less accurate information people have about you, the better. I find it best for people to think that I'm not well-off financially."

From the door opposite us, a tall, slender woman in her forties emerged. Her long, shimmering dark hair complemented her glowing gray robe perfectly. This had to be Hammurabi's wife, Teragonna, and she was even more stunning in person than I had pictured her in my imagination.

"Rabi, you old scoundrel, what trouble have you gotten our family into this time?" she said.

Hammurabi grinned and embraced her. "Nothing they'll ever catch me for."

"And who are these gentlemen?"

"The shorter one is Mopansin Trantinviavax III, more commonly known as Geoff. He manages Lord Hartin's finances and organizes his many tournaments."

"A pleasure, my lady." Geoff kissed her hand. "Your elegance is only outdone by your magnificent decorating touch. Why, this entire home is but an extension of your style and splendor."

For what was probably the first time since I'd met him, I was terribly jealous of Geoff. I would have to outdo him with my famous sexy eyebrow waggle.

"Why is your nickname Geoff, instead of something closer to your name?" Teragonna said.

I stuck both of my hands over Geoff's mouth. "It's his middle name." That explanation had been ridiculous enough the first time. I didn't want to have to go through it again.

"And this is Harry Olson, a scribe," Hammurabi said.

"Nice to meet you," I said, trying not to stare at her too creepily. I'm happy to say I was getting better at it, as she didn't seem put off at all by my staring.

Is it wrong to fall in love with a character that you created? OK, I guess it is, especially when that character is married. Although . . . I don't think it's wrong to fall in love with the actress who plays the character. I didn't care that she was at least ten years older than I; beautiful is beautiful. I'd have to get her number from the director. He owed me after putting me through this absurdity.

"Weren't you the one Axin and Weel did unspeakable things to?" she said.

"No, that was someone else."

"Could you show them to some guest rooms, Gonna, while I settle in?" Hammurabi asked.

"Certainly. If you two will follow me —"

As we turned to go our separate ways, we could hear a commotion from the main entrance. It seemed like whoever was out there wanted to sell some magazine subscriptions, and the servant didn't want any. All I could make out was the word "Stop!" before the door that led to the entrance area opened. A couple of guards and a purple-robed gentleman with a powder blue sash entered the dining room. These guests were not invited; the weapons and commotion were a dead giveaway.

The robed fellow gave us the kind of look you often see on televangelists right before they ask for a donation. "Hammurabi, I am pleased that you have returned to our grandiose and exalted metropolis. It gives me no gratification to inform you that you are to accompany us to the Meriton."

Hammurabi scowled. "Artenarix, you snake-jackass hybrid. What is the meaning of this? You have no authority to demand anything of me, or anyone else, for that matter."

"Oh, but I most indubitably do. Your mentor, the Grand Meritus himself, presented the order." Artenarix turned to his guards. "If he resists, do not hesitate in the slightest to abuse him."

I should probably point out that in my books, Artenarix is Hammurabi's greatest rival. He loves showing off his ridiculous vocabulary, and I hear he's a lot of fun at parties.

How could they do this to Hammurabi? Sure, the actor was making some rather odd choices with his character, but he was one of my major characters. Someone should do something . . . someone who had more of a stake in this than I. Teragonna was too stunned to react. Geoff looked like he was about to interject, but, not wanting to look even more cowardly than he did in front of her, I jumped in.

"Halt!" I'd always wanted to say that to armed guards.

"And who are you, you plump, pale pumpkin of a personage?" Artenarix said.

"First off, that was an impressive combination of 'p' words. You didn't stumble at all." The others all turned to each other and nodded in appreciation of his accomplishment. "And as to who I am, I'm an expert on Atlian Law. I demand to know what charges Hammurabi is accused of, besides making people wet themselves when he looks at them. Other people who are not me."

"Why, there is an inquiry into his possible involvement in gambling. I assembled the evidence myself. A person in such a lofty position as his should know better. I am absolutely confident that the implications alone will be enough to have you removed from your position." Artenarix radiated a combination of self-satisfaction and malice. I was hoping he might pull something congratulating himself.

"Gambling is not illegal in the Garandian Empire," Geoff said.

"Illegal, no," Artenarix said, "but it is the pinnacle of immorality to Atlians. Your political career will likely be over, Hammurabi, and I can assure you that the process will be lengthy and humiliating. Now, guards, if you will."

"Why are there armed guards if it's not illegal?" I asked.

"True, the constables are for show. I do love pageantry, and this grand parade to the Meriton will be quite triumphant. Perhaps my greatest exploit to this point, however, I am certain there will be a great multitude of such forthcoming."

I pushed in front of Geoff. "Wait. There's procedure to follow." It helped that I had actually written the Atlian moral and legal codes. "Hammurabi is allowed to confront his accuser before being brought before the House Tribunal." I could almost see myself smirking.

"Very well. I am his accuser. So, confront me, Hammurabi."

"Why did you do this, Artenarix?" Hammurabi asked.

"Because I loathe you. There, confrontation over. Now that the procedure is complete, let us finish this charade and depart."

"Wait. What evidence do you have?" I said. "You couldn't possibly have seen him gambling with us on the ship." Have I mentioned that I say stupid things when beautiful women are present?

Artenarix's eyes lit up. "I was actually unaware of that event. As you are, therefore, a material witness, new fellow, your presence before the House Tribunal will be requested shortly. Do not leave the municipality. Now, if your stalling is concluded and you do not know anything that will further incriminate the 'Illustrious' Hammurabi Joudisz, let us depart, constables."

Hammurabi turned as he was being ushered out. "Teragonna, you know what to do."

A QUEST FOR MY PACKAGE

As they escorted Hammurabi out, Teragonna nodded to his back. "Garandia will never be the same without you, but, fortunately, you left two heroes behind to take your place. Come upstairs, gentlemen. I have a proposal for you."

I looked around for someone besides Geoff and myself in the room, but no one else was there. I was obviously one of the heroes she had mentioned. Under normal circumstances, I wouldn't even count myself as a hero, but this was my world, and, clearly, I was the protagonist. Geoff could not possibly be the second. I mean, he lost fights with butterflies and strong winds. And I, of all people, frightened him! Going up the steps, he tripped no less than five times. The only way he got up there was by me carrying him. Clearly, she'd been counting me twice.

After we'd entered what had to be the study, Teragonna shut the door behind us. As much as I hated this ridiculous parody of my world, I couldn't help but stare at Teragonna. Her strong, calm voice made me hang on to every word she said. She had that kind of presence that made me want to do everything I could to impress her. Fortunately, with Geoff there as a comparison, impressing her wouldn't likely be too hard. I reached down and put my hand on his shoulder to show her how much taller I was.

Teragonna fought back tears as she spoke. "I wasn't expecting to have to tell you both this so soon, but Artenarix has forced our hand. I had hoped to get to know you both a bit before presenting you with such a task, but I will have to trust Rabi's judgment. He is rarely ever wrong, but I would feel better if I knew either of you even a little."

Geoff looked like he was about to speak (the way he pretty much always looked), but I kicked him in the shin lightly to prevent the likely stream of nonsense. As he bent over halfway to stem the very minor bit of pain I had inflicted on him, I stood on tiptoe to give her a better look at the far superior hero.

"Whatever the quest, I accept, fair lady. Your two heroes are here." I flexed both of my arms and very kindly tripped Geoff with my foot. He fell behind me to very considerately give her an unobstructed view of my heroic left arm, Baby Dragon Slayer, and my dashing right arm, Not in the Friend Zone Anymore.

Relief flooded her face. "Don't you want to hear what the task is, first? We need you to deliver an important package to the capital."

"I do have quite a few questions," Geoff probably said. (I was too caught up with my two friends to notice.) "For instance, why wasn't Hammurabi going to deliver the package himself? And if it's so important, why would he trust it to two people he only met yesterday?"

She nodded slowly. "The numerous enemies of Garandia are on the lookout for this package, and they know Hammurabi has it, so he couldn't give it to a known associate. He told me in his last letter that he would find two honorable and trustworthy men, and, most important, not known friends of his. Two travelers who have never been to our city before are not likely to draw a connection to him."

"But I'm Artenarix's star witness. I'm not supposed to leave the city." I said that mostly because it had the word "star" in it, and I had never been called a star anything before. I puffed my chest up to show her how big of a star I really was.

"His extra attention does complicate things a bit. But you need not worry about being needed as a witness; Hammurabi is going to admit his wrongdoings to the Tribunal. So, please don't worry about your mistake. We forgive you, Harry."

"To save his family from dishonor. Of course." I hoped she was impressed enough by my immense knowledge of Atlian law to overcome that little slip-up, though with Geoff there as a comparison, I had little need to. He began to rise, so I nudged him a little.

She winced as Geoff tumbled back down. "As for cover, we already have that taken care of. You two, or, rather, two men dressed exactly like you, were seen being thrown out of this house in an angry exchange with Hammurabi's brother, Ragitsiom."

"Where could you possibly find two men who look like us in this city?" Geoff said.

"It was fairly simple. We just found two white guys and slapped a beard on the tall one."

"That doesn't sound like a very convincing disguise," I said.

"You all look alike. No one will notice."

My chest deflated a little. Geoff leaned on me for support, and I held him up. I figured I'd more than proven my point, and Teragonna nodded in approval. I was starting to get the hang of this whole hero thing.

"But Hammurabi only met us by chance," Geoff said. "How could he possibly know that two people who were strangers to him and had just happened to board the same boat as himself could be exactly the two modest but spectacular heroes he was looking for?"

I'd like to put it on record that I thought of that question first, but I didn't ask because this whole thing was ridiculous. Plus, Geoff really did need the morale boost.

"A very astute question, Geoff." Teragonna patted him on the head. "Hammurabi had a vision, and his vision told him he would find the brave individuals he was looking for on his journey home."

I'd also like to point out that I had thought of this answer first too, but I was distracted by an intensely shiny light. And, no, I don't know where it came from, nor do I know how it was possible that something so bright appeared out of nowhere and then disappeared. Trust me: there was a shiny light, and it momentarily distracted me. I swear I'm not making this up.

"If you are convinced it will work," Geoff said, "I see no reason not to take the package, especially for such an illustrious individual as Hammurabi. It never hurts to have impressive connections. So, I am also in."

She turned around and opened a chest. "Splendid. As thanks, I'd like give you both one final token of gratitude. These are two swords that belonged to Hammurabi's grandfather, the famed Admiral Kilorabi."

I swung my sword around to show her I knew what I was doing. Those two lessons had really paid off. No one lost a toe this time, either. It had served that guy right for wearing sandals to sword practice, though I'm still not sure where the ostrich came from. Shockingly, Geoff was also fairly adept with the blade, but I doubted he would be quite so impressive if he'd had an angry ostrich and an equally angry nine-toed man screeching at him.

"Splendid," Teragonna said. "It appears Rabi's intuition was right again."

I blew in Geoff's direction out of the corner of my mouth in the hope of knocking him over again, but it didn't work. Perhaps it was because I was too winded from my swordsmanship demonstration. I wasn't too concerned, as I knew I'd nail the evening wear portion of the competition.

Clearly, she must have predicted that, as she handed me—and not Geoff—an object in a dark red velvet bag. It probably helped that Geoff was unlikely to be able to carry the thing, as it weighed a hefty five pounds. I peeked inside the bag but only found an elaborately decorated wooden box.

"The contents of the box are for the king's eyes only," Teragonna said. "You are to deliver this to the king himself. The fate of Garandia is on your shoulders, gentlemen. Do not worry too much, though. The guides you are to meet are some of the finest in the land. I only wish Hammurabi was here to see you off. He didn't expect Artenarix to move quite so fast."

"He expected to be arrested?" I said. "I mean, I expect that all the time, for . . . protecting the innocents from the evil sheriff of Nottingham, but Hammurabi usually has a clever way of wiggling out of trouble."

The actress was truly amazing. She didn't even wince at my obvious Earth reference. Geoff didn't either, but after the mockery he had made of my fictitious religion, I was past giving him credit for anything.

"Not this time. That's why he came back home. He was hoping for a few days to say goodbye to his family before he was detained, but Artenarix was as quick as the snake he's often compared to."

"Why does he gamble when he knows how immoral that is to your people?" Geoff asked.

"He has been holding Garandia together since he became our representative fifteen years ago. Berin is a terrible king. He spends lavishly, with little thought for how to pay for everything. It has become Hammurabi's job to somehow find the money. In order to deal with the stress, Hammurabi started gambling and drinking."

I probably don't need to tell you that none of that was even remotely accurate. I mean, kings don't get called "the Great" for being awful. Sure, writers do (when they give up the television rights in their contracts), but not kings. I would normally have been pissed, but the actress had delivered the line with such panache.

She moved to the bookcase on the wall to my far-right and pulled out a series of books one at a time. A staircase emerged from behind the spinning bookcase. As the bookcase slid into the adjacent wall, I swore I could see a small lens breeze by. If I had blinked, I would have missed what I assumed was a camera. They would probably need to remove it in editing.

"Down these stairs, you will find a series of tunnels. They only lead in two directions. The right side leads to the docks, which are being watched thoroughly, but you are to take the left, which leads outside the city walls. Your companions will be waiting for you."

"Couldn't these people just deliver the package themselves?" I didn't really care about their silly quest. I was trying anything I could think of to prolong my time with her.

"These three are mercenaries, very good ones and highly dependable, but still mercenaries at heart. We do not fully trust people whose major motivation is coin. Hammurabi thought it best to put his faith in you two gentlemen. He has a good eye for honorable and trustworthy people."

I winked and pointed my best feature—my forehead—toward her. "I will fulfill your epic quest, milady."

She said goodbye and kissed us each on the cheek. My kiss lasted at least a second longer.

As she leaned back, I whispered, "Perhaps, when this is all over, we could grab a drink. I am a rich author, after all." (I'm not, which is why I charge fifty dollars for an autograph, by the way, but she likely didn't know that.)

I must have been spoken louder than I'd thought, as Geoff responded instead. "That would be splendid, Harrold. Quite the rousing way to celebrate our victory in this coming quest."

She pointed toward the stairs while giving me the dirty look that my therapist had informed me meant a woman wasn't interested, and not "Keep trying, even if I slap you. I might eventually break down and go out with you." I was definitely getting out of this place as soon as I could. Impressing fictional female characters is a lot harder than it looks.

OF FANGS AND BIKINIS

How much longer could this whole thing possibly take, anyway? While I had included a map of Garandia in my books, I hadn't put a distance scale on it. I shuddered to think of what they'd come up with next, all in the interest of "good" television. Vegetarian werewolves and sex-crazed eunuchs weren't out of the question, but I'd let those slide if they were Muppets; everything is better in Muppet form.

As we came to the end of the surprisingly well-lit stairs, Geoff turned toward me with intense worry in his eyes. I darted a look around, wary of some unseen danger, but I could find none. I looked back at him for some further direction to his reaction.

"Do you think I should do something with my hair?" he asked. "I know what I have is a classic look, but after seeing all of those members of the warrior caste, I was thinking of going with a Mohawk. Do you think I have the right hair for that look?"

I smacked myself in the forehead, but as usual, he was oblivious to my actions.

"No one looks good in a Mohawk," I said. "Plus, I think if any Atlians saw you, they'd be insulted." I know, Mr. T rocks the Mohawk, but all of these actors were stuck in character. Geoff would most definitely pretend he didn't know who Mr. T was, which qualifies as blasphemy where I come from. God, how I wished that, just once, I could get one of these actors to talk like a normal person.

"You may have the right of it. What are your thoughts on pigtails, Harrold?"

"Could we walk in silence, please?"

Geoff didn't respond.

"Well, can we?"

"You said to walk in silence."

"Oh, right."

"Are we walking in silence or not, Harrold?"

I nodded.

He nodded back.

When the tunnel turned slightly, I walked into a wall and made a noise similar to the time I'd bounced my friend's hamster off his stomach.

What? Don't look at me that way. I was seven when it happened, and he bit me—the hamster, not my friend. OK, my friend bit me too, but I had just tossed a hamster at him, so he was well within his rights. Please, don't turn me in to PETA. I was seven, and the hamster was fine. I, however, was not. Thanks for asking. I had to get twenty stitches and a shot. It had turned out that my friend was rabid.

"I was under the impression that we were to be silent," Geoff said. "That crash was rather noisy."

"Have you ever silently run into a wall before?"

"Oh, yes. The last time I ran into a wall, I didn't make any noise. When I woke up afterwards, I distinctly remembered how quiet it was."

How had I gotten into this strange TV show? Had I really drunk so much peppermint Schnapps that I hadn't noticed someone moving me to the middle of a field? It had only been half a bottle. Plus, it was afternoon when I woke up, and it couldn't have been past 11 p.m. when I fell asleep. I bet whoever had set this show up had drugged that bottle or my food earlier. There had to be a lawsuit or twelve in this somewhere. I knew I hadn't signed any waivers, though my publisher sure had required a lot of signatures on my first contract. Had they snuck a waiver in there? Note to self: read contracts more thoroughly.

This was all starting to smell distinctly like the work of my rival, Billiam von Cummerbund, and not just because the passageway smelled like wet socks and bath salts. The jerk had written a whole book with the sole intent of mocking the first book in my series. I'm also convinced that he had somehow been responsible for my third book being "mistakenly" credited to Hairy Smallcock on the first edition. As bad as his "parody" had been, this idiotic production was starting to look even worse. Something like this had to involve him somehow.

Well, if they were going to sneak things into my contract, I was going to sneak off their set at the next opportunity. They had foolishly removed Hammurabi from the story, and since there was no longer anyone to scare me into line, I was free to pursue other opportunities—opportunities that paid my bills, like the book I was supposed to be writing. Opportunities that didn't involve rivals with stupid names.

As we exited the tunnel, we saw two armed men in a clearing. I assumed these were our escorts and my new keepers. I would have to wait until later to escape, when they had their guard down. Teragonna hadn't really given us a description of whom we were supposed to be meeting, beyond that they would be outside the tunnel and be three in number. She really should have given us more to go by. A description would have been nice. A secret handshake would have been even better.

I'd wanted to have a secret handshake since I was a kid, but my imaginary friend hadn't had any hands. He'd also said I shouldn't need one since I already knew what he looked like. When I pointed out that I couldn't actually see him, he'd said he'd go find another kid with "more imagination and better hair."

I approached the man closest to us, a very muscular fellow in his late twenties with a sandy blond mustache. He had on shiny bronze armor with an open-faced helmet shaped like the head of some great cat.

"Do you know the secret handshake?" I said.

"Yeah, sure." He reached out and smacked me on the back of my head.

"Ow! That wasn't very handshakey."

"And that's the secret! It's good to have a secret handshake in case we're ever in disguise. If you're ever not sure whether it's me or not, just ask, and I'll be sure to give you the secret handshake."

The second man shook his head. "That's why the rest of us wear helmets. And you made a very ugly woman, Cat."

"Who're you kidding? I was gorgeous." Cat blew a kiss at his companion.

"Wearing the wig over your helmet didn't help."

"You still mistook that woman for me, Wolf."

"Well, she had a mustache, and arms bigger than my thighs."

"And that's why we need a secret handshake." Cat nodded at me.

The second man held his hand out and I shook it. He wore a nearly identical suit of armor to his companion, the exception being that his helmet was shaped like a wolf's head instead of like a cat's. I guessed him to be the leader by both his demeanor and the obvious age difference. A faint scar just above the left side of his jaw broke up his graying stubble. I placed him to be in his early fifties.

"We should introduce ourselves. You've 'shaken hands' with Cat. My name is Wolf, and our newest member is Jackal, who is skulking in the trees somewhere. We are the famed mercenaries, trackers, and bodyguards, the Fanged Trio."

"Ahh, of course. The famous Fanged Trio." They were so famous, they didn't exist in my books. "I'm Harry, and this is Geoff."

Having heard the commotion, the third member of their group came out of hiding. Although her helmet was of the same style, she had little else about her that would draw any connection to her two hairy companions. If she hadn't been wearing armor, I might have mistaken her for a cheerleader, though no cheerleading squad would likely ever let a member wear anything as skimpy as a chain mail bikini in public.

I had put chain mail bikinis into one of my books because they seemed awesome, but looking at one in real life, it was obvious how impractical the thing was. There was no way it could protect her from swords and axes, let alone poison ivy or even a slight breeze.

"That's . . . nice armor you have there," I said.

"My father, Werin the Finder, gave it to me before I struck out on my own. He said it would toughen me up for the harsh realities of the world."

Werin the Finder was the greatest detective and tracker in all of Garandia. I had written him as a gruff, tough man's man. Misogyny wasn't too much of a stretch, but I guessed they were using it as an excuse to put an attractive woman in something skimpy.

"I'd imagine frostbite can be rather harsh. If your dad's not here, why not change out of it?"

"I can't afford anything better. I just joined. Anyway, I go by Jackal now, I guess."

"Cat!" Wolf said. "Where's the armor we bought her?"

Cat pulled a bag out from behind him and handed it to her.

"Nuts. I was going to initiate her. Can I still do the other part of the initiation?"

"Not this time," Wolf said. "We need her tracking abilities. With her knowledge of this area, we can't have her distracted by whatever nonsense you have planned."

"No fair! When do I get to initiate someone?"

"You could go initiate yourself."

Cat rubbed his hands together diabolically. "Oh, goodie! I'm gonna shave my head while I'm sleeping. That'll show me."

"Remember to put the razor away *before* you fall asleep this time. We can't afford to find a healer again."

"What? My nose grew back."

"You're hilarious, Cat," Jackal said. "I think this'll be fun. Mount up, everyone, while I change."

Wolf handed Geoff and me each a backpack and pointed at two horses. There was barely enough room in my pack for Teragonna's silly package.

After about fifteen minutes of trying to get the horses to stand still long enough for Geoff and me to mount, we were finally on our way. It's really hard to climb on the back of something that clearly doesn't want you there, and I got the feeling that the horse could sense my dislike of him.

As Geoff and I were bouncing everywhere, Jackal kindly gave us several tips on horsemanship. Teragonna had instructed her to avoid the main roads for fear of parties interested in our cargo. I had no idea what we were carrying, but I really didn't care, as I thought this might be the perfect opportunity to escape. I could sense the cameras staring at me even if I couldn't see them.

BURNING BUSHES THAT DON'T
REQUIRE A DOCTOR'S VISIT

The thick forest seemed to go on forever. I was beginning to develop an intense dislike of bushes, and with the way they kept poking at me, the feeling was probably mutual. The only wildlife I saw was an occasional rabbit and one particularly naughty fox who tried to bite my ankle off. It wasn't my fault he'd been sleeping where my horse happened to step. Also, why did he attack my foot and not the horse's? Hat had always told me my left foot smelled like artificial bacon, and perhaps that was true. Wolf was kind enough to smack it away with the flat part of his sword.

"Does anyone hear anything?" Jackal slowed her horse and fell behind us.

"No. It's kind of nice," Cat said. "All those birds have finally stopped their chirping. Now, I can finally concentrate enough to figure out where I put my sword."

"It's in your hand," I said. "The better question is what you did with your pants."

"Quiet." Jackal motioned for us to stop, and we complied.

Wolf and Cat dismounted and readied their shields.

"Just like I taught you, Cat, and your father taught me before that. Protect the non-combatants, then, if possible, pick off anyone who lets their guard down. Remember, our first goal is to protect that thing in Harry's backpack."

I couldn't hear anything, but Jackal soon pointed to the left, toward a large bush. We stared at the bush for what seemed like an hour, but nothing came out. Right about the time I decided that I had better things to do and would go charging into the thing because they wouldn't kill their star, the bush finally made a noise.

"Give me the package, and I will let you leave unharmed."

"Did that bush just talk?" Geoff said.

"Erm . . . yes. I'm a large shrub that has developed the capacity for speech. All despair the speaking shrub!" It shook its branches.

Cat lowered his shield. "I make it a point to always listen to talking plants, like when I've been drinking and the trees tell me to pee on 'em. I think we should do what it says."

"Amazing," Wolf said. "You're not afraid to charge headfirst into a trained army of spearmen with no clothes or weapons, yet a bush says a few words and you'll do whatever it says. Your father would be so proud."

Cat stared down in shame. "Pointy thorns are forever the weakness of the pantsless."

For the record, there were no talking trees or any other plants in my world. I wasn't sure if this was yet another inaccuracy, or if there was someone standing in the bush with a megaphone. I had a really wicked idea if it was the latter, but Geoff beat me to the punch.

"I am not the woodsman that my benefactor, the brilliant Lord Hartin, is," Geoff said, "but perhaps one of you could start a fire to dispel this nasty spirit? I would imagine that, even though it is sentient, it still possesses a mundane bush's weakness to flames."

"Your suggestion of flames does not frighten me." The bush

glowed bright green at the word "frighten," causing my companions to jump. I am proud to say that I only jumped back half as far as anyone else. "Err . . . you don't have a fire, do you?"

Jackal pulled out a flint and tinder and began rubbing them together to make a fire. Wolf held a torch from his pack toward her and soon had it alight.

The bush glowed brighter, almost blinding us. "Now, you idiots," the bush said.

Three Mohawked Atlians came charging from the bush, straight at Wolf and Cat. Jackal recovered enough to send off two quick shots from her crossbow, but her hands were shaking almost as much as I was. She missed both shots and cursed. Still, she did manage to slow their charge enough to give Wolf and Cat time to regain their composure. Wolf caught one with a brilliantly executed shield slam right in the mid-section. Cat intercepted one Atlian's sword with his shield and sidestepped the second. Geoff let out a bloodcurdling cry and charged his horse right through the middle of the battle, making contact with no one. At least he was out of the way.

I, not wanting to be murdered on camera in the middle of my own world and not having the time or skill to make a fire, tossed my sword straight into the middle of the talking bush. I really hoped I broke whatever equipment they were using to project that voice, the more expensive, the better.

The bush let out a shriek. The two standing Atlians immediately broke off and retreated into it.

"Brilliant move, Harry," Cat said. "I've always suspected that talking bushes were weak against swords, though I still think they're weaker against beef gravy. Wolf, did you bring any gravy?"

"No. Whenever I make any, you immediately pour it in your helmet, and I'm not paying for another new helmet."

"One of these days, I'm going to make a gravy-proof helmet, and then we'll all be rich."

Wolf put his boot on top of the prone Atlian he had downed. "Go round up the other two while they're distracted, then we can see who Harry hit."

"Err . . . Jackal," Cat said. "I hate to have to ask this, but could you get them? That bush seems to have a *No pants. No shoes. No service.* sign on it, and I'm all out of pants."

"Wolf," Jackal said, "you're our HR rep. Why is he allowed to not wear pants, again?"

"As his unofficial guardian since his father's death, I'm slowly weaning him off some of his worst habits. Every three months, he's required to wear one additional article of clothing."

Jackal crinkled her eyebrows. "Why weren't pants the first thing you made him put on?"

Wolf sighed. "If you saw what he'd shaved into his chest hair, you wouldn't have picked pants either."

"It's a social commentary on the female form," Cat said.

Wolf motioned to Cat, and they changed places guarding the prisoner. Wolf cautiously led the way into the bushes with Jackal behind. I was expecting the sounds of battle and was disappointed to only hear voices instead. My first thought was that the actors were trying to figure out how to explain the scream when my blade had connected with a crewman, but I was proven wrong when the two Atlians dragged Artenarix from the bush instead. I thought it was rather rude of them to not bring my sword as well, but the actor playing Artenarix was fidgeting and moaning piti-fully, so I decided not to hold it against them. (Doubly so since I was sure no one had even bothered to give the other Atlians names).

"As a non-combatant, I demand to know why you propelled your blade at my personage. That is against all of the rules of chivalrous combat." I'd never seen anyone scowl and cry at the same time before, but I usually don't hold mirrors up when I battle the local kindergarteners.

"So is pretending to be a bush." Cat looked at Wolf. "Isn't it? I know I pretend to be bushes all the time, and you've said I'm the antithesis of chivalry. Also, what does 'antithesis' mean?"

"It means the opposite," Jackal said.

"Oh, good. That makes even more sense. I've always thought he was calling me chivalry's Aunt Thesis. If anything, I'm its adopted second cousin."

"I'm guessing this man is an enemy of our benefactor," Wolf said.

I nodded. "His name is Artenarix, and he really hates . . . the guy or woman who hired us."

"Oh, there's no need for games." Artenarix paused to spit out some fake blood. "We all know that the recently exiled Hammurabi Joudisz hired you and that you are in possession of an important item."

"I thought a woman gave us the package," Cat said.

Artenarix wheezed out a laugh. "Well, now I know for certain that you do indeed have the item I am searching for, even if it will do me little good in this state. If this were any other time, I would despair at such an injury, but I can survive anything now that I know Hammurabi has been finally exiled. Fortunately, there is one thing I can do." He held up two fingers, and one of his men ran off at full speed.

Jackal ran after the man, but Geoff came crashing through the brush before she could get her shot. After she had finally calmed his horse, she looked back at us and shook her head.

Artenarix tried to laugh again, but it came out as more of a cough. "You may have defeated me, but I am not the only one."

His eyes closed, and the only sound around us was the sobbing of his lone conscious companion. Wolf grabbed the man's sword and knife without him even seeming to notice.

"Should we tie him up?" Jackal said.

"I don't think it's worth the effort," Cat replied. "I think he's dead."

Wolf slapped his forehead. "She means the other one, Cat, and no. His insignia indicates he's one of Artenarix's Life Guards. Life Guards are sworn to return their fallen masters to their next of kin after death."

"And to pull them out of the pool if they get cramps."

I would have punched Cat for making fun of my brilliant concept of the noble Life Guards, but he was bigger than I. Also, he wasn't wearing any pants, and I have a strict "no wrestling with partially naked men" policy.

Cat pointed down at the unconscious one. "Can I at least tie up this one?"

"No," Wolf said. "Their master said there are others out there. We need to get out of here now."

"Could I bring him with me and tie him up as we go? I need the practice for my knot-tying merit badge." Cat gave Wolf his sweetest smile.

Wolf turned around and mounted his horse. "How many times do I have to tell you that mercenaries don't have merit badges?"

"Seven and a half."

"Seven and a half." We turned back toward Artenarix. It appeared the actors had overplayed the whole dying thing. His Life Guard leaned him forward. "Why, that's precisely the number of minutes I give you to survive. Do you honestly think my employer will allow such an important object to be delivered by the likes of you?"

"Employer?" Cat grabbed hold of Artenarix and shook him. "Who do you work for? What do you know?"

The Life Guard let go of his master and forced Cat to stop, but it was too late. Artenarix's eyes stopped moving, and his tongue rolled out. The drool really sold it. There was no way someone as fastidious as he would let his robes get that wet.

Wolf and Cat mounted up without another word, like they had the sort of psychic communication that often develops between people who've worked together for a while, or they had read the script. As they moved out of the clearing, Jackal stayed behind to help Geoff and me get our horses moving.

"At least I will die knowing that my cohorts will succeed," the not-quite-dead Artenarix said. "I hope you are quick, because they should be here shortly. Do you want to know who you are about to face?"

Jackal shrugged and mounted her horse. "No."

"One will lurk," Artenarix coughed out.

"If this lurker is as dumb as you, we'll be fine," I said. "I mean, come on, man. You have the power to animate fighting trees, and the best you could do is a shiny bush."

With that, Jackal led us back into the woods, making sure to double back and go in a different direction than we had left from. I thought it was pretty clever of her, as there was no doubt in my mind that he would alert his allies of our direction. Unfortunately, there was no one to do the same for the cameras I knew were out there but couldn't quite see.

ANOTHER REASON WHY I HATE HAMSTERS

We heard the occasional distant sound of pursuit, but we had so far managed to avoid our pursuers. Jackal had expertly directed us through side paths and had changed course repeatedly to throw them off.

After a few hours, thick foliage began to cover our small path. "I think we should leave this soon," Jackal said. "I know of an old goat trail a little way to the north. Unless they've hired a local guide, they won't know it's there. Does that sound good?" She looked to Wolf for the validation her father had evidently never given her.

Wolf nodded in agreement. "Jackal, you're doing great. You don't need to ask permission. We trust your expertise."

"Oh, OK. You both know so much more than I do, and I did kind of screw up when those two Atlians charged us earlier. It's so much easier on the practice range."

Wolf smiled. "You did fantastic. You recovered faster than any of us and had the wherewithal to fire not once, but twice before we even moved. If you hadn't slowed them down, I doubt we would have had our shields up before they struck."

Cat patted her on the back. "Yeah, then there'd be four Atlians staring at a very beautiful, pantsless corpse right now."

Jackal smiled at the sentiment while making sure to keep her eyes up. With a renewed sense of confidence, she easily found the old trail. It wound through an ancient collection of hills, and the vegetation slowly grew less and less dense.

With all of the danger and the very pleasant banter of my companions, I had completely forgotten about escaping this silly show. I was actually having a good time. While I still had misgivings about their having invented all of the characters I was currently with, they were interesting people that I enjoyed being with. Of course I had forgotten about Geoff, as he had been so far too busy writing about our surroundings to speak.

"How far does this path proceed?" Geoff said. "Being so deep in the woods makes me a tad anxious. I have never been what you would call a woodsman, though my benefactor Lord Hartin is exceptionally skilled in that area of expertise. He once killed a raging boar with only a small whittling knife."

"I once killed a boar naked," Cat said, "using only my God-given weapons."

"That wasn't a boar, Cat. It was just a really hairy street urchin, and you didn't kill him, you gave him pinkeye," Wolf said.

By midday, the vegetation had disappeared completely, replaced by a "varied" combination of dirt, rocks, more dirt, and even more rocks. I think I even saw some rocks in there.

"I would assume there aren't many people in these parts," Cat said.

"There are no settlements for at least twenty miles near the Terngarin Mountains," Jackal said.

"These are mountains? Aren't mountains usually, you know, tall?"

"Time has taken its toll, yet the name remains."

"In about five miles," Jackal said, "we'll arrive at the old road that used to attach two cities of the original inhabitants of this island, the Bulmians."

"The Bulmians were all wiped out by the Litotians, the predecessors of the modern Shrannin," Geoff said.

"The Shrannin live in the south," Cat said. "What were they doing all the way up here?"

"Our ancestors drove them south, to the Lowlands and beyond. They used to control the whole island."

"Quite the feat, that was," Wolf said. "The Shrannin are huge, savage warriors. I don't know how the ancient Garandians managed that. We didn't even know how to ride horses then, let alone fight in an organized manner."

"We had recently taken up our faith in The One," Geoff said. "Zealotry and fervor are a powerful weapon."

"That, and hamsters," Cat said.

"Hamsters?" I said.

"St. Bertius, with his trained and holy pack of hamsters, guinea pigs, and chipmunks, drove the merciless King Helfind and his hordes away from the beleaguered crusader army, who had just fought a bloody battle at Diferend," Geoff said. "So terrified was King Helfind of that adorable and vicious swarm that he abandoned the land all the way to the Lowlands in the south."

Oh, yeah. That was why I wanted to escape. The Trio seemed nice, but Geoff by himself had done more to ruin my magnificent world than the rest of the characters combined.

"Where did you hear that ludicrous story?" I said. "How would someone train hamsters to fight? Even if that were possible, how would hamsters drive off a horde of massive barbarians?"

"The village priest told it to me when I was a child," Geoff said. "He said that with enough faith, even the smallest of creatures can overcome the largest of foes. Also, St. Bertius sharpened their teeth and taught them how to leap really high."

"Jackal, please help me," I said.

"He called it the 'leap of faith,' but St. Bertius didn't teach them that. The Almighty did."

"And I'll bet the armor he put them in really evened out the odds," Cat said.

I held back my tears. "Really? He built armor . . . for guinea pigs, hamsters, and chipmunks?"

Cat nodded. "My church still has a few of them on display."

I really needed to get them to stop talking. If my headache got any stronger, my whole head would explode. I had to escape. "Could we stop for the night? I'm not used to the saddle, and I'm rather sore."

"All right. We should be out of danger for the time being," Jackal said.

"Only if I'm not here to strangle you all in your sleep," I muttered under my breath.

RUNNING AWAY CAN BE A VERY REWARDING EXPERIENCE

We set up camp, had our meal—which looked a lot like Hot Pockets—and climbed into our bedrolls. I convinced them that I needed to sleep away from camp by complaining that Cat was a snorer—which turned out to be true—and I had trouble sleeping around so much noise. The fact that there had been no objections made me a little suspicious, so I made sure to walk past all of them to see if anyone was awake about fifteen minutes before my escape. As no one had reacted to my little test, when the time came, I jumped up and ran toward the distant forest. Given my difficulties with mounting and the fact that my horse kept giving me dirty looks, I had abandoned the idea of riding away. I also left my pack behind, as it would only slow me down.

When I reached the concealment of the forest, I made sure to run in an erratic, zigzagging pattern so I would not be easy to find. I could feel the constant glare of the hidden cameras lift, and a nice concealing mist rolled in. It was refreshing that something was going right, even if it made it a little hard to see in front of me. After I ran into the third tree, I decided to slow to a jog. With that much concealment, I could afford a little slackening of my pace.

After a few hours of fast walking, I knew I had to be safe from pursuit, so I slowed to a normal walking speed. My arms were getting scraped up pretty bad from running into bushes, but I didn't care. The only question was whether I could find someone not involved with this production to help me get back home. My prayers were answered when I saw the familiar blaze-orange of a hunter through the mist.

"Excuse me, sir. I'm lost, and I could use some help getting back home. Could you direct me to the nearest town or lend me a cell phone?"

The figure in orange turned, but I still couldn't make out his— or her—face. The glare of what had to be the scope of his rifle shone toward me, so I stopped. I couldn't see any cover nearby, not that my legs were working, anyway. As is my way, I had escaped from one terrible thing and run straight into something worse. I hoped he would at least stuff my body and point me toward the TV for all of eternity.

"Please, sir. I could pay you. I'm a famous writer. I could even sign things for you."

The glare from his scope moved over my left nipple —my favorite nipple. "Like your baby—"

The glare pointed at my head.

"Your forehead?" I asked.

The glare moved down to my crotch.

"I'm not going to sign that. That's absurd."

The glare from the scope was directly in my eyes now.

"Fine," I said, "but I'm going to need a special pen for that . . . and could you not tell anyone about this?"

The glare moved between my eyes.

"Fine. You can tell one friend, as long as he doesn't work for any news outlets."

"And where could one get one of those special pens?" the hunter said.

"The special pen store, obviously." You'd think I'd know not to taunt the guy with the gun, but I couldn't resist a setup like that.

"You'd know where to get special things, given that you're such a special boy, Harry." He really put some extra menace into the last "special." You'd think he wouldn't need to sound so menacing with the gun pointed at me, but some people are over-achievers.

"A clever quip for a clever man, I suppose. Who are you, stranger? It'd be nice to know the name of the man who's probably going to kill me."

"Some call me the Wizard of New Atlia, which I've always found odd, as New Atlia is full of wizards, but I guess the guy who does nicknames was on vacation that week."

I stepped forward defiantly, which for me means I only shook a little. "You can kill me, but do you have to appropriate the title of my favorite character? You, sir, are no Hammurabi Joudisz! Also, the nickname is a double entendre, because he's a financial wizard and he can do actual magic. The guy who made it up is actually really smart. Not that I've met him or anything, but that's what a lot of people say."

"If I'm not him, then who is?" His face began to glow so that I could finally make it out, and it was, in fact, Hammurabi Joudisz (or the actor who was currently playing him, anyway). The way the light barely lit up his already frightening and unnerving face would give me nightmares for weeks.

"What are you doing here?" I asked. "Did I catch you on a smoke break, or were you out hunting?"

"Why, I'm out hunting for you, of course."

Couldn't he say something in a manner that didn't make me want to wet my pants? I'm mean, the guy was like six foot six and had one of the most intimidating faces I had ever seen, but no, he still had to have a voice so frightening that it scared the crap out of me even when I couldn't see his body.

"Fantastic. I finally escape that travesty of a TV show, but then I get murdered, and not by a normal guy. No, it has to be by the guy who's playing my most iconic character."

I think everyone can agree that it was perfectly within my rights to tear up a little here, even though you probably couldn't see that on TV and would never have known about it unless I told you in the book I wrote about this show. The book you're currently reading. The book written by me, in which I could write anything and you'd believe me. Note to self: fix this in editing.

A thought occurred to me, and, yes, I can still think while I'm crying. "Wait. Did you mean you're here to hunt me for sport, or you're hunting me to bring me back to the show?"

"Harrold, I don't know why you think this is some sort of play. It is very much real." The fog suddenly disappeared, and so did the bright light I had mistaken for a scope. His fingers glowed green, and a waist-high sapling appeared beside him. "See. Magic. If this were a play, I wouldn't have been able to do that." He backed away from the sapling. "Touch it."

I did as commanded, not because I was afraid or because I believed him, but because I like touching tiny trees. It was incredibly life-like. It even smelled like a tree, not that I'm one of those weirdos who gets off by smelling trees. "That doesn't prove anything. They can do some really neat things with special effects nowadays."

The fog reappeared, and his face glowed a reddish tint, further enhancing his snarl. "Whatever. It doesn't matter if you believe this is real or not. What matters is that you get the job done. I'm here to send you back."

"Teragonna said that if either Geoff or I survived, it'd be all right, and Geoff's still bravely going forward with the mission. So, can I go?"

"Have you met Geoff? We both know he's going to die in the next day or so. I only said that to make him feel better. You are the important one, according to my magic, and my magic is never wrong about this kind of thing."

"What about the time—"

"I don't know who told you about that, but it isn't polite to talk about that kind of thing to another man. I assumed you would do the right thing, but I guess you're obviously not who I thought you were."

I looked around at the excessive amount of mist, then looked at Hammurabi's anachronistic blaze-orange outfit. "Is this a dream? Are you my conscience?"

"Do you usually dream about—no, I don't want to know."

"So, I have to go back. What makes you think I'm going to listen to you? There are lots of woods out here, and I'm a fast runner."

With the light shining on him that way, I expected him to tell a ghost story, but what he said was worse than any scary story. "Dear Harrold, do you take me for a fool? We both know you're not in the best of shape, and you've been walking for hours. I am quite certain that you're only capable of a slow walk at this point, whereas I am well-rested. I'd catch you in under a minute."

I expected him to smirk, but he only maintained his steady look.

I hate it when they're so confident they don't even bother to gloat. I also hate it when they're right. I was so tired, I couldn't even manage a moderately saucy saunter or a light bit of skipping. At best, I had a respectable old man hobble in me.

"So, is this the part where you tell me dire things will happen to me if I don't complete this silly quest?"

He maintained that same unwavering gaze. What was with this guy? Surely, that question deserved at least an eyebrow tilt. "'Dire' seems like a bit much to me. How about, 'not so nice' things will happen to you? Anyway, the kingdom needs you, and Geoff is less than reliable. Shouldn't that be enough for you?"

"I'll continue for a fifty percent cut."

"Fifty percent of what? There's no money involved." He looked like a sinister jack-o'-lantern with the light bouncing off his face that way. "You're really not going to do this out of dedication toward your country? I did not waste my last day in Garandia before I begin my exile for this."

I paced back and forth. "This isn't the country I created in my imagination. The country I imagined is a good country, a happy country—but not so happy that the knights sing, because that's just ridiculous. OK, some of the knights do sing, but it's gruff war songs, not anything resembling a barbershop quartet or an a cappella group. And that country is a great country ruled by a great king, not a bumbling zealot like you've described. Also, in that country, the creator of the world would not be slapped repeatedly, unless it was while he was naked and by a beautiful lady, and then only if he asked her to. Slapping outside of the bedroom has no place in my Garandia."

My brilliant speech finally got a reaction out of him: stunned bewilderment. The expression looked wrong on him.

"If you won't do it out of dedication to your country, what can I offer you instead?" he asked.

"Fine. I'll do it if I get to go out on a date with the actress who plays Teragonna."

His eyes erupted in flames. The scope-like light reappeared between my eyes but eventually lowered back down to my midsection. "You're very lucky that I need you, little man. My wife is off-limits. Think of something else."

Jeez. This guy was way too into his character. They weren't even married in real life . . . although they actually could be. I guessed I could cut him some slack in case that was true. "Fine. I want to be the hero."

"You will be the hero if you complete this mission."

"No, I want to be made to look heroic. You know: digitally add a bunch of muscle, cover up my gut, and give me a cool scar. Also, I want you to edit out all of the cowardly and inept things I've done so far."

"I can't really change the past, but we could build a statue in your honor or something. The chancellor and I are still friends. I'm sure he could throw together a parade."

"That's a start, but I want to win all of the fights from now on and have every woman fall in love with me."

He grumbled. "The chancellor might have some men about that he could have lose some fights with you, and those might lead to women falling for you. That's the best I can do."

I considered pushing for commercials featuring all of my brave exploits, but when someone's eyes are on fire, it's probably a good idea not to push your luck. He looked like he'd crush my hand if I shook it, so I nodded in agreement.

The flames and the light died down, and he abruptly disappeared from view. The way he disappeared was pretty cool, though the effect was somewhat lessened by his grumbling out new and refreshing insults about my manhood. What had the little guy ever done to him?

I shrugged and walked away. The sooner this was over, the sooner I'd be back home and would get to see how awesome this whole thing made me look. Plus, I was afraid he might come after me.

"The fate of the kingdom rests on your shoulders," he shouted at my back.

I hastened my pace and called back, "This isn't my kingdom, so you'd better make me look good," as I got out of hearing range.

At least the mist faded when the sun began to rise, and I could finally see where I was going. I soon saw the occasional indication that humans must have traveled this way: a soleless shoe here, a broken bow there, though nothing in a Garandian or Atlian style. At first, I thought that must be an indication that I was headed away from the show, but given the show's blatant inaccuracies, I realized it really didn't tell me anything. The fact that the forest was thinning should have told me where I had gone, but the exertion of running made thought difficult.

With my eyes glued to a particularly shiny object, I ran face-first into the back of a particularly hairy man. As we tumbled down, I landed on top of him. While he was rather soft, he also smelled like burnt popcorn and rotten fish. I assumed this must be some sort of homeless man, until I saw the rusty sword lying next to us. He appeared to have small twigs in his long, shaggy black hair.

I quickly stood up to avoid the smell and was finally able to take in the scene around me. Cat was engaged with another one of the smelly extras, while two more seemed to be pretending to be dead. The fake blood was really lifelike, too. Geoff was furiously attacking an opponent who was unseen and possibly non-existent. Wolf must have had quite the struggle with an exceptionally large man—judging by his sword's temporary residence in a tree and very real-looking cuts on his knuckles—but Jackal turned the tide by emptying her quiver into the giant's back.

The smelly man in front of me took advantage of my distraction and reached for his sword. I drew my blade, but it slipped and went flying into a nearby bush. A scream echoed from the bush, indicating that I had either hit some unseen opponent or that the sound effects guy was having an off day. When I turned back around, I saw that my opponent lay sprawled on the ground. I had either inadvertently hit him or the actor was pretending I had. As Cat finished off his last opponent, he nodded to me in respect and gave the prone, stinky man a kick before he could get to his weapon.

When my heart stopped pounding, I turned around but saw no new opponents. The sounds of battle died soon after that. I guessed they hadn't had time to tell the actors to make me look heroic yet. The party regrouped as Geoff finished off his imagined partner, and I ran into the bush and retrieved my sword. Fortunately, the "dead" man released my sword relatively easily from his chest. He was either too dedicated to playing dead to struggle or had fallen asleep.

"Mine's dead," Wolf said.

"Three here," Cat said. "Harry caught one trying to get me from behind. Good work."

"I must have fought off twelve of 'em," Geoff said.

Jackal smiled condescendingly. "I saw you get at least fourteen."

"I told you Harry hadn't abandoned us, Wolf," Jackal said. "It was all a ruse so he could perform an elaborate flanking attack."

Cat giggled. "They charge extra for that it in Sculan."

"That's not what a flanking attack is."

Wolf shook his head. "No, but that's what Cat thinks it means. After years of working with him, I find it easier to go with his definition rather than argue with him. We lost one of the previous Jackals while I was arguing with Cat over what a flower was."

"Flower is another word for penis."

"According to him, almost everything is another word for that."

Cat stuck his hands over Jackal's ears. "How can you say 'word' in front of a lady, Wolf? Have you no manners?"

Jackal shook Cat off and pointed at my slowly rising captive.

Wolf pushed Stinky back down with his foot. "So, there are no known settlements out here?"

"They must be bandits on the run. Why don't we ask him?" Jackal said.

Wolf removed his boot from Stinky's mouth. "Whatence you wantzen?" Stinky asked.

"Who are you?" Wolf said.

"I isen Blackie." He stuck his finger in his nose.

"Okay, Blackie. Who are your people? Why did you attack us?"

"Weez isen, Bull Moose. You isen, Lito. No Lito lives in Bull Moose landen."

"Any of that make any sense to anyone?" Wolf said.

"I think he said they live here and kill all trespassers on sight," Jackal said.

"Never mind. What should we do with him?"

"Kill him," Cat said. "He tried to flank me, and I only let the ladies do that to me."

"Wait," Jackal said. "We can use him as a guide to safety, or a hostage if need be."

"I don't know," Wolf said.

"Look, it appears my knowledge of this area isn't as good as I thought it was. We need an expert, and he's the closest thing. Now, how do we get out of your clan's territory?"

"Thisens way," Blackie said, pointing straight up. When we all responded to him with confused looks, something seemed to click, so he stuck his other index finger in the same nostril and then pointed off the path with his left foot.

THE ABOMINABLE CHIEFTAIN

As we slowly climbed the large, boulder-strewn hills, Geoff ceaselessly pestered Blackie about his people. I considered tossing my newly returned pack at both of them. I won't annoy you by giving an exact account, as Blackie's speech pattern was incredibly annoying and often incomprehensible. I was deathly afraid they were using leftover Jar Jar Binks lines. The highlights were: Blackie's people had lived in this unexplored rock garden for as long as their history went back, they had remained undis-covered by killing all trespassers, and he really liked pie.

"Doens you havens pie?" Blackie said.

"No, Blackie," Geoff said. "Now, are there other tribes or clans that live in these hills?"

"Yeses, there ins da Grey Moose, da Left Moose, da Blue Moose, and da Bull Moose."

"Are all of the hill people called the Moose?" Geoff asked. "If not, what do you call all of your collective peoples?"

"There ins da Grey Moose, da Left Moose, da Blue Moose, and da Bull Moose."

"Never mind. How do you feed yourselves? This terrain is too rocky for crops."

"Enough, Geoff," Jackal said. "Are we heading into the territory of another clan, Blackie?"

As if on cue, the sound of drawn blades echoed across the highly acoustic landscape. I suspected that Jackal's line had been, in fact, an actual cue to attack. The hill people sprang from behind the numerous boulders and easily surrounded us, so there would be no fighting our way out of this one. They were very dirty and dressed in the same mish-mash of bedraggled clothing as Blackie's associates, though their hair was of a lighter shade. Remembering my agreement with Hammurabi, I drew my sword from its sheath, but Jackal begged me to drop it, so I agreed. She must have gotten word from the showrunners that now was not the time.

The tallest one, who seemed to be in charge, gestured for his men to take our weapons and horses, and they soon began to grab and push us forward on the path. The nearly toothless fellow escorting me smelled strongly of a mixture of alcohol, urine, and cupcakes. To this day, I can't eat a cupcake without remembering that smell. Needless to say, I don't eat a lot of cupcakes anymore. Do you think I can sue for that?

Their leader grunted for us to speed up. Now, normally, I don't like to be grunted at. My usual response to a grunt is, "Use your words," but after Blackie's barely coherent gibbering, I wasn't complaining. I now almost look fondly on being grunted at. By the way, when you smile at someone who has grunted at you, it generally doesn't draw a friendly reaction. Their leader gave me a smack on the side of the head, fortunately not in the same spot as Cat's secret handshake.

"Blackie," Geoff said, "which tribe is this, and what do you think they'll do to us?"

"Demses da Left Moose. Meeses no know. Chiefsas of Left Moose ees crazy."

After about fifteen minutes of fast marching, minus a few

breaks for us to vomit from the smell, we arrived at the Left Moose village. I use the term "village" very loosely. A better description is: slightly organized pile of junk assembled by a pack of eight-year-olds. The buildings didn't look very sturdy; they consisted of rocks and random scavenged large objects stuck together with any available sticky substance. The walls surrounding the village were of a similar quality but a few feet taller than the buildings. Clearly, the Left Moose Tribe had not heard of building inspectors or fire codes.

Colonel Grunty lead us to the center of the "village" and limped toward an even taller man who I assumed must be their king, given his crown—even if it was made out of one cup from a very large bra with a hole in the middle. He was also the only person I could see with two shoes on, though each was on the wrong foot and they were from different sets, one a dainty slipper and the other a sandal.

Grunty and the leader talked quietly together, with much gesturing and head-shaking. After what felt like an hour, it seemed like the leader had won their exchange.

Grunty stepped toward the group. "Yousss preesoners step forrrrrward."

Oh, great. Stuck in a town full of people who talked like Blackie. I wondered if they'd scavenged a few bottles of aspirin.

The leader nodded, and we all did as we were told. I was deathly afraid that if my closest escort, One Tooth, stuck me with his shovel, I'd get tetanus.

"Yousss in presenccccce of Archibald Feniworth IV, chiefsss of Left Mooses."

"I say, dear Elworth," Archibald Feniworth IV said. "You muuust get that throat looked at. You sound positively like a serpent."

I wasn't sure why this actor thought that using a 19th century, upper-crust English accent was appropriate for his character, but at least it was intelligible and several degrees less annoying than Blackie's gibberish. My headache began to fade, so I decided not to complain.

"Ssssorry, bosss," Elworth said. He then left, hopefully to find a lozenge.

"Now that that business is out of the way," the leader said, "let's have a look at you. Hmm . . . We have some veeery well-accoutered knights here. Bravo on the armor, gentlemen. It's smashing. And what are your names?"

"Wolf and Cat," Wolf said. "Now, what are you going to do to us?"

"In due time. In due time."

The leader walked over and stood in front of Geoff. "Your glasses are a delight. And I do admire that wonderful hairstyle of yours. I simply muuust get the name of your stylist."

He patted Geoff on the head, then moved in front of me. "My, you're a strapping fellow. Not a fan of that beard, however. Not. At. Awlll. You reeeally should grow it longer. It is the fashion." This guy was like a cartoon of an English gentleman. He must have gotten his lines from an episode of *Scooby-Doo*.

Next, he came to a stop in front of Jackal. "My heavens! What a vision! Release the prisoners, immediately! My sincerest apologies, my dear lady. I was unaware that I was in the presence of a goddess." He then leaned in and kissed her hand gently.

This gesture would normally have been very charming, but remember: this man had half of a bra on his head, was coated in dirt, and smelled like he used garbage as deodorant. Jackal recoiled and put her other hand over her mouth. Smart move, as the hand he had kissed probably needed washing with an entire bar of soap just to stop smelling like a dead cat. Her eyes began to water, and I was greatly impressed that she managed to hold back her urge to retch.

"My dear, you look like you might be coming down with

something. Perhaps I should call for a doctor. I can't have you falling ill as I begin to court you. Momentum is everything in this sort of situation."

"No, I'm fine, really." She waved him away, but in doing so, moved her smelly hand a little too close to her nose.

I hadn't been aware that vomit could be blue.

The leader shook his head. "The fairer sex is always the same, never wanting the help of a man unless there is danger abounding. Nonsense! I shall send for One-Eye at once. Reginald, summon the healer." He nodded and one of the tribesmen ran off into the village.

"I really just need to move around a bit," Jackal said. "This isn't necessary."

"Your modesty and fortitude are astounding, but Alistair is a wonder. Ah! Here he comes now."

From around the other side of a house (three boulders with an old bedsheet over it), Alistair wandered towards us. I thought the other members of this tribe were dressed ridiculously, but Alistair One-Eye was outrageous even by his tribe's standards, with skin dyed bone white on one side, purple on the other, and glowing red hair shaved completely down the middle with each side stuck together into a large spike. As both of his eyes bore patches, he used a small child on a leash for navigation. True to form for his style-challenged clan, he was wearing a pale blue ball gown with frilly lace, and his underwear was bunched around his ankles.

Jackal stood there for several minutes, clearly at a loss.

"Good heavens! The sickness has spread and seized her voice from her," Archibald said. "What can you do, Wise One?"

"Copious amounts of excrement should alleviate this ailment."

"No. No. No. No. No," she said. "I can speak perfectly fine. I think the smell of excrement is what caused this in the first place.

I just need some fresh air. Thank you for your concern, but please leave me be."

"The only cure for excrement sickness is to cover your body in excrement," One-Eye said. "It is a cure that has been set down through the ages. Please take your clothes off so we can begin."

"Yes!" Archibald said. "We must do this immediately. Allow me to assist."

"If you try that, I'll punch you," Jackal said.

One-Eye shook his head. "Hmm . . . uncontrolled anger. Filling the ears with excrement usually cures that."

She backed away. "Is there any ailment that isn't cured with excrement?"

"Sadness."

"And what, pray tell, cures that?"

One-Eye put his hand on his chin. "A nice smile and a kind word. Excrement usually makes it worse."

She frowned. "Well, I'm sad, then."

"Oh . . . you have very pretty boots."

"Why, thank you."

"Do you feel better now?"

"Yes."

"Splendid." Archibald slapped One-Eye on the back. "The doctor is a marvel, is he not?"

"Quite."

"My lady, may I have your hand again? This is a tad embarrassing. I am not happy with the quality of my first kiss and would like to request another attempt. My sincere apologies."

Panic overwhelmed Jackal's still watery eyes, which darted around looking for anything that might excuse her from more contact with the smelly chieftain. She quickly found one and pointed toward Geoff, who had his hand raised like an obedient student.

Archibald rolled his yes. "Yes, yes. What is it, chap?"

Geoff lowered his hand. "Where do you acquire your sustenance? This soil does not look like it can maintain much in the way of crops, and with so little plant life, I doubt there can be too many animals about."

"That brings up a splendid idea. Why don't we show you all how it's done? This will provide me with ample opportunity to display my masculinity to my future consort. Ready a hunting party. To the peaks!"

"Huzzah!" the tribe yelled as one.

Chief Archibald grabbed his spear, an old broomstick with a rusty nail attached, and most of the men in the village hoisted equally decrepit, inefficient weapons. Our war party marched out of the village with what seemed like every able-bodied man present—somewhere around a hundred total.

We headed toward the crest of one of the tallest hills while our hosts sang one song after another, all of which sounded like children's songs from the eighteenth century. While we technically were not captives, our group was positioned firmly in the center of the party, with no way of getting out. Jackal was trapped in the constant, flirtatious attention of Archibald, never getting a moment to gather her thoughts.

Mercifully, Archibald motioned for a stop when a large cave came into view. "In order to answer your dapper friend's question, my dear, I thought it best to show you how we gather our nourishment. Shortly, my men will scare out the great beasts and, with me in the lead, slay one of the mighty behemoths that feed our tribe."

"Huzzah! Huzzah! Huzzah!" the men said as they thumped their weapons against the ground. Three of the smallest tribesman detached from the group and scurried into the cave.

"Now, shortly, my dear, those men will draw the mighty yetis from their cave. I must warn you, they are quite massive, terrifying beasts. I will not hold it against you if you faint, as it is the way of the fairer sex."

I found it much more likely that she would faint from the smell of the tribesmen.

Within moments, the small tribesmen bounced out of the cave like rabbits. I was deathly afraid of what was about to come—not a fear of the beasts themselves, but because there was no such thing as yetis in my world. I had no intention of including them in my future books.

While this show had, so far, been tragically inaccurate with almost everything, the costumes and special effects had been of the highest order, so, when the yeti emerged, I was horribly disappointed. The beast was a few inches taller than Archibald and I, and significantly wider. It was covered in ragged, exceptionally dirty white hair that appeared to be coming loose.

"Behold the yeti!" Chief Archibald said. "Is it not terrifying?"

In response, the yeti let out a "terrifying" yawn. It then moved its hands upward, and the entire Left Moose party recoiled and assumed a defensive crouch. It languidly rubbed its eyes.

"Men, encircle it. It is preparing its classic attack."

The men at the edge of our party began to jostle and push each other in order to get "volunteers" to move away from our protective formation and complete the encirclement.

After several minutes, the yeti completed the rubbing of its eyes, smacked its lips slowly, and let out a few short yawns. The tribesmen in front of us continued their internal struggle, and eventually one of them was pushed forth to engage the beast. The man was completely naked save for a sock on his man parts and a boot on his head. He quivered and held his exceptionally old sword by the blade as he hesitantly stepped forward. When he stopped, his friends ran forward and gave him a push. The momentum carried him toward the yeti, and when he arrived, he barely remembered to swing his sword. The hilt caught the yeti in the side of its stomach, and the sword immediately shattered.

The yeti stared at the spot of impact for a few seconds, then let out a yell that sounded like "Heeeeyyyyyy!"

"My gods, it's a tough one," Archibald said. "Quickly, men, attack it as one. Show your future queen your tribal unity." He then pushed a few of the men in front of him forward.

The yeti, finally awakened from its stupor, grabbed the weapon of the tribesman closest to him—an umbrella missing its canopy—and beat the implement's former bearer to death. The yeti then turned and clubbed all the other tribesmen who were too slow or unable to escape its reach.

"Behold our bravery, my dear. See how we unify in the face of such a ferocious beast."

"Yes, it's fantastic," Jackal deadpanned.

"What unity?" Cat said. "You're all just cowering."

Being an expert on the subject, I almost interjected that this was some of the most pathetic cowering I had ever seen. They weren't even scrunching up in a protective ball or hiding! Their weapons were still mostly in their hands, too. A truly great coward knows to drop anything resembling a weapon, or else your potential attacker might mistake you for a threat. I decided against pointing that out because someone might hit me for it.

"We are not cowering," Archibald said. "That is merely the legendary attack stance of the ferocious Left Moose tribe. It is, after all, the reason that our tribe is the terror of all of the other Moose tribes."

"Yarp," Blackie said.

"So, when are you going to attack, then?" Cat asked.

"In a moment. At the present, it is not tactically prudent."

Tired from smacking tribesmen to death at will, the yeti sat down and rested its head on its knees.

"Now looks like a good time," Cat said.

Chief Archibald pushed a few more of his men forward, but the yeti didn't seem to notice. After taking a few tentative steps forward, one of the men tapped the yeti on the head with his weapon, a long stick with a beanbag tied to it. When the yeti's body moved infinitesimally—probably from taking a deep breath—the tribesmen scurried back to the formation in terror.

Archibald frowned. "It seems, my darling, that we have encountered a particularly ferocious one this day. It is unfortunate that you will not get to see the slaying of one of these magnificent beasts, but sometimes even our peerless bravery cannot overcome such overwhelming bad luck. Men, gather the dead and retire."

While I considered whether it was worthwhile to slay this yeti, Cat knocked over the tribesmen holding him and pushed toward the center of our band. "You've got to be kidding me. Give me back my sword, and I'll show you how it's done."

"What a lark!" Archibald said. "To think you could personally match the bravery of my entire tribe. Besides, I cannot risk the safety of one of my beloved's companions."

"Cat, don't," Wolf said.

Cat quickly located the tribesmen holding our weapons and marched toward them. When one of them pointed his lawn rake at him, Cat grabbed it from his hands and snapped it in two. The tribesmen holding our supplies dropped them and sprinted off in the direction of the village. It all happened so fast that before any of the tribesmen could react, Cat grabbed his sword, pushed through them, and approached the still crouching yeti. Upon hearing the sound of Cat's steady approach, the yeti stood to face him. I almost grabbed my sword from the ground but decided that after the pathetic display from the tribesmen, I wouldn't really look all that heroic slaying the pitiful beast.

In reaction to the yeti's movement, the tribesmen grabbed their dead and ran down the hill in terror. "There's that legendary discipline, men," Archibald said. "Now, regroup back at the village. Songs will be sung of your brave deeds this day."

In under a minute, our party, minus Blackie, stood alone with the yeti. They had left our equipment, including the package, in a pile.

"Cowards," Cat said. "Now, it's time to slay a yeti. I've always wanted to slay a yeti."

"Have you even heard of a yeti before?" Wolf said.

"Well, no, but if I had, I'd have always wanted to slay one."

"That makes no sense whatsoever."

Cat raised his sword. "It'll make sense when I slay it."

"Not really," a booming voice said. "That sounds like a logical fallacy to me."

"No, it's just common stupidity," Wolf said.

"I'll show you stupidity," Cat said. "with my sword!"

"Truer words have never been uttered," the booming voice said.

Cat turned his back to the yeti and pointed his sword at Geoff. "That wasn't a very nice thing to say."

Geoff jumped back. "I didn't say a word."

"Then, who did?"

"That was me." The yeti clapped its hands to get Cat's attention. "Sorry if I'm not that mellow, but poor reasoning really irks me."

Cat scratched his forehead with the point of his sword. "You can talk?"

"Why wouldn't I be able to speak?"

"You're a yeti, and yetis don't speak."

The yeti gave him a questioning look. "You just said you didn't even know what a yeti was before now."

"Well, now that I do, I know they can't speak."

The yeti scratched its head in confusion.

"Don't worry about him," Wolf said. "He has that effect on people—and yetis."

"Why do you guys keep calling me a yeti?"

"The tribesmen told us you were a yeti," I said.

"I don't know if you noticed, but they're not the brightest group out there. My name is Dave, by the way." Dave held out his hand in friendship.

Wolf shook his hand and introduced our group.

"If you're not a yeti, then what, pray tell, are you, sir?" Geoff asked.

"I'm just a dude living in a cave."

"Men don't have white fur," Cat said. "Only yetis do."

"It's a coat. It gets cold up here." Dave pulled the coat off, revealing a Hawaiian shirt and shorts.

"Have you abided here for very long?" Geoff said.

"My scattered people have lived up here for generations. The tribesmen come up here every so often to hunt us."

"Why not move, if you are in such danger?"

"I don't know if you've noticed, but they're not exactly a threat. I don't think they've succeeded in a generation. Their leader is wearing my grandmother's brassiere, though, which is rather annoying."

"That is truly terrible," Jackal said. "I'm sorry for your loss."

"Thank you, but she died of old age a decade ago. They took it from her grave."

"If they're not successful in hunting your people, then where do they get their food?" Geoff said. "My apologies if this is a sore subject, but I am an amateur historian, and this question must be answered."

"I'm not exactly sure," Dave replied. "We do kill a lot of them, and they never leave a body behind."

"What do your people do for food, Dave?"

"There are some rather large bats in the cave systems around here. Their meat is delicious and gluten-free."

"Where did your people come from?"

"Geoff, I think you've pestered Dave the non-yeti enough," Jackal said. "We have a rather important mission to complete."

"Let me write all of this down," Geoff argued. "I need to keep careful notes. This will be a landmark discovery! Don't reveal anything more, Dave, until I'm ready."

"My full name is Davefucius, by the way."

At least they were plagiarizing something that wasn't copyrighted, I thought. This was still pretty awful, but it could be worse. They didn't have copyrights in ancient China, did they?

"So, are you a philosopher or something, Dave?" Wolf said. "Is that why you live up here in the isolated mountains?"

"No, man. My people are actually all Parrot Heads. We're all fans of Jimmy B—"

"No way am I letting you finish that sentence," I said. "I don't want to be sued."

"I think he was going to say 'uffet,' Harry," Cat said.

"Thanks a bunch, Cat."

"It's actually pronounced Boo-fay," Dave said. "That's how real fans pronounce it."

Oblivious to our conversation—and my gentle sobbing—Geoff finished his notes. "Two whole lost peoples. There are so many unanswered questions, and I, a simple but brilliant scribe, am the first to meet them. Why, I could write a book on my experiences with them. *Geoff of the Hill People: With the Fanged Trio and Some Other Guy*, I would call it. I can already picture the fame and wealth. I might even get to go on all of the talk shows."

I wisely decided not to question Geoff's mention of talk shows. I just wanted to get away from there. "Geoff, we have to go. You can come back later."

"No, no. Someone else might arrive and get the entire story before I do. I must do this now."

"But—" Jackal attempted to say.

"No, no. You heard him. He wants to stay." I quickly tossed everyone their packs, except for Geoff. "He has some very important things to do, and so do we. Now, it was really nice working with you, Geoff, but, you know, important package to deliver and stuff." I pushed Jackal down the hill in the opposite direction from the village. "This way, right, Dave?"

"Yes," Dave agreed. "You should see a lake at the bottom of the hill, and there are farms not too far from that."

"Harry, wait," Jackal said. "We might still be able to talk Geoff out of this."

I shook my head. "You heard him. Dave's people need to be studied, and he's the only one who can do it. Isn't that right, Geoff?"

"Well, actually—"

"See, he has to stay." I continued pushing Jackal as fast as I could. "Now, there's a lake down there. We can get all of this stink cleaned up. Won't that be wonderful? You'll be able to raise your hand to your face without retching."

"That does sound nice," she said, "but I'd hate to leave Geoff."

"Oh, we're too far away to hear him now, but I heard him say he'll be happier there and that he's just slowing us down, anyway."

"I didn't hear him say that," Cat said.

"He also said that Cat is the greatest warrior who's ever lived, and he's jealous of all of his muscles."

"Oh, yeah. I'm going to miss Geoff. He was a really great guy."

"I'm really going to miss Geoff, too," Jackal said. "Do you think he'll be all right?"

"Of course," I said. "Besides, I heard him say how much he likes living in caves and roughing it."

Don't say anything, OK? This was my only chance to ditch the terribly annoying Geoff, and I wasn't going to have it ruined. If you mess this up for me, I'm not going to continue, and then you'll miss out on more tales of my heroics.

Good. I'm glad we're in agreement.

HOW MANY CYCLOPS DOES IT TAKE TO CHANGE A LIGHT BULB?

We finally left the barren, hilly terrain of the Terngarin Mountains to a stand-in for the lush forest that dotted the northern coast of Garandia. I never wanted to be near another hill, yeti, or oddly speaking person ever again, which will be unfortunate for my lispy French neighbor who likes to dress as Bigfoot when I get back home.

A few miles in, we came upon a clear, wonderful pond.

"Oh, thank The One," Jackal said. "Some clean water. I have to get this stink off me."

"We all could, but I think the lady should go first," I said.

"Thank you, Harry. If you could all leave me some privacy, that would be great. Please make sure Cat doesn't peek."

"Don't flatter yourself, stick girl," Cat said. "You're not my type. I prefer older women. Women with more experience."

"Women with more hair, especially around the mouth and legs," Wolf said.

"Exactly."

We gave Jackal some privacy and moved a respectable distance into the forest.

"I can't wait to get cleaned off and finally take my underwear off my face," Cat said.

"No one told you to do that," Wolf said.

"I thought we might need a disguise to get past the tribesmen."

"Their village was in the other direction."

"Oh, well. I like the feel of the wind on my junk, anyway."

"A monster!" Jackal's scream pierced my brain and might have shattered a nearby tree.

I felt guilty that the sound of a woman in peril was actually a relief, but pretty much anything was a relief after thinking about Cat. Cat trailed behind us with his underwear still partly stuck to his helmet. As we exited the woods, we could see a tall, one-eyed monstrosity staring from across the pond. Behind the cyclops was a thin man with a dark goatee and eyes that never seemed to stay focused on any particular spot for more than a second. Cat and Wolf both drew their swords and cautiously approached the cyclops from the edge of the pond.

"We should kill this thing fast, or it might alert more of its kind," Cat said.

"Please, we mean you no harm," the goateed man said. "We stumbled upon this woman by accident."

"The monster has him under his spell," Cat said. "Watch out for the cyclops' magic eye."

"He's not a cyclops," the goateed man said.

"Your trickery won't work on us, monster," Cat said.

"Wait!" I said. "There aren't any cyclops in this world!"

"Just because no one has proven they exist," Wolf said, "doesn't mean they don't."

"Yeah! Like dragons, or lawyers with morals," Cat said.

"I know they don't exist because I created this world," I said.

"Are you saying that you are The One?" Wolf asked.

That wasn't a smart thing for me to say. While I had given

very specific descriptions of The One's earthly guise in my books, and I did have the rugged handsomeness and all-knowing eyes I had mentioned, I neither spoke in a Jamaican accent nor did I look Mongolian. They obviously didn't care about accuracy, and I couldn't risk feeding that further. I quickly ran through my knowledge of Vyenra to find some way out of this predicament.

"I'm not him. I . . . err. . . can only speak to the Creator."

"You mean you're a prophet?" Cat said.

"Yes, I'm a prophet. That's it."

"So, that's why you appear to talk to yourself sometimes. You aren't talking to yourself at all. You're speaking to the Almighty!"

"That's it exactly."

Talking to myself helps me organize my thoughts. I'm not crazy. If the insanity of this place continued, I might become crazy, but at this point, I wasn't crazy.

"And why haven't you mentioned this before?" Wolf asked.

"I don't like to brag."

"Who wouldn't want to brag about something like that?" Cat said. "If I could talk to The One, I'd tell everybody. Think of all the free stuff people would give you, and the ladies would be falling over themselves to be with you."

"Their expectations would be really high, and people would be bothering you all the time," Wolf said. "I'll bet that's why you didn't tell us, Harry."

Thank God Wolf had thought of that. The only thing I'd come up with was that accents interrupted my communion with my fake god. "Yes. As I was saying, cyclops—the monsters—don't exist. This must just be an ugly, one-eyed man."

Upon hearing the tone of our conversation change and seeing my companions' swords droop, the goateed man approached us. "Your friend is right. Brodus is only a man, but please don't tell any of our customers that."

Jackal had used our distraction with the cyclops to get dressed. "Customers?"

"We are members of a travelling circus. Brodus is our 'cyclops,' though, in actuality, he is just a tall man with one eye."

Brodus was still hunkered down at the other end of the pond, cringing. I couldn't get a good enough look to verify his partner's claims.

"That's unfortunate that he lost an eye in an accident, but inspiring that he uses his disability to his advantage," Jackal said.

"He didn't lose it in an accident. He poked it out to make himself more employable in the circus industry."

Brodus nodded from afar.

"Couldn't he have not poked it out and found other work?"

The goateed man shrugged. "You try being a seven-foot-tall mute in this economy. It's really hard to get work when you can't answer questions on a job interview. However, if you only have one eye and you're seven feet tall, you don't have to answer anything when you apply for the cyclops position."

"Surely, there has to be another way . . ."

While we were busy with the conversation, Cat inched away from us.

"So, what is your job in the circus?" Jackal said.

"I am the proprietor, the famous Jalev." He bowed, while not taking his eyes off of us.

Jackal's eyes lit up. "*The* Jalev! I've always wanted to see your circus since I was little."

"Well, we're just past the hill over there, but we're in the process of packing up for the next town." Jalev rose back up and gave us a very long look. He spent a lot longer on me, and especially on my very sexy back, than on anyone else. "What, exactly, are people such as yourselves doing here?"

"We're a band of mercenaries. We were travelling through

these woods on our way to the capital when we were waylaid by strange tribesmen."

Wolf appeared about to speak, but Jalev silenced him with the simple wag of an eyebrow. "That is fascinating. Perhaps—"

At the other end of the pond, there was a loud splash, punctuated by a scream. The cyclops was whimpering in a ball, and Cat was standing over him with his fists balled up.

"Cat, what are you doing?" Jackal asked.

"He kept winking at me."

"What do you mean, winking? He only has one eye. Are you sure he wasn't just blinking?"

"When you quickly close only one eye, it's called winking. If he was blinking, he would have closed both eyes. He only closed the one eye, therefore he was winking. And I'll hit you again if you wink at me like that. You're not my type."

Brodus began to cry.

"He doesn't have two eyes to wink with, idiot!"

The small part of his brain that Cat used for reason must have finally clicked on. He actually looked bashful. "Ohhhhh. Sorry, mister cyclops. I forgot you only have one eye. Here, let me help you up. My mistake. Won't happen again."

Jalev was already on the other side of the pond, holding the sniffling cyclops on his shoulder. I wasn't sure how he'd gotten over there that fast. "Let's get you back to the camp, big guy," Jalev said. "I'll make you my famous soup, and you'll feel all better. Perhaps these fine mercenaries can make it up to us by performing a job for us, yes?"

Wolf shook his head at Cat in disgust. "If it's short. We can only spare a day. I suppose we do owe it to you, and we promise Cat will stay far away from Brodus. Won't you, Cat?"

"I promise. Sheesh. I only punched him, like, five or six times."

"Splendid." Jalev was somehow right next to us again. "I'd

like you three grizzled warriors and the guy that Axin and Weel did unspeakable but completely consensual things with to look around. We've had reports of a string of small, possibly unrelated incidents in our peaceful and honorable circus. Nothing major, mind you; an uptick in thumb wrestling, a couple of drunken brawls, an outbreak of nipple-twisting on men, and a few deaths by electrocution. Pretty normal, everyday things for a circus, but there seems to be a bit too many of those going on. Worst of all, there seems to be a lurker around, and I would like to know what he's looking for."

Cat puffed out his chest. "I like the way this guy talks, Wolf. He really seems to get how grizzled I am." Then Cat whispered in my ear, "What does 'grizzled' mean?"

"I'm not sure what we can do about those," Wolf said, "and a death by electrocution sounds pretty serious."

The pit of my stomach dropped. I had visions of cell phones, televisions, and computers running rampant in my medieval-inspired world.

"Oh, we have those all the time here. Our new motto is, 'Now with twenty-five percent fewer deaths by electrocution.' It really does draw in more business. You're probably asking what any of this has to do with you. Well, I'd like your crew to go around and see if there is any special cause for all of that. It's probably just a few random occurrences, but my gut tells me to investigate. Having you walk around should, at least, calm everyone's nerves. In exchange for your services, we can provide you with transportation. What do you say to a little bit of easy work that gets you to your destination faster?"

Jackal had walked Brodus over to us and had given him a handkerchief to wipe his eye with. "You're such an idiot, Cat. Let's get the poor guy back to his camp."

"Can we at least clean off this stink?" Wolf said. "Cat really needs it."

"I'm at the height of ripeness, just waiting for someone to pluck me."

"It's over that ridge," Jalev said as he led Jackal and Brodus away. "Meet me there when you're done."

Wolf pushed Cat under the water and held him there, maybe a bit too long.

"Wow, that was refreshing," Cat said. "The water feels great on my junk."

We quickly finished our bath after Cat had recovered the rubber ducky that he had pulled from I didn't want to know where, and changed into clean clothes. We burned our old clothes for fear that they might kill any wildlife that accidentally wandered near them, and then headed to the circus.

A QUEST FOR A NEW CHAPTER TITLE

The circus was a bit of a letdown. Most of the tents were down, and all of the animals were in their cages. None of the clowns even had any makeup on, though some of them were still wearing their big floppy shoes. Not that I could blame them. If I had floppy shoes, I'd wear them all the time, too.

One of the workers sighted us immediately and took us towards Jalev's trailer. If she hadn't found us we would have easily gotten lost through that sea of trailers, wagons, and cages. As soon as we sighted Jalev's trailer, our guide excused herself and ran off. Brodus sat off in a corner dozing under a large blanket. Wolf rushed us to Jackal's side, probably to prevent her from revealing anything important. He had nothing to worry about, as it was almost impossible to get a word in around the highly animated Jalev.

"Ahh, excellent," Jalev said. "I was just telling your young friend, here, about our operation. She would be perfect for several positions we have open, but, alas, she has informed me that she is not looking for a new occupation."

"I didn't know they had a—" Cat tried to say before Jalev stopped him with a wink.

"I'd like you to start by interviewing our strong woman, Weyma. She saw this lurker last night. Though, as it is getting late, that will have to wait until tomorrow. For tonight, I will show you to your trailers. This way."

Before we could speak, he pointed at the sleeping Brodus and then pointed in the opposite direction. We followed him silently until we were sure we were out of range.

"You will find Weyma a bit brusque, although, with your mustachioed companion, I am sure you are used to that."

Cat smiled. "This guy just gets me. Are you guys looking for a handsome lead?"

"I think they make the gorillas wear pants here," Jackal said.

Cat gave Jalev a questioning look, and Jalev nodded in response.

Wolf pretended Cat hadn't said anything. "So, Jalev, what exactly does this lurker look like?"

Jalev directed us to make a left to avoid the center area, where they were taking down the main tent. "Ahh, well, that is a bit of a problem, as there have been several conflicting reports. The most recent sighting described him as wearing a black, wide-brimmed hat, a small mask, and a cape."

Fantastic. We were looking for either Zorro or the Hamburglar.

Wolf chuckled. "That sounds like the legend of the Tickling Bandit from my childhood."

"If it's from your childhood, that'd mean he'd be at least 150." Cat started counting his toes. "Err . . .151. How many leap years have there been since you were born?"

"Cat, I'm three years younger than your dad, and he's fifty-four. Well, he would have been. Sorry."

Cat slapped him on the back. "That's OK, Wolf. And I think you're a little off. Dad would have been 237 next week."

Jalev had uncharacteristically stopped speaking and was

taking a bit too much interest in what they were saying. His eyes made it look like he was mentally taking notes of everything they said, while still managing to take the time to eye my back in between pauses.

"You know," Jalev said. "There are some who say that the Tickling Bandit was a real person, and those legends do place him as active in the Forest of the Thumb, which happens to be nearby."

Wolf laughed. "Like one man could take out an entire squadron of elite royal knights guarding the king's niece. That would take a whole group of men, and there's no way a group of people who were that skilled could collectively fail to do anything noteworthy for fifty years."

"I know I couldn't," Cat said as he "inadvertently" knocked over a cage, letting a large snake loose.

"I'm sure you're right," Jalev said as he shooed the snake back into the cage. "We have also received reports that this lurker is a rather attractive blonde woman, and others that describe him as having a red mustache and a 'Professional Lurker' sash, though I would think that if either of those was true, someone would have spotted this person rather easily since then."

"My money is on it being an invisible man," Cat said. "The last circus I was at had one. He was even intangible."

"If he was invisible and intangible, how could you tell he was there?" I said. "It could've been someone projecting their voice."

"No, he was a mute, too. It was amazing."

Jalev brought us to a stop in front of two rickety-looking wooden trailers with paint so faded, it didn't seem to be there at first glance. I couldn't see any horses nearby to move them with, but then again, I hadn't seen any near the other trailers. I figured they had to be kept in a central location until it was time to move. My shoulders felt like they were about to fall off, so I set my pack inside one of the trailers. Cat and Wolf followed suit.

"As it's about to get dark, you can start in earnest in the morning. We'll likely get moving around ten tomorrow. Dinner can be found around the small bit of smoke you see coming from over there." Jalev pointed behind him. "I'll leave instructions that you are now our guests."

"Ahh, so, not the big smoke coming from over there." Cat pointed to Jalev's left. "Is that some sort of closing ceremony?"

For once, Jalev's eyes focused on a single spot for more than a few seconds. His mouth dropped. "No, it is not. With all of the cloth tents and wooden wagons, I would never allow something so big."

WHIP IT. WHIP IT. OWWWW

Chaos ensued. The fire was growing rather quickly, and the sound of a very respectable ruckus grew closer. A number of workers came sprinting past our shabby wagons in a state that I can only describe as passably disorganized. It took Jalev several attempts to get one of them to stop long enough to get a response.

The middle-aged woman did a pretty good job of seeming out of breath. "We're under attack!"

Jalev glanced back at us, probably to tell us to gather our weapons, but we were all well past that stage, so he turned back to the woman. "By the townsfolk? With our numbers, they shouldn't give us much trouble."

Her feet wanted to keep moving, and her upper body seemed to agree, but Jalev's gaze was enough to keep her in place. "No. These are professionals. Merf and Gurb tried to stop them, but the big one took them down with one swipe of his blade."

"Merf and Gurb are . . . were our security personnel. They both served in the Garandian army. They would have also been the ones to lead our workers in any skirmishes with an angry populace. How many of them were there?"

"Three that I saw, but they weren't no amateurs." Her feet finally overruled Jalev's gaze, and she took off.

Jalev shook his head as she ran from view. "Well, it appears quite fortuitous that your little band arrived when it did."

Wolf motioned Cat to stand next to him. "As long as 'fortuitous' pays extra. We did not agree to fight your battles for you."

"Yes, all right. Whatever your usual rate is fine, but we must hurry. If my circus is destroyed, I'll have nothing left worth paying you for."

Jackal stopped to tie her boot. "Go on. I'll catch up."

We ran toward the fire. It was easy to find where we needed to go; we just ran in the opposite direction from everyone else. It took quite a while to move the quarter of a mile to our objective, as the bodies moving away often exceeded the space between the narrow trailers and wagons. The occasional escaped animal also slowed us down, though, fortunately, even lions and bears are afraid to fight a mostly naked man. (More than likely, they were just trained well, but I was not going to argue with Cat.)

We eventually came upon the source of the disturbance. Standing over a very dead circus worker—who must have tried to oppose him, judging by the sword nearby—was a large man in red and black armor. The man laughed maniacally and stabbed the corpse repeatedly, apparently in case we weren't sure he was the bad guy. If it had still been in fashion, I imagined they would add some boos to the tape to give even the densest person a clear idea that they weren't supposed to root for this guy. I mentally inserted the boos so I could at least get a laugh out of something to maintain my sanity.

Jalev was nowhere to be seen.

When the man finally looked up from his game of Stab the Corpse, he gave Wolf a broad smile. "Ha! Look who it is, Fox. It's Wolfie and Kitty."

A stout man in similar armor stepped out from behind him.

"Fox left with our friend. Also, I think their names are Wolf and Cat." He had that whiny voice that belongs to people who like to correct every tiny error, like what shade of brown Arik's belt is or how I spell my name.

"Bah! Oh, well, more fun for us, Platypus. I wonder how much extra we'll get paid for offing the Fanged Trio." He advanced on Wolf, who locked his shield with Cat's.

The one called Platypus (who I now noticed was wearing a helmet in the shape of the animal of the same name) pulled two large metal paddles from his belt. "There is nothing in the contract about it, but with less competition, it should prove most beneficial in our future contracts. I'd still kill the pantsless one for free since he took my bit."

Wolf stuck his head above his shield. "The Toothy Three will always be a cheap knockoff of the Fanged Trio, and we're really getting tired of proving it."

"Yeah," Cat said, "and you totally missed the much cooler names of the Tooth Fairies or the Maws of Doom."

The taller one scowled at Cat. "But those don't tell you how many people there are in our group."

Wolf laughed. "Manatee, that's exactly why you'll always be in our shadow. Think outside the box, man."

Manatee growled—not at all like an actual manatee—and charged. Wolf took his strike easily in the shield and counter-attacked, but Manatee dodged. Cat squared off against Platypus. Jackal aimed her crossbow at the melee but couldn't find an opening as the combatants danced back and forth. I considered jumping in, but my skill at throwing swords at bushes didn't seem to apply to this situation, and our opponents were clearly more skilled than I at the more mundane arts of war.

When Manatee backed off to catch his breath, Wolf glanced over at Jackal and me. "Go find a middle-aged woman in a fox helmet. She's the brains of this outfit and is sure to be looking for their real objective."

"Nuh-uh," Manatee said as he brought his long, thick blade down on Wolf's shield yet again. "Our objective is to kill indiscriminately, and we do not at all have an objective to steal anything in particular, especially not something in a velvet bag."

Jackal stood like a statue. "But, Wolf, this is my first mission. I can't do it alone."

Wolf staggered back as Manatee slammed a particularly hard blow against his shield. "Jackal, you did fine against Blackie's tribe. Great, even. I probably would've died if you hadn't hit that big guy. We're counting on you. Harry can't do it alone."

"Hey," I said. "I can too."

Jackal grabbed my shirt sleeve and pulled me away. Her uncertainty was still there if you looked real hard, but I decided not to point it out. The character (and probably the actress) needed this. We headed back the way we had come.

"Do you know the way?" I said. "Where's Jalev?"

As if he had been summoned—or the actor had been waiting for us—Jalev appeared from around the corner. "Need to get back to your wagon? I'll lead you there."

Jackal's face scrunched in confusion. "How?"

Before I could ask about the part that would make me look heroic, a whip snapped just above my head. I was disappointed that its owner was not a Harrison Ford knockoff in a fedora and was instead a muscular, middle-aged woman wearing a fox-shaped helmet. Behind her, a man with a red mustache slunk out of view yelling, "Lurk, lurk, lurk!" as he went. I was intensely jealous of him since that was my move, but the only direction I could currently slink was back to the other battle, which involved twice the number of people who wanted to injure me. I had learned long ago that even when people try to fake-injure you, it still leaves bruises. I flinch whenever I see a butter knife, and newspapers give me night terrors.

Jackal fired her crossbow. The bolt landed dead center of where her attacker's face had been, but Fox had effortlessly dodged it. The whip lashed out again, catching Jalev on his right arm, and then struck Jackal's bow, ruining her effort to reload. There were no bushes to toss my sword at, so I tried to slash the whip. Unfortunately, whips are really hard to hit, especially when their owner doesn't want you to. The wagon behind Fox would never mess with me again, though, especially since my sword would likely never leave its side. I gave up after a few strong tugs.

Fox tried a few more slashes, but my companions were too quick for her. "I'm going to guess by the jackal-shaped helmet that you are Wolf's and Cat's newest companion."

Jackal tried to load her crossbow but fumbled the bolt again as Fox's latest blow landed inches from her face. "Yes."

Fox reached her whip back for another strike. "A pity, as you remind me of myself when I was your age. I was hoping to be the one to kill my old squamate and our captain's son. It gives me shivers to think about the old letch rolling in his grave."

I was separated from Jalev and Jackal by the length of the wagon. Being that I was unarmed, the least dangerous person there, and not very interested in the battle, Fox had given up on me after I had lost my sword. I wondered if this was their way of giving me an opportunity to finally be the hero. It would be just like these morons to put my heroic moment right after the part where I lost my sword to a wagon and to let it be by hitting a woman. Granted, she looked like she worked out and could probably take out a mountain lion in a fair fight, but still, it was wrong to hit a woman. Unfortunately, I didn't see any knockout gas nearby, and even if she agreed to a battle of wits, I was sure it would end with me getting slapped. Fortunately, my mind is a highly tuned tactical machine, and I came up with a brilliant idea in the nick of time.

"Hey, Fox, over here." I waved my arms like I was doing jumping jacks to let her know I was serious.

Her whip caught my left pinky to let me know she was also serious. "What is this? Bring Your Idiot Brother to Work Day?"

"No, we're not related," Jackal and I said in unison.

Fox gave Jackal a pitying look. "It's OK if he is. I have a son just like him, minus the beard and pants."

I wasn't sure what fault she found with my pants. I mean, sure, they weren't the kind of things a noble might wear, and you could still kind of see where I had wet myself earlier, but they were way more stylish than anything the other peasants were wearing. Maybe she meant the opposite, and she really liked them. Whatever her meaning, I took it as an insult that fueled my anger and charged.

Unfortunately, being angry does not fuel the whole "thinking" thing, and I forgot the earlier lesson about not charging in a straight line if someone is aiming at you. Her next strike caught me right in the calves, and I tumbled to the ground. My legs burned horribly, and I doubted I would ever be able to wear shorts again.

"You bitch," Jackal said. "You've crippled poor Harry."

I couldn't see what happened next, being as I was having my daily face-to-face meeting with my old friend the ground, but it sounded like Jackal's next bolt found its target. There was definitely screaming involved, and my mouth was full of dirt, so it wasn't me. The next thing I knew, I was being hoisted up by Jackal and Jalev.

"That was very brave of you, Harry," Jackal said.

"Bravery and stupidity do seem to mean the same thing to you warrior types," Jalev said, "but it did work."

I was very glad that I had so much dirt covering my face, as it completely hid the tears. "Where did she go?"

"Your friend's bolt caught her right in her whip arm, so Fox fled. Which means she has a head start on the wagon, though, fortunately, she went the wrong way."

Jackal looked down at the ground. She seemed to focus on some blueish scraps of paper littered roughly every few feet. "But I left a trail, and she's headed right for our wagon."

Jalev's eyes darted back and forth between the direction we had come from and the direction the scraps of paper pointed. "Err . . . yes. It seems I got mixed up in the excitement. You are quite correct. Your wagon should be just around the corner, there. As you should be able to find it easily, and I am not much use in a physical confrontation, why don't you go on without me and I'll . . . go look after my circus. I am sure my people need my leadership to direct them in this time of crisis after all." He bowed and then darted back the way we had come.

After I was sure he was out of earshot, I stopped Jackal before we rounded the corner. "I think he's up to something. Did you see the way he kept eyeing my bag before? I'll bet he ran back here and took it while we were busy with Platypus and Manatee."

Jackal cocked her crossbow and gave me a wry smile. "Then he'll be very disappointed when he discovers that the package isn't in your bag. I stopped to tie my boot and took the package out of your pack. I have it now."

I, of course, had known that all along. I'd just wanted to give her a chance to take credit for all the hard work she had done. The character, and by extension the actress, had seemed like she needed a boost in self-confidence, and I was more than happy to give it to her. As I've shown, I was overflowing with self-confidence and had more than enough to spare. I was also well aware that she'd still had her pack on the whole time.

Jackal pointed around the corner and made hand signals like

they do on military shows. I had no idea what her signals meant, but I wasn't armed anyway, and even if I had been, there likely wouldn't be any bushes to fight.

"So, if we have the item, why are we going back to our trailer?"

"Because that's where Jalev wants us to go, and I want to throw him off the fact that I have the package." She scratched her forehead.

"But we don't actually have to go back there. He already thinks that's where we're going."

She stepped away from the corner. "You're right. We should go get the others and get out of here. Hopefully, with the chaos, no one will even realize we're gone."

"So, we'll just follow your trail back to them."

"Unless they've moved. If they've moved, where do you think they'll be?"

Suddenly, a new flame shot into the sky, twice the size of any of the previous flames, followed by screams of "Where are his pants?"

"Cat!" we said in unison.

WHAT'S THE RETURN POLICY ON VILLAINS?

It didn't take long to find the source of the noise, as a giant flame is pretty easy to follow. It's like a crude version of the glowing arrow you have to follow in video games. The sound of all of those voices made it even easier. The hard part was overcoming my natural instinct to run in the opposite direction of either of those things.

After we cleared through the smoke, we found a large group of people congregating in front of Jalev's trailer. The trailer was an absolute wreck; all of the windows were broken out, the door was ajar and missing one of its hinges, and most of its contents seemed to be strewn over the ground. Wolf stood next to Jalev, who was kneeling down, massaging the forehead of the prostrate Brodus. A capuchin monkey held Brodus's hand. We pushed through the crowd that always seems to form whenever there's a crime.

"Where are Platypus and Manatee?" I asked.

Wolf shook his head. "We disabled both of 'em, but before I could tie them up, Cat thought he saw an invisible man take the package and run off."

Jalev turned from massaging Brodus's head with a wet cloth.

"And the gentleman in the panther helmet must have followed him here."

"I thought his invisible man was also intangible?" I said.

Wolf grimaced. "Cat's not much of a thinker."

"I'm a doer," Cat said as pulled himself out of a nearby pile of debris.

"Whatever his reasons," Jalev said, "he inadvertently charged straight into a very visible, very tangible person as he was assaulting poor Brodus."

"Is Brodus all right?" Jackal said. "Will he live?"

"He appears to be fine. No noticeable damage. Brodus, what did he do to you?"

Between sobs, Brodus gestured toward his armpits and belly.

Jalev inspected both areas. "I don't see any damage besides a little redness, and it's fading quickly. What exactly did he do, Brodus?"

Brodus rubbed his eye and regained his composure. He then reached out with one finger in a slight hook shape and tickled Jalev's right armpit.

Jalev giggled. "Stop it, Brodus. This is no time for levity. My goodness, do you mean—? No, it couldn't be. Not the bandit!"

Brodus nodded.

"It's the Tickling Bandit! Oh my God. Hide the children. Pull out your armpit protectors. Carry a fresh pair of pants whenever you leave your house!"

The crowd gasped and began to talk animatedly amongst themselves. Some of the people even ran away in terror. The monkey screeched and jumped up and down. Clearly, this was supposed to be a big deal. What was I to do without a fresh pair of pants to put on? This villain might be a threat for Big Bird and Elmo, but he had no business being in my world.

"But, how could it be?" Wolf said. "He hasn't been seen in over fifty years."

The monkey shrugged.

Evidently, they had recruited this crowd from a children's show. In no other place could someone called the Tickling Bandit actually induce terror instead of mockery. I guessed Gargamel and the Trix Rabbit were otherwise occupied.

"How, exactly, did someone tickle a seven-foot cyclops into submission?" I said.

"The Tickling Bandit is a master of the martial art of Tickle-Shen," Jalev replied. "According to legend, a Tickle-Shen master can knock out a knight in full plate armor in half a second. It is a lost art from the east, allegedly from Zelahadon, which was thought to have disappeared over 200 years ago, until the bandit appeared."

Isn't it against the Writers' Guild rules to employ a class of kindergarteners? That would be a violation of child labor laws, wouldn't it? My guess was that the bandit was Jalev wearing a mask, like on *Scooby-Doo*. "That's . . . awful, Jalev. At least they didn't get anything important."

"Unfortunately, they took your package from Hammurabi," Jalev said. "You see, I swiped your bag."

Jackal gave him a big smile. "Actually, I pretended to tie my boot and took it. It's in my bag now."

Jalev sighed. "Look again, dear. I swiped it from your bag while you were fighting Fox."

Jackal set her pack down and pulled the contents out. She rolled her eyes at him as she pulled out the velvet bag, then gasped when the bag turned out to contain a brick and not a wooden box.

"You really should have protected it better," Jalev said. "The fate of the kingdom rests on that. How couuuuuld you lose it? Do you want us all to die?"

"Well, maybe just Cat," Jackal said half-heartedly.

"If I were dead, who would have captured the invisible man?"

"By The One, Cat, there is no mute, invisible, intangible man."

Cat scratched his head with a fork. "Then what, exactly, did I catch?"

"More stupidity?" Wolf said.

"You can't catch that. It's a fast runner."

"That's fascinating, Cat," Wolf said, "but let's get back to the important part. Jalev did take our package. Who do you work for? Was this whole Toothy Three attack just a distraction so you could take it, and then they double-crossed you?"

Jackal pointed her crossbow straight at Jalev's head. She was only a few yards away, and it would have been nearly impossible to miss at that distance.

Jalev raised his hands in surrender. "If I took it to sell or give to some evil organization, do you think I'd inform you? I could have just told you that Brodus's assailant took it, without the part where I had my hands on it. I may be a thief and a con man, but I'm a patriot first. I would never do anything to threaten the safety of my homeland. Sure, I may steal now and again and again and again, but losing this could doom our country. Besides, Hammurabi sent word of you travelling through here. He paid me off so I wouldn't steal it, and I swore to help you all on your way. I'm an honorable thief, after all. I'll even let you borrow Mr. Monkey to help you out."

Wolf lowered Jackal's weapon.

"Fine, but I'm not calling him Mr. Monkey," I said. "That name is awful."

"Cat Junior?" Cat said.

"No, we'll call him Mr. Plot Device, because that's obviously what the writers put him in here for."

"Ohh, I like it. It has a really nice ring to it."

The monkey beamed in agreement.

"So, then, who took it?" Wolf said.

Jalev put his hand on his chin. "I did notice a man with a red mustache talking to Fox before you clashed with her, and as you'll recall, that matches the description of the lurker we've had in our fine circus. Plus, he kept saying 'lurk, lurk, lurk,' so it's safe to say that's your guy."

Cat dusted himself off. "I did feel a mustache brush against me when that guy got in my way of taking out that dastardly invisible man. I also remember thinking about how red the mustache felt."

"How exactly can a mustache feel red?" Jackal asked.

"When you run around naked as much as I have, you get more sensitive to these things. Try it and you'll see. Red will never be the same after you've felt it on a mustache or a horseshoe."

Jackal edged around behind me. "I'll take your word for it."

"So, we know who took it," Wolf said, "but where did he go?"

Mr. Plot Device, true to his name, pointed off into the nearby forest.

"Do you have to tinkle, little guy?" Cat said.

"No, Cat," Jackal said. "He means the bandit ran off that way."

"Let me show you the evidence I found, first," Cat said.

Jackal began walking toward the forest. "I am not falling for that."

A FIGHT INVOLVING ME AND NO TICKLING?

Jalev sent runners to gather our things and gave us some food and other supplies as an apology for losing the package. He couldn't afford to spare any horses, as the Toothy Three had let most of them go as part of their initial attack. The trail those mercenaries had left went off in the opposite direction from our thief, so finishing them off would have to wait for another day.

In under fifteen minutes, we were ready to go. We headed off to the "Forest of the Thumb"—so called because during decades past, most of the Tickling Bandit attacks had occurred nearby. When I asked why "of the Thumb" when most people don't tickle with their thumbs, I was told that "of the Index Finger" didn't have quite the same ring.

"Who is the Tickling Bandit?" Cat asked. "I've never heard of him before."

"That's right, "Wolf said. "You didn't grow up in the north. He would attack any group who passed by the area carrying anything valuable. It didn't matter how secret the item was, how many guards there were, or how big it was; he would always take it."

"All of the accounts I've heard vary greatly with regard to

anything substantive about him, beside the fact that his tickles can effortlessly incapacitate or kill. Some think the Tickling Bandit is more than one person."

"He might not even be a he," Jackal said.

Cat laughed. "Like a girl could do all that damage."

Mr. Plot Device shook his head as Jackal pushed Cat into a tree.

The trees in the forest were entirely evergreens; of what type, I'm not sure. The fresh scent made me think of my cabin, where I would much rather be. The ground was sprinkled with crinkling pine needles, reminding me of my walks with my grandfather in my youth. The constant crunching made it very difficult for anyone to sneak up on us, but also made it unlikely that we would be able to do the same. The needles also made it fairly easy for even a novice tracker such as myself to follow our prey.

Eventually, our trail led us back out of the woods to a modest farm with three cows, a few chickens, and an old barn. A clean-shaven man with salt and pepper hair waved from the porch. He didn't get up to greet us, so we walked to him instead. As we got closer, it became apparent why, as his right leg was in a splint.

"He looks just like the Tickling Bandit," Cat said. "I told you he had a red mustache."

"Is Cat color blind?" Jackal asked.

"He sees what he wants to see," Wolf said.

Mr. Plot Device made a gesture with his hands that I'm not going to describe. Let's just say I hate monkeys and leave it at that.

"Hullo there, strangers. What brings you here?" The farmer pointed a crutch at me. "Ain't you the boy who let Axin and Weel do all of them unspeakable things to him?"

"No, that guy still has a speck of self-esteem left," I said. This was really getting old. As if this show wasn't bad enough. I didn't need that rumor floating around.

"My mistake. You do fit the description, though."

"We're looking for any other travelers who might have come this way," Jackal said. "Something of ours was stolen recently."

The concern on the farmer's brow vanished. "Ahh, no, sorry. Only travelers in these parts are locals. Most were heading to that circus. You might wanna try there. Maybe they can help ya."

"No, that's where the theft occurred. It was the Tickling Bandit. He knocked out the seven-foot-tall cyclops and took it."

"The Tickling Bandit! Thysla, Wolo, get out here!" the farmer called out. "They need to hear this, and then we need to tell the neighbors."

A man, who the farmer identified as Wolo, appeared shortly after from the fields, but after several more yells, Thysla never arrived. The farmer was unconcerned since, at four years old, Thysla was unlikely to be much help anyway.

The farmer had taken Wolo on as an extra hand after his son had been killed in a recent bandit attack. Wolo had to be around thirty, with red hair, a mustache, and an eerily familiar build. I'd seen more difficult mysteries on *Sesame Street*. I could even see the corner of his blue sash sticking out beneath his shirt.

"What do you want, boss?"

"Hey, he has a red mustache," Cat said. "That must be him."

"Subtle as always, Cat," Jackal said. "You might as well have just told him to start running."

"Him, who?" Wolo said as Wolf circled behind him.

"Where is our item that you stole?"

"I didn't take nothing. I swear."

"Look at his fingers," Wolf said. "They're all bent, and the ends point upwards."

"Just like my p—" Cat said.

"Shut up, Cat!" Jackal and Wolf said in unison.

Wolo said, "So, now you accuse me of a crime I didn't

commit *and* make fun of my fingers. You're not that perverted gang who goes around tickling people until they pee, are you?"

"I wasn't making fun," Wolf said. "What happened to your fingers?"

"They got messed up in my lumberjacking days. I tried to slow down a tree that was going to fall on the little kid who was working with us. He was one of those dying kids whose last wish was to be a lumberjack. I told them it wasn't safe for him to be out there. My fingers haven't been able to bend much since, but it was worth it, saving the kid."

"Could you try to tickle me?" Jackal asked.

"I can't really bend my fingers," Wolo said, "but I can try." As I had suspected, the only reaction he got was a slight "Ow!" from Jackal.

"So, it appears we owe you an apology," Jackal said. "Someone is clearly trying to frame you."

"Or he has an accomplice," Cat said. "I'll bet it's the little girl."

Jackal smacked him in the helmet. "Sorry. I thought it was time for the 'secret handshake.'"

Wolf examined the farmer's splinted leg closely. "There's no way he could have travelled that kind of distance with his leg like this. So, where is the little girl?"

The farmer stared into the forest. "She must have wandered off. She's always liked to be alone."

"Do you know where she usually goes?" Jackal asked.

"Yeah, some old lean-to near the creek," Wolo replied.

"Show us the way. This is the closest thing to a lead we have now."

We followed Wolo through the forest, the crinkle of the pine needles giving the little girl ample warning of our approach. The farmer hobbled slowly behind us on his crutches. I had the distinct impression that we were walking into an ambush, but what sort of ambush, I had no idea. I assumed the girl was going to her accomplices. Perhaps this was my chance to finally display my heroism.

"It should be coming up in about a minute," Wolo said.

Almost as if that had been a signal, the farmer and Mr. Plot Device fell like they'd been hit by knockout darts. There was no rustling from the trees near them to indicate where their attacker was. Seeing the tiny monkey doubled over like he was asleep was so adorable that I almost forgot I was in pretend danger.

The rest of our group was in a near-panic. Wolo hunched into a ball—the classic defense maneuver of both the armadillo and me, but I performed my best superhero pose, right out in the open. There was no way they would dare hurt their star. Cat and Wolf drew their swords and assumed positions on either side of me.

Jackal coolly bent over and checked our fallen comrades. "No puncture wounds or darts, but they seem to be unconscious and breathing normally. I see the same red mark under their armpits as Brodus had."

"Are you saying someone knocked them out from up close with no one seeing them?" Wolf asked.

"That can't be," she said. "Thysla, are you out there?"

A childlike cackle erupted, seemingly from all around us.

"See, I was right," Cat said. "Sometimes, I wish I wasn't so smart." Cat went down, again with no sound or movement from the trees.

"We need to form up in a close circle," Wolf said. "If we're close enough together, whatever is out there won't be able to get to us easily."

"Good idea," Jackal replied.

We were too slow. Jackal and Wolf went down before they could even move, but our opponent seemed to be ignoring Wolo, who was sitting off to the side. My heart was racing, even though my mind was saying that none of this was real.

I cracked my knuckles for what I knew was coming. Surely her big, strong accomplices would emerge soon, so I could finally get one of my agreed-upon heroic scenes.

"Come on out and face The One's chosen champion and part-time prophet, you vile thugs," I called.

Thysla appeared about a couple of yards in front of me and frowned. "You're a prophet?"

"Yes. The One speaks to me, and he wants you and your thugs to leave us alone." I took a half-step back, an involuntary reaction learned from years of being bullied by people smaller than I.

"I'll show you my thugs." In less time than it takes to blink, she had charged forward and leapt with her index finger pointed at my right armpit. Again, my highly-tuned reflexes took over, and I tripped over the leg of the prostrate Cat. As I fell, my left leg stuck straight out while my right leg got caught on Cat. That caused my body to twist with my left arm flailing forward, hitting Thysla on the back of the head. We both hit the ground face-first, a position I was well practiced in.

When I stood, I noticed that my small opponent appeared to be just as unconscious as everyone else.

"All right, you evil bandits. I've taken down your tiny messenger. Now, it's your turn."

Wolo peeked out like a turtle. "I'm not an evil bandit."

"I didn't mean you, Wolo. It's nearly impossible to engage in banditry when you curl up into a ball whenever there's danger. Not that I have personal experience with that. I was referring to her accomplices."

"Oh. I don't think she has any."

"Couldn't be. She's just a little kid." I looked around at the forest and waited for the big hulking attackers I knew were hiding all around us. I thought I saw movement near one of the trees to Wolo's right, but it turned out to be a sudden gust of wind.

"I think you scared them off."

"Must have," I said. "Come and help me tie her up before she wakes."

He popped up out of his ball. "D-D-Do you have any rope?"

"Cat has some in his pack. Don't ask what he usually uses it for."

Wolo hog-tied her like a cowboy. I was glad he was the one who tied her up, as I didn't want to be arrested for child abuse. The tape will clearly show I hit her by accident.

After a few minutes, we'd managed to rouse the rest of our group. While they were groggy, they appeared to be unharmed other than a few scrapes.

"Great job, Harry," Cat said. "You continue to impress me. I may have to appoint you as my new protégé."

Jackal patted me on the back. "Really well done, Harry."

The farmer crawled over to his crutches, and Wolf helped him stand.

"Let me guess: you're going to tell us that you didn't know she was the Tickling Bandit?" Jackal said.

"I found her on the Tangholds' farm," the farmer said. "Real tragedy. They was a young family. Didn't know 'em well. Come to think of it, I didn't even know they had a daughter till we found her."

"Hmmm. Interesting," Jackal said.

"All right, let's wake the Bandit," Wolf said. "We need some answers." He poured the contents of his water bottle out on her and she started to wake.

Once again, when you file your child abuse claims, I did not pour a water bottle over an unconscious child.

"Stop, stop," she said. "I'm awake already."

"Now, who are you really?" Wolf asked.

"I'm Thysla Tangleholder. My parents died in a bandit attack."

Jackal looked at the farmer. "Didn't you say it was the Tang-holds who died?"

"Yup. 'Twas the Tangholds, Bricheff and Neora."

"That's what I said," Thysla said. "Tanghold."

"No, you didn't," several people said in unison.

"Fine. I'm the spirit of the last Tickle-Shen master, WayShun, who was also the first Tickling Bandit. While wandering as a spirit, I came across this poor girl who was dying alone in the forest. I inhabited her body to save her and gain vengeance against those who had slain me."

"But I didn't find ya in the forest, Thysla," the farmer said. "You was in a burnt-out home."

"And how does taking our item grant you vengeance against the people who killed you?" Jackal said. "Wolf was the only one of us who was even alive when the Tickling Bandit was around, and he was a child."

"Ahh . . . umm . . . crap. Okay, you got me, though the spirit thing is true. The spirit was my grandpa. Someone hired me to take your package."

"Who?"

Thysla shook her head. "Thief's code. I'm a professional, and I have a reputation to maintain."

"Back on topic," Jackal said. "Where is the item you stole from us?"

"Up his butt," Thysla said, pointing at Cat.

As expected, he bent over and stared between his legs. "I knew there was a reason I felt sore."

"By The One!" Wolf said. "It's not up your butt. She's just being a pain."

"Oh! You mean like when you said you can hear the ocean in my ears."

"I'm not convinced that I can't, but you have the right idea."

Jackal gathered our group together. "How are we going to get her to tell us where it is? We can't torture her, she's just a little girl. A deadly little girl, but still a child."

"Why is everyone suddenly looking at me?" Cat said. "I agree, we can't hit a kid."

"Oh, sorry. We assumed your utter lack of morals would extend to this."

"I would never hurt a child. I'll have you know, I was a proud member of the Big Brother program in my village. My little brother, Jaxus, would never have learned how to be a man without my guidance. Who else would have taught him how to push girls he likes or beat up the local wuss, Sterlton Penwhicker?"

"A fine role model, you are. Wait—isn't Sterlton Penwhicker the leader of the rebel armies?"

"And to think," Cat said, "when I was beating him up all those years, I was performing my patriotic duty and I didn't even know it."

"Didn't he say something like, 'Why is everyone being so mean to me? I'm going over to the rebels because they know how to appreciate their soldiers'?"

"Ha! He did. He was even a weenie when he grew up."

"Hey!" Thysla said. "I have a proposition for you."

Jackal sighed. "Go ahead."

"I'll show you where the item is if you let me go."

"Ya're not welcome back at the farm," the farmer said. "Ya little beast."

"Fine by me, gramps," Thysla said. "You were only cover, anyway. I have a nice mansion back east."

"How do we know we can trust you if we let you loose?" Jackal said.

"I'm a practitioner of Tickle-Shen. My word is my honor, and I give you my word that I will not attack you again."

Jackal motioned us back together. "What do you think? Can we trust her?"

Mr. Plot Device gave several spastic hand signals to Cat. "Tickle-Shen is an ancient art," he translated. "Its practitioners are known for their focus and honor. Her word is good enough for him."

"That was very eloquent, Mr. Plot Device. Can we replace Cat with the monkey?" Jackal turned to Thysla. "You have a deal, but we're keeping you tied up until we have our package."

"I'll carry her," Cat said. "I wanna see if she's ticklish. Bwa-ha-ha!"

"Make him stop!" Thysla said.

"This'll teach you to knock me out. No one knocks me out but me!"

The farmer hurried over to the girl. "I won't let you do that to her. She's just a child!"

Apparently having learned a lesson from his adopted daughter, he tickled Cat until he dropped the girl. Thysla hit the ground hard, and I heard a popping noise from one of her joints. She grimaced in pain, but her now-dislocated shoulder allowed her to slide out of her bonds.

"Ha! I'll see you suckers later. My super toddler healing factor will heal that up in no time." She sprang to her feet and sprinted off at an incredible pace.

ABSOLUTELY NO WEREWOLVES

The sun went down completely. With Thysla's ultra-fast pace, we had little chance to catch her. Our only hope was that something would slow her down. In the dark of night, there was always a slim chance that she would bump into something or, at the very least, get lost.

I was really hoping for a toy store in the middle of the woods. Don't argue with me about how that would make no sense; nothing had made any sense at this point, anyway. Really, Santa Claus was just as likely to be behind the next tree as a knight.

The evening of the next day, we came upon a sleepy village of about twenty buildings. Apparently, we had marched all the way back to the main road.

"Do you think she went through here?" Cat said. "What should we do, Harry?"

"No idea. I think The One is sleeping."

"She didn't leave any trail," Jackal said. "Might as well ask around. We have no other leads. Let's split up into two groups. Harry, you're with me. The rest of you, go to the tavern. People are always talkative there."

Cat saluted. "Yes, ma'am."

"We're here for information, Cat," Wolf said. "Don't drink too much."

"I won't drink anything. Mr. Plot Device is a recovering alcoholic, and I need to show solidarity."

Cat and Mr. Plot Device walked away laughing, their hands flickering in constant communication. Wolf shook his head and followed a good distance away.

"Where to?" I said.

Jackal turned away from Cat and started walking. "We need to find the local busybody or someone else who might have seen Thysla."

"There's somebody. Let's ask him." I pointed to a man standing in the center of the square. I was in a hurry, so I ran toward him before she could answer.

"Stop!" she called. "I think I saw him bite a dog a few minutes ago."

My mouth was open before I had fully registered his tattered clothes or the pungent mixture of filth and alcohol. "Excuse me, sir. Do you have time for a few questions?"

He attempted to pee on my shoe. His accuracy was quite impressive, given that he still had his pants on, but I managed to dodge. He gave me a broad, stupid grin.

"Myargh." His tongue drooped out of his mouth.

"He can't help us, Harry. He's clearly the town idiot."

His eyes widened at the sight of Jackal. Was that embarrassment I sensed? Clearly, at least part of his brain worked.

"No," I said. "He's just a little too good at being an idiot. Now, if you could answer a question, fella, I'll give you this shiny coin. Have you seen a small girl coming from the forest recently? I swear, I won't tell any of the townspeople that you're not an idiot. I also promise not to return fire."

Big strings of drool dribbled from his mouth. He was still

peeing, too. I didn't think it was humanly possible to pee for that long. He had been going for over a minute.

"The girl is around four years old, with blonde hair in braids, and can move at an incredible pace."

He stuck his right hand out, indicating a person of roughly Thysla's height, as his eyes gave me a questioning look. All the while, he continued to drool and pee.

"Yes, around that height."

He pointed toward the entrance of a building across the street.

"Thanks," I said. I pressed a silver dollar into his left hand, at which point he fell over. He had still been pointing his right hand out, and the act of holding his left out as well unbalanced him. His falling over did not, however, stop the stream of urine.

"Let's go, Harry," Jackal whispered in my ear. "I don't want to be rude and not help him up, but I also don't want to get wet."

We ran across the street to the indicated building.

The building had an old, worn sign with letters that were completely illegible. I thought the sign had a horse or a centaur on it. As I entered the building, I peered back, and the village idiot was still going, now surrounded by a large puddle of yellow.

The building was dimly lit and a little dusty, though more from age than a lack of cleanliness, I decided. Most of the furnishings were well-maintained but worn. Knick-knacks covered the walls.

Jackal immediately rang the bell on the counter to our right.

A young, pimply-faced man ran in from a door in the back. "Can I help you?"

"Have you seen a small blonde girl with braids recently?" Jackal asked.

The young man's eyes bugged out for a second, but he quickly regained his composure. "Naw, nobody like that. You're the first customers I've had today."

"I said 'recently,' not today. I think you're lying."

The boy immediately turned and ran through the back door.

Jackal followed. "Why do they always run?"

Caught off-guard, it took me a few seconds to process everything. Before I could run, the front door opened, and a well-dressed man entered.

"Excuse me. I'd like to purchase a two-legged donkey."

"I'm not an employee, and I really need to get going. I'm chasing after the guy who works here."

"Oh, sorry. When you catch him, could you send him back over here? I really need a two-legged donkey. It's an emergency."

I took a step forward, then stopped. "Did you say a two-legged donkey?"

"Yes, I did."

"Why a donkey with only two legs?"

"Well, donkeys are more stable than horses, especially on uneven terrain, and I need to haul some stuff over the mountains."

"OK, but why one with two legs, instead of the standard four?"

"Well, this is the Two-Legged Donkey Store. It says so on the sign."

The hundred questions rolling around in my head completely subsumed any other thoughts. I completely forgot I was supposed to be chasing someone. I decided to let the first one out and let the others roll out as they came to me.

The questions had to come out, or my mind would overload.

"Why come here? Couldn't you get a better donkey with more legs at another store?"

"Two-legged donkeys are the best. It says so in the store's jingle. 'Two legs are better than four. Get one at the two-legged doooonkey store.'"

"How are they better?"

"The jingle says so."

"You can't believe everything you hear in a jingle."

"Sure you can. It says so in the jingle for jingles. 'Everything in a jingle is truer than the truest true.'"

I decided to run as far away as fast as I possibly could. I was afraid I might catch his stupid. I know you can't actually catch stupid, but why chance it? As I exited through the back door, I remembered I was supposed to be chasing someone. What a coincidence that I was already running, and in the right direction, to boot.

I entered a yard with patchy grass enclosed by a tall white fence with a gate. Neither Jackal nor the pimply-faced boy could be seen anywhere. There were a few donkeys milling about, doing normal donkey things: eating grass, staring into space, and passing gas. They did, in fact, all have only two legs—one in front and one in back. I stopped and stared, mesmerized. How did they move? How could they even stand up? Were they actually defying gravity? I wished I had a physicist or whatever type of scientist this phenomenon required to explain this to me. There should be studies done on these donkeys. They might unlock the secrets of the universe, or revolutionize chair-making.

"Harry, some help?" Jackal yelled from nearby.

"Where are you? I'm behind the store."

"Come out the gate, then make a right."

I did as instructed and found Jackal standing with one foot on the chest of the boy from the store. She had her crossbow pointed at his head. A few feet away, the Tickling Bandit was giving Jackal a rather spectacular glare.

"Let go of my cousin, and I'll let you live," Thysla said.

"Only if you tell us where our item is," Jackal replied.

"Why would I do that? I could knock you out easily and still have it."

Jackal pressed her boot down harder on the boy. He began to whimper rather pathetically, though not as pathetically as I would have. Whenever I see a child whimpering to get a toy, I whimper back. I'm so good that the parents usually buy me a new toy.

Thysla's face was bright red. "Leave him alone! I'll give you three seconds, and then I'm coming for you. One . . . two . . ."

Jackal pressed down harder, and the boy screamed. "Give us our package, or I'll start breaking things in him."

Thysla took a few steps back and paused. She was surprisingly worried. I'd had her pegged as someone who didn't care about anyone. "All right. I'll get it if you stop hurting him."

Jackal released the pressure a bit. "You'd better hurry. My stomping foot is starting to feel extra stompy."

Thysla ran off at her typical ridiculous pace.

"I'm here, Jackal," I said.

She turned slightly. "Good. I'll need you to get the package from her while I stay on top of Pimples."

"You can stand on me as long as you like, beautiful," the boy said. "The view from down here is spectacular."

She pressed her foot down harder.

"Worth every broken rib. The pain will go, but the images will never leave me."

She rolled her eyes. "Why do men always have to be so disgusting?"

Thysla appeared in front of us carrying our box and anxiously eying Jackal's foot. "Here's your stupid package. Now, stop hurting him. Are you all right, Banthin?"

"I'm fine, Mula."

"Mula?" Jackal said. "That sounds like a cow's name."

"Shut up. I was named after my great-grandmother."

"Whatever, Muuuuuuuula. Was your grandmother also a cow?"

"Stop antagonizing her, Jackal," I said. "I can't believe I'm about to say this, but be careful, or she might tickle you." I think my IQ dropped three points from saying that.

"Sorry, it's a funny name. Muuuuuuula. Go get the package from her, Harry."

"If I ever see you again, you fashion show reject," Thysla/Mula snarled, "I'll tickle you till you wet yourself, and then kill you." She handed the package over without even looking at me, so intent was she on glaring a hole through Jackal.

"Is the box still locked, Harry?"

"Yes." I gave it a shake. "And it's the right weight, too."

"Good. Now run around the corner to the main street."

Thysla/Mula stomped her foot. "Hey, we had a deal."

"I'll get off of him when Harry's safely around the corner. You won't attack Harry in broad daylight with witnesses around."

"And what about you, Jackal?" I asked. "You know she's going to go for you when you let go of her cousin."

"Let me worry about that. Now, go."

I considered doing the brave thing and telling Jackal I'd take on Mula to save her, then I remembered that they were only actors. Taking on a toddler who tickled people as her primary method of attack didn't strike me as worthy of my bravery, especially not a second time. So, I did as instructed and ran around the corner. Fortunately, even though it was getting late, there were at least fifteen people in full view. This part of Jackal's plan would probably work, but I wasn't sure how she could get herself out of there. I wondered if her safety just wasn't important to her.

"Now, get over there, Banthin," I could hear Jackal say from around the corner, "and if I ever catch you giving me that creepy glare again, I'll put a bolt through your eyes."

"Just like the love arrows of The One's flying accountant," Banthin said.

"Come here, you loud-mouthed pixie. Time to get your medicine," Mula said.

"No, stop. I love her."

I heard either the sound of two bodies crashing into each

other, or someone smacking two sacks of mashed potatoes together. Don't ask how I know what that sounds like. I wasn't the culprit behind the Great Mashed Potato Explosion in middle school; someone just told me what that sounds like.

Jackal came sprinting around the corner. "Run, Harry! That couldn't have bought us much time."

I pushed myself hard, but Jackal quickly outpaced me. Evidently, I was not in as great a shape as I'd thought, though, to be fair, I was carrying a five-pound wooden box.

"Hurry up. We need to find the others and get out of here," Jackal said.

"I think I saw them somewhere across the street."

"Let me take the box. It's slowing you down."

My exhaustion overpowered my manly instinct to not let a woman carry something heavy. Then, from a block away, we saw a large man fly through the door of the tavern. That had to be where Cat was.

"And stay out!" Cat said through the door.

"Cat," Jackal said. "We need to get out of here fast."

Cat stuck his head out the door. "Oh, hi, guys. I was just teaching this guy how rude it is to let me ogle his woman."

"Not going to bother with the logic of that. Get the others. She's right behind us."

Cat looked up and down the street. "I don't see her."

We both turned around. No small girl or teenage boy was chasing us.

"Maybe she's waiting for us to leave town," Jackal said.

I finally recovered enough to begin speaking. "There's no way she's going to let you go unpunished, Jackal. You really got her mad."

Cat pouted. "Hey, that's my job."

The others came out of the bar. I would have thought they'd come out sooner to check on Cat. Wolf must have been well-used to Cat getting himself into trouble by now and knew he could handle himself.

"Any luck?" Wolf asked. "Not much to report here, other than that we really shouldn't take Cat into a bar, whether he's been drinking or not."

Jackal held up the box.

"Nice job," Cat said, "but you said we really need to start running, right?"

"Yes, the bandit—whose real name is Mula—is around here somewhere."

"Mula," Cat echoed. "That's great. Muuuuuula."

"Stop it, Cat. She might be able to hear you, and I've already ticked her off."

Almost immediately, Mula came charging around the corner from a few houses down. "I was going to let you guys get out of town before I smacked you around, but now you've really pissed me off. No one makes fun of my name. My great-grandma was a saint."

Her cousin came up behind her. "Stop it, Mula. You can't use that here. We need to keep it secret. Remember the family legacy."

"Yeah, remember your legacy," Cat said. "Muuuuuuuuuuuula."

Within half a second, Mula had Cat lying on the ground, laughing his head off. "Stop it. Ha-ha-ha. I'm really ticklish. Ha-ha-ha. Oww, my lungs hurt. Ha-ha-ha. I think I'm going to burst."

"I'm going to make you suffer, you big jerk."

"Not if we have anything to say about it," Wolf said as he drew his sword.

A local in a black hat with the word "Sherrff" written on it in chalk came running over. "What do you think you're doing there, missy? I'll have no violence in my town."

"Just giving him a friendly tickle, officer."

"Well, he doesn't seem to like it much, little one. You need to stop."

"Ha-ha," Cat said. "Yeah, Muuuuuula."

Mula tickled him so hard that he vomited.

Funny, I didn't remember him eating any rutabagas. And how had he eaten them whole?

"That better not be what I think it is," the Sherrff said as he turned toward another villager. "Tumis, some help. I think she's using Tickle-Shen."

"That's right, Sherrff. I'm a Tickle-Shen master," Mula said. "If you interfere, you're next."

"Mula, you've ruined everything," Banthin wailed.

"Not if I use the tickle of forgetfulness on them."

"I was afraid of that," the Sherrff said. "You really picked the wrong time of day to try something here, missy. I'll bet you're no match for us when we transform."

As much as I love the *Transformers* cartoon, those characters had no place in my world. Although, it would be kind of neat to see Optimus Prime take the witness stand in the ensuing lawsuit.

The Sherrff, Tumis, and all of the other townspeople started to howl.

No. No. No. This had better not mean what I thought it meant. As I stared, transfixed in horror—though not for the usual reason someone would in this situation—a bright light flashed, blinding me.

When my vision returned, the Sherrff and all of the townspeople had been replaced with soft, adorable puppies. The puppy that had been the Sherrff began to nibble on another puppy playfully.

I had explicitly stated in the foreword of *Storms of Sculan* that there were no werewolves, vampires, or orcs in Vyenra. I'd thought it was implied that there were no were-anythings.

Evidently, the writers on this show thought "no werewolves" didn't include werepuppies.

Really, puppies? Not werecats or werebears. No, those would be too scary. I figured werebunnies and werebabies were coming up next.

Mula, who was just as confused as the rest of us, completely stopped tickle-torturing Cat. "Well, that was anticlimactic. Who should I tickle next? Not you, stick girl. I'm saving you for last. How about the older guy who thinks his sword is even slightly threatening?"

From behind Mula, we heard a high-pitched scream. Somehow, several of the puppies had taken Banthin to the ground and were nuzzling him aggressively. The puppies didn't appear to be biting or clawing him; they were just rubbing their noses on him and occasionally licking him. It would have all looked rather playful and adorable if Banthin hadn't been screaming and thrashing about like he was being strangled. The kid was either a really good actor or terribly allergic to dogs.

"Banthin," Mula said, "how the heck is that hurting you? They're only puppies."

"The pain. The pain! Make them stop!"

"Seriously? Oh, all right. This had better not be one of your impractical jokes again."

She ran over and tried to pull him out from under the puppies covering him. There was the possibility, I realized, that he was in danger of suffocation. As she pulled his arm out, a look of pure horror spread across her normally unflappable face. While his hand was perfectly fine, the rest of his body was nothing more than bone, picked clean of any skin or muscle.

"Ha-ha . . . huh?" Cat said.

"How about, we don't find out?" Wolf said. "Run!"

With no hesitation, our group followed his lead toward the main road out of town. After a few hundred yards, I glanced over my shoulder. Some of the puppies were indeed chasing us on their stumpy little legs at a surprisingly fast pace. I had hoped that since Mula was the one who had angered the Sherrff that they would leave us alone.

An idea of pure brilliance came to me. If I "killed" myself on this stupid TV show, they would have to let me leave it. Screw my agreement with Hammurabi. I wasn't going to look heroic anyway if the only opponents they were going to offer me were puppies and toddlers.

I came to a stop and lay down to let the puppies have me. Besides, having a dozen puppies nuzzle and lick me sounded like a lot of fun. Someone should get a bunch of puppies together and charge money for that. If any of you readers do that, I'd better get a cut.

Out of the corner of my eye, I could see the village idiot charging toward me. He had finally stopped his fountain impersonation, it seemed, though he was soaked from head to toe. I was glad I wasn't his dry cleaner.

The idea of being tackled by a man covered in urine wasn't at all appealing, so I stood. Why was it that the weirdos were always the ones who were attracted to me? And why did they always have to be male?

"What are you doing?" I demanded.

He bravely stood with his back to me and faced down the angry, adorable horde. When they got within a few feet, he cried, "Yarrrrrgggggghhhhh!" and began to spray their ranks while twisting slightly back and forth.

The puppies stopped their charge immediately and began to whimper in heartbreaking unison. I really hoped no children would watch this scene when it aired, or I'd be getting psychiatrists' bills until the day I died.

As I stood watching in horror, Cat grabbed my arm. "Come on, Harry. He can't hold them off forever."

So flabbergasted was I that I followed without resistance. In retrospect, I missed a golden opportunity to "kill" myself, but then again, I probably wouldn't have wanted to jump into a pile of pee-covered puppies, no matter the result.

When we caught up to the rest of the group outside town, I finally turned back. There were no puppies in pursuit, nor were Mula or the village idiot anywhere to be seen. I should have known that whoever was running this show would make me look heroic in the dumbest ways possible. Of course, everything else about this show had been idiotic, so why would that be any different? They might have even been legitimately trying to make me look good but were just really bad at it.

I hunched over, breathless.

"Did you guys see that?" Cat said. "Harry tried to sacrifice himself to save us. Maybe he can join us, and we can be the Fanged Fouro?"

"The word's' 'quartet,' moron," Jackal said, "but you do have a good point. I'd like to have Harry around after this mission."

"Let's talk about it later," Wolf said. "Jackal, do you still have the package?"

She nodded.

"Good. We need to move fast."

We ran down the road as quickly as we were able, with a few breaks, mostly for Mr. Plot Device and me to catch our breath.

During one of those breaks, I finally got out the question that had been burning a hole in my mind. "Who was the guy who saved me, anyway? I mean, besides the village idiot."

"Oh, he's a government agent," Cat said.

"You mean the man in clothes as dirty as your mind?" Jackal said. "There's no way he's a professional spy. He chases dogs and pees himself in public."

"Nope. He definitely works for the government. All government agents have mustaches."

Jackal rolled her eyes. "Just because someone has a mustache doesn't mean they're a government agent. My elderly grade school teacher who could barely walk had a mustache. Are you telling me he was an agent?"

Cat gave her a coy smile. "The perfect cover. No one would suspect him."

"And what about the Iron Workers' Guild? It's a sign of their guild to have a handlebar mustache."

"Remember the Great Strike of '89? They were on strike for six months. It was a cover so the government could use them to suppress the revolts in Western Shranmel. The strike ended a week after the revolt stopped."

"And what about women?" Jackal asked. "I know there are women who work for the government, and they don't have mustaches."

"I think it's optional for them," Cat said. "I mean, we can't have all of those ugly government chicks trying to be mustache beautiful."

"Your theory is probably the dumbest thing you've ever come up with, which is saying something since you once said all trees are left-handed."

"Actually, he's right," a voice said from some nearby bushes.

"Who goes there?" Wolf said.

A familiar wet figure walked out of the shadows, looking no worse than before. The puppies had not, in fact, cuddled him to death. "Hi, there. My name is Werin, and I'm here to save you." He peeled off a wig and a fake beard.

"Wait," Wolf said. "So, all Garandians with mustaches are really government agents?"

"No, I only said that to make my entrance more dramatic."

Cat shook his hand. "Darn. Another one of my brilliant ideas down the tube, but I won't hold it against you. You're a hero, after all. Harry owes you his life, and so do we."

"All in a day's work. The chancellor sent me. Hammurabi notified him through discreet channels of the importance of your journey."

"Hello, Father." The ice in Jackal's voice was so palpable that it gave me chills. "How did you know to find us here?"

Werin nodded at her and continued like she wasn't even there. "We have several agents out in the area. I figured you'd come this way, so I volunteered to fill in for this village's idiot. Fortunately, he needed a vacation."

"Those are some of the dumbest things I've ever heard," I said.

"That didn't come out of Cat's mouth," Wolf added.

His story was all very nice and neat. He'd clearly thought of everything. Well, almost everything. It had one major hole in it. Without this one key piece of information, his story was nothing but a sham, the kind of thing that could derail everything and prove him to be an enemy agent out to kill us all. The kind of thing that could rock—nay, destroy the whole televised world of Vyenra.

"How did you manage to pee for that long?" I asked.

"I have a device in my pants."

"If I had a trakon for every time someone's said that to me," Cat said. "Yeah, don't go into an alley with someone who tells you that, especially if it's me."

Werin pulled his shirt up to display a tube extending from his left arm to his pants. "I press a button, and it sprays out like I'm peeing. There's two bladders on my thighs with all the liquid. Every true idiot has to have a gimmick, so I thought I'd be the one who pees a lot. Plus, werepuppies are allergic to the liquid. It's a lemon and turmeric mixture."

"You knew you'd run into werepuppies?" Wolf said.

"Oh, yes. The people who are after you infected the villagers days ago. They figured the werepuppies would finish you off, then they'd come get the package in the morning when it was safe. Well, we'd better get going," Werin said. "I think I hear puppies howling nearby, and I'm all out of pee."

Jackal had been strangely silent throughout all of that. She seemed to be trying to blend into the surroundings in the hope that he would forget about her. But with the way he was avoiding looking in her direction, I doubted she needed to make the effort.

THE HAIRY TRAITOR

We marched throughout the night. Surely, there had to be laws that required actors to be allowed to get some sleep. In spite of our tiredness, the constant howling kept us sharp and on edge. Nothing keeps a person more alert than fear, even if that fear is soft and adorable. The image of Banthin's suddenly skeletal body didn't help, either. To this day, I can't see a commercial with a puppy and not shudder.

When the sun rose, the howling ceased, presumably because werepuppies operate like werewolves by changing back in daylight; either that, or their sound person actually got to clock out and sleep, unlike us actors.

What are the rules for werepuppies? Do they only change on a full moon? How do they decide whom to kill and whom to bite in order to create a new werepuppy? If you're born to a werepuppy mom, do you inherit the affliction, or do you have to be bit, like anyone else? Do they prefer puppy food or human flesh? I should explore this in my next book.

Oh, crap. They had me thinking this idiocy was actually logical again. I'd been running around this place for too long and had developed something like Stockholm Syndrome; I was starting to sympathize with my captors. I'm sure psychologists will want to study me and write papers on my experience. They will, of course, have to name this after me: Harry's Syndrome, or Harry's for short. *"What's wrong with him? Oh, he has a case of the Harry's."* Like I hadn't suffered enough. Just once, couldn't they name something awesome after me, like running shoes— *"Harry's, for the coward on the go"*—or beard trimmers? *"You don't have to be a writer to look like one."*

For the first time, Werin motioned our group to a halt. We hadn't stopped to catch our breath at all during the night, our fear being a very effective fuel. "I think the danger has passed. Sunlight usually stops them."

"Good. I'm beat," I said.

"Did you just say—insert something about beating? Sorry, I'm all out of juice for my usual witty play on words," Cat said.

"Did Cat say . . . I've got nothing, either," Jackal said. "Need sleep."

"There should be a campsite over there," Werin said, pointing to the woods. "The red cloth on the branches marks the direction. Agents use those to mark safe spots."

We lumbered through the forest. Mr. Plot Device was asleep on Cat's shoulders. I was already starting to doze, and I don't remember much else of what happened until we arrived at the campsite. The haze temporarily evaporated when we found that the campsite wasn't deserted.

Sitting by the fire was a well-muscled older man with a crisscross of scars covering his bare arms. He nodded and smiled as we approached, not the least bit frightened by five armed people. Werin nodded in return, seemingly indicating that he knew the man. Wolf peculiarly trailed back as we approached, his hand slowly heading toward his sword. When Jackal gave him a questioning glance, he shook his head and shooed her forward.

Werin plopped down across from him. "Jorin, what brings you to these parts? I thought you were assigned to Sculan."

"The king himself pulled me out to come look for five travelers with an important package. Looks like ya found 'em, but I don't remember any of them being a monkey." He nodded toward the rest of us. We stopped a few feet away from the fire, following Wolf's lead. "Sit down, please. We're nothing but friends here."

"Daughter, sit down." Werin turned his eyes toward the fire.

Cat clapped his hands and sat next to Werin. "Please keep standing, Jackal. I want to see a spanking."

Jackal sat as far from her father as she could get. "I'm only doing this to spite you, Cat."

Wolf's eyes never left Jorin. With the others in front of him, Jorin had evidently not gotten a good look at Wolf. Now that they were no longer in the way, recognition, then sadness lined his weathered face.

Werin shrugged, pulled something out of his pocket, then began to roast it in the fire. "We're all on the same side here. Forget about Bagus Bay and remember the mission."

"He's right, Wolf." Cat's sentiment was mostly lost as he made spanking motions toward Jackal. For once, Jackal ignored him.

Wolf finally removed his hand from his sword and sat next to Jackal. "Fine, but I'm not going to sleep as long as I know he's around. We leave once everyone has gotten a few hours."

Werin continued to focus on his meat and the fire. "Five hours, then we head out. Jorin can stay behind and throw some misdirection on our trail."

"It's refreshing to see you order someone else around like a child, Father," Jackal whispered to the ground.

Werin turned slightly toward her, and she flinched.

Jorin nodded toward Werin. "I am more than happy to oblige the great Werin. If I'm doing that, could you drop off a few stragglers on the way?" He motioned toward the trees. A middle-aged man dressed like a shopkeeper holding the hand of a very attractive woman was walking slowly toward the fire. "Their village was attacked by some werepuppies, and I found 'em tramping through the woods. Names are Vartin and Alinda."

"We encountered those beasts, too," Werin said. "Be happy to look after them. Everyone, get some sleep. We leave in five hours."

There was no time to be properly introduced to the newcomers, and everyone was much too tired to care. The newcomers seemed much too scared and unnerved to talk, anyway. Even Jackal dropped off to sleep within a few minutes of the command, though she made sure to put her bag as far away from her father as possible. Vartin, Alinda, and Wolf seemed to be the only ones not interested in sleep.

I was awakened by shouting.

"It's gone. Daughter, why weren't you watching it while we slept?"

"Me? You're the one who's supposed to be the great protector of all things Garandian. How could the great Werin the Finder let something so important slip through his grasp? The great Werin I heard about non-stop would never let something like this happen to him. Maybe we should go find that Werin instead?"

Sleep finally cleared from my eyes, and I could see the two of them, inches away from each other's faces. Jackal had her bag open, and it was definitely emptier than when I fell asleep.

"I knew it was a mistake to let you go out into the world and use my name. I think you should take off that ridiculous armor and put on an apron instead."

"Yes!" Cat said. "Except for the apron part."

"I thought you weren't attracted to her, Cat," I said.

"I'm not. I'm just tired of being the only one on Team Naked."

Sleep deprivation and anger filled Wolf's face as he stomped forward. "Leave her alone. I don't care how famous you are; no one talks to my squad that way, especially not when they're so terribly wrong. This woman next to me is, without a doubt, one of the strongest, most competent people I have ever had the privilege of serving with. If she were my daughter, I would be proud to call her my own. You, sir, are a disgrace to fathers everywhere. Besides, it's obvious that snake Jorin did it."

Werin backed away, not used to people speaking to him that way. In my books, he was never wrong and was the most respected person in the land other than Hammurabi and the king. It was good to see them get something right, especially with the whole sexism angle they had created for him.

"Just because you had a bad experience with Jorin doesn't mean he's a bad guy," Werin whispered. "He's had decades of exemplary service since then."

"Oh. In that case, where is he?"

We looked around, but Jorin was nowhere to be found, nor were his two friends.

"Clearly, they were a team," Wolf said. "If they were smart, they would have split up so we'd have a hard time catching them."

Jackal and Werin immediately looked for tracks. They both found something at the same time and followed it into the woods. I couldn't see what it was they were following, but I hadn't read the script. It didn't really matter, because the clashing of swords was pretty easy to follow. We arrived just in time to see Jorin stab Vartin in the chest. As Vartin slid down a tree, he tossed his dagger with deadly precision straight into Jorin's eye. I wasn't sure how they did that without actually killing the actor, but it was awesome.

I wished Vartin had tossed his dagger into Jorin's mouth instead. It didn't seem very believable that he had time to utter a line before he passed. "They took it."

"See?" Werin said to Wolf. "Jorin was as dedicated to Garandia as I am."

"No . . . no, he's not," Alinda whimpered from the bushes nearby. "I had to make tinkle, and my Vartin came with me in case one of you men tried to peek, especially the perverted one in the cat helmet. Just as we were coming back, Jorin came screaming at us with his sword drawn, and my Vartin drew his dirk to protect me . . . and now he's dead. Dead!" She started to weep.

All of the men got real uncomfortable and immediately began searching the bushes for the package. It was a very important package, so we were well within our rights to go looking for it. Normally, I was sure one of us would have comforted her, especially since she was very attractive and now single, but, you know, package. Unfortunately, we didn't find anything, and she was still crying. After a lot of uncomfortable glances between us, Wolf said probably the most important thing ever said in a situation like this.

"Where is Mr. Plot Device?"

Everyone looked at Cat. "He was there when I went to sleep. I'll bet he took it!"

"Yes!" all of the men said at once. "He must have taken it. Let's go find him."

We immediately all ran off to find him. Clearly, he was the one who had taken the package.

We followed Werin for a bit, but all the trails he could find eventually went cold. Evidently, the monkey had climbed into a tree, and even Werin's legendary tracking skills could not follow a trail in a tree.

"Cat," Wolf said. "Since you two think so much alike, where would you be if you were him?"

"A monkey brothel, obviously, or an all-you-can-eat banana bar."

"Since neither of those two things is real, where else might you be?"

The sound of weeping had died down, which made me feel so much better—because I was worried about her, not because I didn't want to comfort her.

Cat scrunched his chin in thought for probably the first time. "I'd be back at Harry's pack, laughing at what I found—or didn't find—in his underwear."

"No wonder you like my daughter so much," Werin said to Wolf. "In your group, she's the smart one, by a large margin."

Wolf responded with a glare. "You're not wrong."

"Actually," I said, "I think Cat's right. Listen."

It's really fun to observe the expressions people have on their faces while they're focused on listening. Wolf looked like he was trying to solve the final question on *Jeopardy!*. Werin had diarrhea face. Cat's face didn't move at all, and he drooled a little. Jackal . . . had evidently stayed behind to comfort Alinda.

"Laughter," Werin said. "Monkey laughter. And it's coming from back at the camp."

We ran back to the camp and found Mr. Plot Device in the middle of a pile of my things. He was laughing hysterically at the pictures in my wallet. I don't know how he'd gotten it out of my pocket.

"Stop right there, thief!" Cat said.

Mr. Plot Device looked around in confusion.

"I'm talking to you, Mr. Plot Device, if that even is your real name."

Mr. Plot Device gave Cat a dirty look and a hand sign that did not need translation.

"Where's the package?" Werin said.

Mr. Plot Device was perplexed by the question. If you've never seen a perplexed monkey before, it's one of the most adorable things you'll ever see. To cap it off, he shrugged. And after puppies had been forever ruined for me, I was very glad to refill my stock of cute.

"I've got it!" Jackal yelled from the forest. "The package is here."

We ran back to find Jackal with the package in one hand and her crossbow in the other. Alinda lay sprawled on the ground.

"While you four were running away like she had the plague, I decided to check into a few things. Her story was a bit too convenient. Jorin didn't catch them coming back from a pee. He really did see her take the package."

Werin rolled his eyes. "You didn't figure anything out, girl. You got lucky."

Jackal glared at him. "No, Father, I caught the look in her eyes, and so did you, but to throw you off, she immediately started to cry."

"I . . . She did."

"And then, as you scurried off with your tail between your legs, I reached in to pretend to comfort her, and guess what I found."

He nodded and seemed impressed for a second, then covered the look with scorn. "The package."

"No," Cat said. "It was a penis."

"You only hang out with this group so you can feel smart, don't you?" Werin asked.

Jackal shook her head. "Actually, Cat's right. I'm never going to live down saying that, am I?"

Cat gave her a thumbs-up. "Not as long as I'm still alive."

I hadn't really found Alinda to be all that attractive. I was only being polite. She was just all right, but in a mannish sort of way. I had known the truth subconsciously all along, but my conscious mind hadn't put it together yet. I thought she might be attractive to other guys, but not me.

"When I found that she was a bit too happy to see me, I knocked her to the ground," Jackal said.

"It was the will of The One," Alinda said. "He cursed me with masculinity, and I don't know why." She started to weep uncontrollably.

"I think she's suffered enough," Werin said. "We have the item. That's the important thing. We should go."

"Seriously?" Jackal said.

"Look how much she's crying. She's obviously suffered enough. I'm in charge here. Let her go."

"You men have no defense mechanism for a crying woman, do you?" Jackal said. "I guess it doesn't matter that this isn't an actual woman, as long as he looks like one. This should help." Jackal pulled a handkerchief from her pocket and dabbed a little spit on it. She vigorously rubbed Alinda's face like she was a toddler who'd attacked a bowl of ice cream.

When she pulled back, Alinda looked nothing like she had before. She went from looking like a passable woman to one of the ugliest men I'd ever seen. "Her" face seemed to get longer and "her" nose much bigger, which I'm sure it was just my imagination.

"Ferelic, my old nemesis!" Werin said. "I should have known."

Ferelic spat at him. "Nemesis? You finally defeat me, and you stoop to calling me that? We're arch-enemies, and you know it."

Werin explained, "Ferelic and I graduated from the Garandian Academy of the Hidden together, in a tie for top of our class. Our rivalry continued throughout our careers, until he decided to leave the service and become a mercenary. I've been trying to capture him ever since. He's been responsible for some of the greatest catastrophes in recent history."

"Likfe wha?" Cat said through a mouthful of popcorn.

"Where did you get that?" Wolf demanded.

"I always keep it in my underwear in case someone tells a good story. Want some?"

Werin began to pace back and forth. "Do you remember the Great Fire that wiped out the Sculander capital building? Ferelic's work. He impersonated the duke and ordered it burned."

Ferelic shrugged. "So what? My clients paid good money for that."

"Did you have to burn the orphanage, too?"

"The orphans kept taunting me with their downtrodden eyes."

"Normal people would feel sympathy for that look. He's also responsible for the Pantsing of the Ambassador of Lithia, the Reasonably Large Suspender Riots, the Great Baby Strike, the Shaving of the High Minister of Cheese, and the Prolonged Staring Contest."

"I did not cause the Great Baby Strike. I only encouraged it. Those babies were on the verge, anyway."

"Well, I know you personally started the Prolonged Staring Contest. Production in New Atlia ceased for over two months because of you."

"I can't help it. It'd be immoral not to use such a fantastic gift. If I wasn't supposed to use it, The One wouldn't have given it to me."

"Regardless, it's illegal, and it gives me great pleasure to finally arrest you," Werin said as he tied Ferelic's wrists. "You have the right to say anything stupid you want. Anything you say, think, or might say can and will be used against you in a court of law. You have the right to an attorney. If you cannot afford one, then you're in trouble, because we're not paying for one. Do you understand these rights?"

"No."

"Even better. You can try to figure them out for the next hundred years in a dark cell."

H.O. PHOINE HOME?

Surprisingly, the journey to the capital went without incident. I guessed the showrunners felt they had enough material or had run out of ideas for how to make this any more ridiculous. Even I couldn't think of how to top werepuppies and deadly toddlers. Werin managed to find us an escort and a nice wagon to sleep in. Much to Cat's dismay, Mr. Plot Device decided to go back to a previous job, teaching at the university. Cat's decision to blame the monkey for the theft had evidently strained their friendship too far.

Werin and his daughter stayed their typical "as far apart as humanly possible while still being part of the same group" for the beginning of the journey, but as the trip progressed, they slowly got closer and closer to each other. When the capital came into view, it looked like they finally might speak, but the closest they got was a few glances and nods that one might call unobjectionable. Given that they had only looked at each other with hatred or condescension so far, it was a big step.

Werin escorted us to the palace but had to part ways with us to take care of his prisoner soon after. He was eager to put his captive in a very dark cell. I can relate, as my rivalry with Billiam von Cummerbund is a thing of legend in the literary community. I'm still not sure how that scumbag convinced the judge that his piece of crap was a parody of my beautiful first book. I guessed I couldn't hate him as much anymore—as this show was a thousand times more insulting—but that likely meant he was somehow involved.

As Werin rounded the corner to the dungeon, Jackal paused expectantly but finally gave up when the sound of his footsteps faded completely. I felt bad for her, as, even though she was only an actress, I had the feeling that this was all real to her. Perhaps the actress had a similar situation with her real father. I jumped with a start, and in reaction so did Jackal, when a finger tapped me on the back.

"This isn't the time, Cat," I said.

"I'm not Cat," the person behind me said. "He's down the hall, drawing phalluses on all of the armor. I don't know what the point is when most of them have codpieces, but it's keeping him out of real trouble, so I didn't interrupt. You should probably go stop him or join him. I don't care, but I'd like to talk to my daughter alone."

Werin must have used one of the numerous secret passageways to get behind me; either that, or he had walked around the edges of the set. I nodded in agreement and scurried around the corner, but barely enough so I still could hear.

"You did . . . good with Ferelic," Werin said to Jackal. "I'm sure I would have eventually figured it out anyway, but . . . yeah."

"Does that mean you're proud of me, Werin?"

"Why can't you call me Dad like all of the other kids? I said you did good. What more do you want?"

"That you're proud of me? That you love me? That you're glad I'm your daughter? Heck, that you even like me."

"Just like a woman to cry when I offer even a small compliment. Listen, daughter, you did good, but you know how much putting Ferelic in a cell means to me. I have to go."

The word "go" echoed down the hall. I think it still haunts me to this day. I'd never known my dad, being that he and my mom had died when I was little, but my grandpa and grandma had made every effort to let me know how much they loved me. I made a vow to tell any future children I would have how important they were at least three times a day.

When I heard Jackal's slow approach, I immediately turned to get as far away as possible. I didn't want her to know I had been listening. Even if she was only a character, I would likely have to deal with her for several more days, and I didn't want her to have to act like she hated me.

Once again, someone had snuck up on me from behind, and I ran smack into Wolf's large chest. Wolf pointed toward a side chamber, and we ran inside. The chamber looked like it was used for storage.

"God, Werin is an asshole." He punched the beard right off a nearby painting.

"I didn't write him that way." I poked two nipple holes in the one nearest me.

"I'll make it a point to only take missions as far away from him as possible from now on."

"I think I'll kill him in my next book."

"I'd kill him for real if I thought it would help, but I think that would only make it worse."

I patted him on the shoulder. "I don't think she'd ever forgive you if you did."

"You're right. I never had any kids, but I think I could be the father she's always deserved."

"Don't you already do that for Cat?"

"I guess I do, but for him it's mostly making sure he only does minor damage." He sighed. "We should probably go. I'm pretty sure kings don't like to be kept waiting."

We rushed back to the receiving area outside the throne room. Cat had evidently tried to draw something on Jackal's face, and she had responded by breaking all of his pens. I cringed at the sight of pens in my medieval world, though they were at least made of crude metal and could theoretically have been produced by their level of technology. Ink was dripping from Cat's hands, and as the guards opened the door to the throne room to let us know it was time, he quickly cleaned them on the nice white tablecloth under a nearby vase.

We were escorted into the throne room by guards wearing some of the most elaborate and blindingly shiny armor I'd ever seen. Cat had to walk backwards to avoid the glare, while Jackal stared down at the floor.

The throne was atop a dais roughly ten feet above the rest of the floor. To either side of it was a smaller chair on a lower tier. I stared into the shadow-filled corners of the room and decided the cameras had to be hidden there. The throne wasn't occupied, but the two other chairs were. The less elaborate one contained an old man with a long, flowing white beard and robes that very nearly matched his hair—fitting my description of the high chancellor— and the other chair held a teenage boy dressed in royal blue from head to toe, sitting sideways with his legs draped over the side. The young man seemed very bored, to the point that he was nearly asleep. He had to be the prince and heir to the throne. Except for a couple of guards, no one else occupied the chamber.

"Bring the package forward," the high chancellor said.

Jackal placed it before him and stepped back into line. The magnitude of being in so important a place had eroded any signs of what had transpired with her father only moments before.

The chancellor smiled warmly. "As I'm sure Werin has told you, Hammurabi informed us of the importance of this package.

Unfortunately, this item is for the king's eyes only, and the king left for Sculan before we received word of your journey."

"Of course he did. They just couldn't let me out of this show easily, could they?" I said, staring toward the dark corner and the cameras I knew to be there.

"Hammurabi has no right to order us around," Prince Ambric said. "He isn't even the New Atlian representative anymore."

"While that is true, Royal Highness, the man has never steered us wrong in the past. He has shown nothing but the utmost diligence and brilliance in his decisions."

"When I am king, I'll sack the lot of you," the prince grumbled as he groomed his nails.

"I know you don't mean that, Highness. Now, on to the matter at hand. Your contract states that you must deliver the package to the king, I believe."

"It does," Wolf said with a hint of a glare in his eyes.

"Then I charge you to deliver it to the king at Caltisport. I'll have a ship waiting at the docks in the morning. I know this must be frustrating, but I am sure His Majesty will compensate you further for this complication."

The prince paused in grooming his nails. "What's in this package, anyway?"

"I don't know, Highness," the chancellor said. "Hammurabi said it is of utmost importance to the king, and we must trust his judgment."

I had clearly done more than enough service to my imaginary kingdom. Teragonna had only instructed me to deliver the package to the capital, after all. I hoped the chancellor would let me have the Phoine and go home immediately. The Trio didn't need my help to deliver it over the sea. I decided to act while we still had the chancellor's opinion high in his mind.

As I opened my mouth, Cat blurted out, "I think it's a sandwich." And with that, any goodwill toward our group surely evaporated. Jackal groaned, and Wolf rolled his eyes.

"Did he say a sandwich?" the prince said, suddenly perfectly at attention.

"I believe he did, Highness," the chancellor said.

"How could something mundane like a sandwich possibly save the kingdom? Is it magic?"

"You'd be amazed at the kind of damage I can do with ordinary household objects," Cat said.

"Oh, God, not the grape story," Wolf said.

"Nice setup, Wolf. We're like a well-oiled machine. One time, Wolf and I, along with one of the previous Jackals, were cornered by a gang of thugs. We had left our weapons elsewhere as we were travelling undercover as a group of grape salesmen."

"No," Wolf said. "You were undercover as a grape salesman, though no one told you to get into disguise, and you threw our weapons in the river because 'they don't look like grapes.'"

"Are you going to let me finish? The only thing I had close to a weapon was four grapes. So, I put them in my mouth and spat them at our well-armed attackers. I took the first one's eye out—"

"The old Jackal did that with his fingers," Wolf groaned.

"I disarmed another one with a trick shot—"

"You distracted Jackal, which caused him to get stabbed."

"—and the guy's weapon got caught in Jackal's body, which disarmed him." Cat pretended to try to pull an imaginary sword out of Wolf. "The third one tripped when I bounced a grape under his feet."

"He tripped over the clothes you took off."

Cat pretended to choke. "I choked another man when I spat the last grape straight into his mouth."

"No, he had a stroke when you started to shake your manhood at him."

"And due to my mastery of mundane objects, they all ran away." Cat winked at the prince.

"No, it's just that no one wants to wrestle with a naked man."

"As you can see, even a seemingly mundane object can turn the tide of battle in the right hands—and I'll bet the sandwich is a club on rye."

"No, no," the prince said. "It has to be a panini."

"I believe it's a bacon sandwich," the chancellor said. "Bacon is amazing."

"Our country is doomed," Jackal whispered to me. "I hear Lithia is beautiful this time of year."

I shook my head. "Lithia does sound nice, but I really need the Phoine. Do you think he'll let me have it?"

Jackal shrugged.

"Chancellor," I said, "regardless of what's in the package, Hammurabi gave us strict instructions not to open it. However, he promised me that the Phoine of Destiny would get me home. I have more than fulfilled my part of the bargain and will be of little use on the voyage to Caltisport. Seeing as how the Phoine is here and it makes little sense for me to travel across the sea and then come back, I ask that I be allowed to use it now, great and honorable high chancellor."

"I would like to see it, too," the prince said. "I've heard it radiates a glowing light that's so beautiful, it'll make even the vilest of individuals weep."

"I've heard it can peer into your soul," Wolf said.

"No, it can make two enemies fall in love," Jackal said.

"I heard it's a cake," Cat said.

"What kind?" The prince leaned over in great curiosity.

"Cat, are you hungry?" Wolf said.

"No, why?"

"Regardless of what it can do," the chancellor said, "I'm

afraid I cannot fulfill your request. The king took the Phoine to Caltisport."

I almost broke down and wept. They clearly weren't going to show me any mercy and let me leave. Couldn't they continue the show without me? The only thing I added was a good shot of a regularly disgusted face. They could use footage from before for that and have a stunt double fill in.

Someone really hated me and wanted to abuse me mercilessly.

MORE THAN THREE IS NOT A TRIO

After a good night's rest in the palace, we were escorted to the docks and a very speedy-looking ship. It looked pretty aerodynamic, anyway, unlike the bulky cargo ship that had brought me to this island. The ship was manned by professional-looking men dressed in the royal colors, complete with a taciturn captain whose only interests were his ship and his duty. He immediately had us escorted below and out of the way.

The chancellor had arranged for an extra complement of men-at-arms and archers to accompany us, as well as two escort ships. This would turn out to be one of the few times in this entire adventure that I felt like I was being given the recognition I deserved.

Fortunately, there was no game of cards going on below deck, unlike my previous maritime journey. There did not even appear to be any other passengers. I assumed the chancellor didn't want even the slightest breach of security, so important was our mission.

"So, besides Cat, what do you think this stupid thing is?" I asked.

"An all-powerful weapon of some sort," Wolf said. "Perhaps the Sword of St. Maxentious or the Breath of The One."

"The box isn't big enough for a sword," Jackal said, "but it could contain a vial or a bottle. I think it's a scroll or a book with detailed plans for how to defeat the Sculanders."

"I'm going to guess it's the Phoine of Destiny or something else that could get me home," I said, "though with how things have been going, Cat's probably right."

Jackal put her hand on my shoulder. "You really miss your home, don't you, Harry? What do you miss most?"

"I miss writing. And my next book isn't going to be anything like what's happened over the last week. There will definitely not be any werepuppies."

"Yeah, I doubt anyone would believe half of the stuff we've seen. Well, maybe they'd believe it a little more if they met Cat."

"I *am* too good to be true, aren't I?" Cat said. "Who would believe all of this awesomeness could possibly be present in one package? Hee-hee. I said 'package.'"

Jackal groaned. "You're a package of something, all right."

Cat grinned stupidly. "So, Jackal, how did it go with your dad? He seems like a great guy. I was trying to draw dongs on all the armor with charcoal, but it wasn't the right medium, so he showed me where they kept the pens."

"Don't ever mention him again, please." She lowered her eyes.

"Cat," Wolf said, "this isn't like how I told you not to mention what you did in Meraboern, and you bring that up every time I say I'm going to the bathroom. This is something you really shouldn't bring up."

I decided to save Jackal and the actress playing her from having to speak about something that was obviously very painful and changed the subject. "So, how long have you three worked together?"

"Cat and I have worked together for five years now," Wolf said. "This Jackal replaced the previous Jackal when he tried to fly off the top of a fifteen-foot-tall tower."

Cat smirked. "Now, that was an idiot. I told him jackals don't fly, they levitate."

"He was a truly exceptional idiot. Cat looked like a genius beside him, but he could find anyone or anything even if there was no trail or clues. We figured if anyone could replace him, it would be the daughter of . . . sorry."

Jackal shrugged and stared at the deck.

The Fanged Trio was really the only bright spot of this show. I was considering actually including them in my next book, but I'd have to recast Cat with someone less ridiculous, because no one would believe half the things he'd done. "So, when someone dies or leaves the group, you replace them. Are there always only three of you?"

"Yes," Wolf said. "Cat replaced his own father. Old Tamin was the most skilled swordsman I've ever worked with. I figured if anyone could fill his shoes, it would be his son."

Cat slapped Wolf on the back. "The joke was on you. My feet are way too big to fit in those dainty foot coffins he called shoes. My dad never taught me anything about sword-fighting, either, or much of anything, actually. I only saw him four times in my entire life. He did teach me the value of nudity, though—a gift I give to the world every time I go outside. Thank you very much."

Wolf did a really nice job of mixing pity and disgust in one facial expression. "Cat, I worked with your father for twenty years, and I never once saw him naked in public."

"Oh, right. My imaginary second dad taught me that. I made him up for Bring Your Dad to School Day. He took his clothes off in front of the class and gave all the other kids imaginary nightmares for months."

Wolf pretended he hadn't heard Cat. "Tamin was a great

mentor to me. We served together in the Garandian Army, along with Jorin and Fox from the Toothy Three. When Cat replaced him in the Trio and displayed such terrible skill with the blade, I felt it my duty to teach him everything his father had taught to me."

Cat smiled. "He even taught me how to grow this beautiful 'stache."

Jackal glanced at Wolf's clean-shaven though stubbly face, then back at Cat. "Cat tried to convince me when I joined that it was a signature of our company to grow a mustache. I should have known it wasn't part of the franchise agreement."

"Sorry," Wolf said. "The first thing I should have told you is not to believe anything he says. The other Fanged Trios have an orientation packet they give to new members, but Cat traded all of ours for . . ."

"Magic underwear. Too bad it turned out I was allergic to it. Say, remember when we ran into the Lithian Fanged Trio? Seeing their Cat was like looking in a mirror." Cat rubbed his chin wistfully.

"The Lithian Fanged Trio's Cat was Ipanian and a woman."

"She made me wonder what it would have been like if I had decided to be Ipanian and a woman. If I had, I would have looked just like her."

"And if you had a fully-functional brain, too."

"Yeah, makes you wonder, doesn't it?"

Wolf turned away from Cat. "So, where are you from, Harry? We don't really know a lot about you."

"I'm from a far-off land called Minnesota, though I grew up in Ohio."

"I've never heard of either of those places," Jackal said. "What is your home like?"

"Cold and snowy this time of year, but I do love how peaceful it is up in the woods." I almost teared up, and barely held it back.

"I love the snow. It stays yellow when you pee in it." Cat tried to hand out snow cones, but there were no takers.

"I wish I knew how to housebreak him, like the cats I have back home," Wolf said.

"They, however, did not turn yellow when I peed on them," Cat said. "What? I had to mark my territory."

"So, that's why they always give me a dirty look whenever you're around."

"Speaking of dirty looks, when do I get to meet your mom and dad, Wolf?"

"I think we should finish this journey in silence."

I SWEAR I DIDN'T SPANK HIM, OFFICER

Our journey finished without further incident. Cat even put underwear on without arguing. Evidently in his mind, being granted an audience with a king required just enough dignity to put on underwear but not enough to wear pants. We were escorted by a contingent of eight of the Garandian Empire's finest—or at least finest dressed—to the citadel and command center of the town. Once there, we were told that right outside the town, the king was attempting to rally the army, which had just returned from a massive defeat. As our party turned around to find the army, we bumped into some old friends of mine, my two favorite knights from my books—though not really this show—Arik and Verix.

"Look, Verix, it's old Blue Fingers!" Arik said.

Verix patted me on the shoulder. "Harry! I guess Axin and Weel finally got tired of you and let you go."

"No, I managed to outwit them."

I swear I could see Arik snickering behind her hands.

"Good to see familiar faces, I guess. Arik, Verix, I'd like to introduce you to my associates. This is Cat, Wolf, and Jackal, known as the Fanged Trio, and the rest are our escorts, led by Captain Idon'trememberhisname."

"I've heard of you guys," Verix said. "Didn't you three once charge naked into an entire squadron of Sculander knights and still manage to capture their leader?"

"There were only six of them, and Cat was the only one who was naked," Wolf said.

"Being naked makes me quicker," Cat said. "And it provides me with an extra weapon."

Arik and Verix stared at each other in disbelief.

"Hey, this is usually when Jackal calls me stupid or hits me," Cat said. "Come on, Jackal, it's our thing. I say something witty, then you hit me for it."

Jackal leaned down and pretended to tie her boots.

"We're on our way to the king," I said. "We have a delivery for him."

"What a coincidence," Arik said. "We've been assigned to his personal guards. We're heading that way now. If it's all right with your escorts, we'll join you."

Captain Idon'trememberhisname nodded.

"We were just coming from the royal armorer here in the citadel," Arik said. "Our armor got pretty banged up in the last battle."

"We're famous now," Verix said. "The Duke of Trobanton said he'd commission a song of our exploits. I personally requested a gangsta rap or a sea shanty. Do you think they can do both?"

"I do love a good rap," Arik said.

"There is definitely not any rap in this world—gangsta or otherwise." I bit my lip in frustration. "Seriously, who's writing this crap?"

"So, what have you been up to, Blue Fingers?"

"After I last saw you, I escaped to New Atlia where Hammurabi sent me to deliver an important item to the king."

"It's a sandwich," Cat said.

"No, it's not," Wolf said.

"You can't prove that."

I sighed. "So, what's been going on since I left?"

"Well, we won the Battle of the Butt Cheeks," Arik said. "Marshal Scritz praised Verix for his quick thinking. With Dyfantus on trial for all sorts of crimes, mostly against fashion, he couldn't steal our glory."

"Unfortunately, our army faced a second Sculander army a few days later, and we were mauled pretty handily," Verix said. "Their general, Sterlton Penwhicker, is a genius, and for some reason despises Garandians even though he is one. I wonder why he hates us so much?"

"That's odd, isn't it?" Wolf said, looking at Cat, but Cat was busy restocking the popcorn in his underwear and wasn't listening.

"Fortunately," Verix said, "Arik rallied a force that barely held off the main pursuit and allowed us to regroup here. Her scowling was very effective at keeping the enemy at bay."

Arik showed us her best scowl, completely missing the sarcastic tone. "The king has brought much-needed reinforcements to help us, but it may not be enough."

We entered the army's camp, which seemed fairly ramshackle and disorganized. Most of the soldiers we passed were too busy staring at the ground to make eye contact. The healer's tent was flickering with a steady glow. Untold numbers of wounded were tossed almost carelessly in a line that stretched all the way from the center to the outside of the camp. This army was definitely on its last legs, and victory in the next battle would require a miracle.

Perhaps that was exactly what the king was hoping to accomplish with whatever was in the box. Not that I cared. My plan was to be back home before any of that occurred. Observing the next battle would provide a great opportunity to have the ending for my next book planned out for me, but at this point, I was exhausted and frustrated beyond words. Besides, my faith in the writers of this show wasn't exactly high.

"We're just going to deliver our item, then be on our way," I said. "Better to leave the soldiering to the professionals."

"Can we stay, Wolf?" Cat said. "I've always wanted to see a battle."

"I've seen more than my share of battles, Cat, and you're not missing anything." Wolf looked around at the soldiers we were passing. "Besides, you really don't want to be here for this particular one. Trust me. We need to be on to our next job, anyway."

"I don't think I'll be joining you," Jackal said. "I need to find a different line of work."

"Is this because of me?" Cat said.

"Cat, no more talking until we're out of the camp," Wolf said.

Cat shrugged and gave Wolf a thumbs-up.

"Can we talk about this after we're done, Jackal?" Wolf asked.

She sighed. "Sure."

Off to our right, soldiers were running constant sprints in pairs of two. I wasn't sure if this was some form of fitness training, or perhaps a punishment, like my teacher used to give me for being bad at all things sports. Seriously, making someone run just because they're bad isn't going to make them better; it's only going to make them hate it more—especially when he was supposed to be teaching me math.

"Shouldn't they carry weapons while they're doing that?" Jackal asked.

"They told me they'll practice running toward the enemy when they get paid," Verix said.

Arik smirked. "The infantry has always been a bunch of cowards. Where is their sense of honor and duty?"

"Easy for you to say when you have a big castle and peasants to fight the hard fights for you," Wolf said.

Arik's mouth dropped. "They don't have that?"

Verix shook his head in bewilderment. "No, they do not, friend."

"Not even a little castle and a few peasants?"

"Only if they're toys."

"Maybe we could give them some."

"I guess I'll have to explain how the feudal system works to you later." Verix patted her on the back.

"I'd like to hear that, too," Cat said. "And could you explain the birds and the bees to me afterwards?"

"Is he serious?" Verix asked Wolf.

"You've only touched the tip of the iceberg on that one, my friend," Wolf said.

Cat scratched his forehead. "Where does the bird stick his penis in the bee?"

With the royal tent in sight, I realized that my journey would finally be coming to an end. I would have enjoyed my experience on this show if they hadn't gotten everything so horrifically wrong, except for the names and the basic descriptions of my characters. I had pretty much given up on them making me look heroic, and no, defeating a toddler—no matter how deadly they had made her look—and bravely getting my sword stuck in things didn't count. For someone whose greatest physical accomplishment had been not finishing last in most of his college track meets, this had still been a truly epic experience. I was going to miss the Fanged Trio. So what if they were just actors? They were also my friends.

With Arik and Verix at our side, no one questioned us as we entered.

The tent looked like it had been attacked by an army of Smurf decorators. It was covered in royal blue, and I do mean covered—everything from furniture to clothing to even the food was pure blue. Are raspberries that are dyed blue still called raspberries?

You can't call them blueberries, can you? The guards' skin was even dyed blue. I was so glad I hadn't made the royal color black. I did not need racism added to the long list of things wrong with this show.

Seated on a throne eating blue-dyed raspberries was the king of Garandia, Berin the Great, the first of his name. He seemed to be in good spirits, chatting amiably with his advisors and generals. Fortunately, he hadn't required his advisors to dye themselves, only his personal guards. I would not enjoy becoming a Smurf in order to converse with the king, even if he was the greatest king in the history of my fictional world. While they were conversing quietly with Berin, one of the generals took notice of us and pointed his gaudily ringed finger in our direction.

"Marshal Scritz, Your Majesty," Verix said, "the people behind me come bearing an important package from Hammurabi Joudisz. May they present it?"

The king clapped. "Hammurabi told us of this important object. They may." When the king spoke, his lips, tongue, and teeth were almost indistinguishable in their blueness.

Wolf walked forward and bowed, then handed the box and the key over to one of the guards. With a signal, the guard unlocked the container, opened it, and displayed it to the king.

Berin gasped in astonishment, dropped his bowl, and leaped from his throne. Since the guard had his back to us, everyone had to crane their necks in odd directions in the hope of seeing what the box contained. Fortunately, our wait was short, as the king pulled the item gingerly from the container and held it up. At first, none of us could see what it was except that it was small, metallic, and shiny. Cat deflated in obvious disappointment. I was surprised that in his bizarre mind, a sandwich could not be shiny or metal.

"Amazing!" the king said. "I thought this ancient relic had been lost since time untold. Can you believe it, Arik?"

"Uhh . . . no, Your Majesty."

"Such a thing to find! It's a shame that Hammurabi had to be removed from his post. Marshal Scritz, do you think the New Atlians will allow him to be appointed to an exclusively Garandian position instead of as their representative?"

"He is in exile, Majesty," Marshal Scritz said. "We'd have to find him first."

I still couldn't make out what the item was, and judging from the intense squinting of those around me, neither could anyone else. Cat had lost interest now that he knew the item was not a sandwich and had grabbed a handful of blue oranges from a nearby bowl.

"Is that man eating at a time like this?" King Berin said.

"I wshnen eafin," Cat said through his blue mouth.

"Young people have no priorities, which is probably why we are losing this war. Behold! The very paddle that slew our Lord in his worldly form."

The entire room gasped except for me. I wasn't sure what they were talking about. In my books, The One was slain by the blows of a massive heathen horde.

"You mean the Padalus Rexiconum?" Verix said.

"What was that story?" I said through gritted teeth and untold mental tears. I regretted asking as soon as the words had escaped my mouth, but curiosity got the better of me.

"When the Paruxians, our Lord's own people, rose against the small but infinitely devout cadre of followers of the new religion of The One, they caught our Lord at prayer and captured him," King Berin said. "To shame our Lord, they sold him to the chieftain of the horse people, Hung'Lo, who bent him over his knee and paddled Our Lord with this very object over one hundred times. Our Lord would not submit, for the spiritual wellbeing of his followers was more important than the pain of an infinite number of spankings."

The king paused, then went on, "Tiring to the point of collapse, Hung'Lo called for someone to continue with the spankings. No one would come forth, seeing that Our Lord's conviction and honor were immeasurable and that his heart was pure. Finally, after the fifth call for assistance, someone did come forth: Jaenia, our Lord's own wife. The shock of her betrayal was too much, and Our Lord succumbed on the very next spank."

None of the king's story was even remotely close to anything I had written. The One, in his human guise, was not even married in my books. And who would follow a religion where God was spanked to death?

"Aren't paddles usually made of wood?" I asked, because I don't know when to shut up before I make things even worse.

"A wooden paddle wouldn't really challenge Our Lord's faith," King Berin said. "A metal one was needed to penetrate his holy posterior."

I decided to change the subject before this somehow got worse. "Wouldn't a chest full of money help your cause more than this thing? I heard the army hasn't been paid in a while."

"Hammurabi said that as well in his letters," King Berin said, "but I thought that finishing the shrine to St. William the Overly Dramatic would inspire the men so much more."

"Hear, hear," the best-dressed of his advisors said. "The gold plating will be particularly inspiring."

"As will the thousand inlaid diamonds, Your Majesty," said the shortest and fattest advisor.

"I like the silk toilet paper in the lavatories," said the advisor who was so much of a toady that he actually looked like a toad—one that was dyed blue.

Berin stepped forward dramatically, monologuing away from everyone else toward what had to be a camera. "When the men see this great relic, they will be assured that The One is on our side and will overrun the enemy with renewed fervor. I would imagine that within days, this little rebellion will be finished, and I can continue my work of improving the holy places of the empire."

The best-dressed advisor started a slow clap, and soon all of the advisors had joined in with a brilliant display of yes-manning.

What had these idiot writers done to King Berin? While I had made him rather devout in my books, they had gone completely over the top in that aspect and had ignored everything else about him. I bet this Berin wasn't even an award-winning banjo player.

When the clapping died down, Berin set the paddle in his lap and smiled at us. "Now, let us see the second item that Hammurabi talked about."

I turned toward my companions, who were just as confused as I. Teragonna had only given us the one package. Wolf had been handed back the container, and he turned it upside down. Nothing else fell out. Out of ideas, my companions shuffled their feet nervously.

With nothing really left to lose, I decided to speak up. What was the worst they could do to me anymore, anyway? "We were only given the paddle, Your Majesty. Would you accept the gift of song as the second item?"

My voice is terrible. I was hoping that after a few notes from me, they'd be forced to end the show. My only regret was that I didn't see a gong.

"I don't think that is the thing we are looking for, but I will have to consult with him first." The king pointed to a group assembling in the entrance.

QUITE PROPHETABLE

A small, modestly dressed priest pushed his way through the throng of advisors to clear the way for the priest behind him. The second priest reminded me of a mixture of the pope and Elvis. I wasn't sure if I should ask him to forgive my sins or to see his blue suede shoes. Judging by the reverence the king showed him, I assumed he must be someone important, which in this messed-up version of my fake religion likely meant he was the one in charge of administering the holy wedgies. Perhaps he was the director of this travesty.

"All bow before the Holy Archon, Shlong'Dong Yuranus the Forty-Second," the first priest said.

"Holy Archon," King Berin said as he bowed, "it does us great honor to have the head of our entire religion present to bless the Shrine of St. William. While you're here, could you tell us what the second item is?"

"You may all rise. In the history of our religion, there have only been six of these, and, given that fact, I needn't tell you what I'm talking about."

Cat spat out something blue in surprise. I didn't want to know what it was, especially after it had crawled away. "Is it the number of morally trustworthy priests we've had?"

The Holy Archon and the seven priests accompanying him all gave Cat a dirty look.

"You're right. There's no way we've had six of 'em. How about the least number of holy days we've had in a week?"

"As much as I hate to agree with this imbecile," one of the advisors said, "it is hard to get anything done with our one-day work weeks."

"One day?" the king said. "We had eight holy days last week. Which two did you not honor?"

The guards seized the advisor and took him away. I wished they had taken me as well. I wasn't sure how there could be eight holy days in a seven-day week.

The Holy Archon cut Cat off before he could say something about a sandwich. Surprisingly, Cat did not try to talk over the archon and shut his mouth. "What we have before us is a prophet."

There was a gasp from the crowd. The short, fat advisor fainted. The toad-like one yelped, then swallowed a fly. Verix and Arik made the sign of the cross—which was completely out of place for their religion. Someone from the back shouted, "Testify!"

"My word!" King Berin said. "There hasn't been a prophet among us for over a century. Why, whoever could it be?"

Cat stepped forward and waved to the crowd.

Jackal whispered to me, "Harry, that's you. Do something."

Two of the priests stepped forward and put a robe on Cat.

"Please! Before he proclaims mandatory sexual harassment and makes pants optional."

"Ohhhh, no," I said. "I know how it goes with prophets. They're declared a witch and burned at the stake. Cat can have this one."

"Think about it, Harry," Jackal pleaded. "We'll have a generation of mustachioed idiots running around interrupting tearful last words with fart noises, stabbing everything in sight, and doing unspeakable things with their manhood to pretty much everything. You'll never be able to eat out again and will spend most of your time washing your hands. Think of the children!"

While I do like to do what's right, I am not what anyone would call a hero. I'm usually frightened by loud noises, the thought of danger, and hummingbirds. Plus, this was all a TV show, so none of it even mattered. It wasn't like real people were going to die. However, I thought, if I "died" in this show, they would have to let me go home. They'd probably burn me alive with special effects, and I wouldn't even be hurt. "Your Majesty, I am a prophet of The One, and I can prove it. If I'm not, I'll let you burn me at the stake."

"My word," the king said. "That is quite the claim. Will your challenger make the same claim?"

Cat flung off the robes and ran to the back of the crowd. "Oh, look, blue peaches. Sorry, I'm too hungry to be a prophet right now."

"Great," I said. "So, what do I do? Say something wise and inspired? Then someone betrays me and I get killed, right? Where's the best place to stand to start my speech? Come on. I'd like to get out of here by dinnertime."

"While I appreciate your enthusiasm," King Berin said, "the Holy Archon has to prove that you are in fact a prophet and not just some fat guy who craves attention."

"I am not fat!"

One of the priests scurried in front of the archon and held out a large, elaborately decorated book. The archon turned the pages a few times—likely at random—and gave a reverent nod to the crowd, asking for silence.

"The great book outlines threeeeeeeee characteristics that a prophet must possess, and only threeeeee. We will not get into the fourth one that the heretics who follow The One and a Half believe."

"Yes, Your Holiness, those blasphemers actually believe that a prophet can be a woman in even-numbered years. Ridiculous." At least the last word was right.

"Our crusaders should have that heretical sect destroyed within the year. How fortunate that they are all allergic to water. Now, on to the Three Holy Attributes of a Holy Prophet of Most Holy The One. According to the Book of Marlon the Goofy: 'A prophet must be over the height of six feet, but not exceeding six feet and seven inches, as that would be a little weird.' Is this man within the height criteria? Brother Fungus?"

A small, rather flustered man scurried forth and attempted to measure my height with a measuring tape. Unfortunately, he could only reach my armpits, and after a few minutes of shouting from the Holy Archon, a stool was brought forth and he concluded that I was six feet, three inches tall. I must have grown an inch.

"As this man meets those criteria, let me continue: 'A prophet of Our Lord must also hear voices guiding him in all matters spiritual, but not doing things like telling him winning lottery numbers or where he left his wagon keys.' Does thou hear voices?"

"Yes, I do." I actually didn't, besides the usual, like my grandma telling me not to pick my nose in public or stare at women's breasts when they might notice.

"Do you know yesterday's winning lottery numbers for the Garandian National Lottery?"

"No, I do not."

"Take a guess."

I rolled my eyes. "1-13-37-44 and the Special Ball of 14."

"Brother Inflammation?"

"That is not correct!"

The Holy Archon put his hand on my shoulder and gave me a serious look. "And where are your wagon keys?"

"I don't have a wagon, and I don't think they usually have keys, anyway."

"Very clever of you to have sold that. Prophets are often crafty. Now, we must determine if you can hear the voice of the Lord."

"Brother Stink Eye, bring forth the cup."

Another priest shambled through the throng of advisors, this one holding a small cup encrusted in gold with engravings of tiny fat kids poking each other. The priest handed me the cup, which was empty. I stared at it for a few minutes, but no one came forward to fill it.

After a lengthy, painful silence, the Holy Archon said, "Ahem. You have to urinate in it."

"Really? How is that going to show that I hear the voice of The One?"

"Well, I know that I usually have some of my best ideas when I'm in the bathroom."

"I thought up the plan for the Battle of Awkward Hippos when I was doing number two," one of the generals said, "and that was a great victory."

"That was!" King Berin patted the general on the back. "Our current fiscal policy was thought up while I was urinating after my coronation." I thought I heard someone cough that the policy really was just a bunch of something, though not urine.

"And it is written in the Great Book that Our Lord created the Fifteen Holy Suggestions on How to Live a Better Life when he had a case of the runs," the Holy Archon said. "Now, please, pee in the cup. We also need to test for performance-enhancing drugs."

"Oh, no," the king said, "using those would be terrible. We must run a clean religion here."

"Quite right, Your Majesty," said the fat advisor. "Leave the drugs to the followers of The One and a Half."

In order to get this over with, I turned around in the corner and peed into the cup while Brother Stink Eye watched. After I was done, Brother Stink Eye took the cup and scurried off to test it. I wasn't sure what kind of tests he was going to do—he probably just tossed it into a bush—but I was confident that I would pass all of them.

"Now, please grace us with a prophecy," the Holy Archon said.

What do you say to that? Obviously, I wasn't a prophet of any kind. Whatever I said could affect the lives of a lot of people. Generations might stick with whatever came from my mouth right then because I was on TV.

"How about, 'Love thy neighbor as yourself'?" I suggested.

"That's stupid," Brother Fungus said. "What if your neighbor is a jerk?"

"Or what if you don't like yourself much?" Brother Inflammation said. "Are you supposed to hate your neighbor then?"

"It's supposed to be a metaphorical neighbor," I said. "Neighbor means anyone besides yourself."

"Ha!" the Holy Archon said. "The One would never send that as a message. In the Book of French the Steward, it says: 'Beat thy neighbors with sticks to prove how much better thou art, unless they are bigger than you, then you should bake them pies, so that they might leave thou alone.'"

The Holy Archon continued. "Now, try again. I'll give you one more try, and then we'll burn you at the stake or slap you around a little if we can't get a fire started. You may have just had indigestion, which we all know can affect prophesizing."

"Yes," Brother Inflammation said. "The prophet Blandulese

once prophesized that hurting another person is a sin after he had a bad sausage, and look where that got him."

"The Paruxians beat him to death with sporks shortly after that," Brother Stink Eye said. "But he was responsible for the prophecy of no underwear Saturdays as he lay dying."

Brother Inflammation nodded vigorously. "The freedom of no underwear on Saturdays carried the early followers of The One to countless military victories over the heathens. Our faith would have never spread without that prophecy."

Okay, so inspiring religious statements from the Bible didn't seem to work. These people did seem to like ridiculous, nonsensical things, so maybe they'd like No Shave November, or Pig Latin, or I could "invent" the fanny pack. No, that was too stupid.

Wait! Why did I care? I *wanted* to be burned at the stake.

"Beans, beans, the magical fruit, the more you eat the more you toot." My four-year-old self would be so proud that I'd said that on television.

The crowd was stunned into silence, so dumb was my statement. I beamed a fantastic grin and mentally patted myself on the back. No one said anything for at least a minute, a feat I can usually only accomplish unintentionally. The majority of them stared at the Holy Archon for guidance. Most likely, he was trying to figure out if he could burn someone at the stake twice.

After a few aborted attempts at speech, the Holy Archon finally blurted out, "Brilliant! The Almighty has finally given us guidance at this low ebb of spirituality and desperation."

"Of course, Your High Holiness," Brother Fungus said. "The bean is indeed a magical fruit, though I had always thought of it as a vegetable. If The One says it is a fruit, then it is a fruit. I must find some parchment to record this holy statement."

He skipped off to find something to write my moronic wisdom on. He probably could have found it carved into the walls of the nearest men's bathroom.

"I thought it was a legume," Cat said.

"If the prophet says it is a fruit, then it is clearly a fruit," the Holy Archon said. "I shall issue a proclamation that henceforth, all legumes are now fruits and are magical. And all armies of The One shall consume mass quantities of beans before engaging any heathen armies."

"Isn't there a third criterion?" Cat said. Wolf and I both gave him an incredibly dirty look, which, as usual, was lost on him.

"Oh, I know this one," King Berin said. "From the Book of Adam of Sand: 'All prophets shall be considered by the majority of their peers to be idiots, but in a loveable way and not in a pitiable way, like, 'Aww, that's so cute, but now I feel bad for him.'"

Perfect. I was definitely lovable. I was obviously not an idiot, though this group probably would consider me one, as they likely wouldn't know a good idea if it hit them in the genitals. They had, after all, thought my earlier statement was genius. This requirement might have thwarted my plan of being burned at the stake, however.

"That is what it says in the general public's version of the Holy Book," the Holy Archon said, "but in the secret copy only given to the high clergy, it says something different. We keep this version of the text out of the general public's view so that false prophets don't fake all the steps."

Brother Inflammation walked forward and opened the comically oversized book in front of the Holy Archon, who turned it to a marked passage.

"According to the secret Book of James, who only became famous because of his more talented brother:

Adam does not know what he is talking about. The Lord only talked to him as a joke, to see what people would actually believe. It was on the Day of Fools, after all. He really should have known better.

All Holy Prophets of the Lord shall have dark beards and glasses. They shall also be not quite overweight, though they could stand to lose a few pounds.

"So sayeth The Lord. Amen." The Archon closed the book dramatically and Brother Inflammation left, probably to set the book down and get his back looked at.

After a few minutes of hushed conversations amongst the crowd, the Holy Archon silenced them. "And I'd appreciate it if everyone here would keep the whole 'secret book' thing quiet. Brother Fungus will have you all sign holy non-disclosure agreements before you leave. I think it is clear that this person does not fit the last criterion."

Huh? That was exactly what I looked like. In my last book, it even said that word for word in my dust jacket bio. (I really should have reviewed that thing before they printed it.)

"Quite right, Your High Holiness," the toad-like advisor said. "This man is a clean-shaven redhead and is rail thin." The gaggle of advisors all nodded in agreement.

"Umm, Your Holyship," Cat said, "that sounds exactly like him. His hair is most definitely dark brown." He then poked me in the stomach a few times, which I found rather comforting. "And, see, he does need to lose a few pounds."

The advisors shook their heads in disagreement and gave Cat disgusted looks.

The Holy Archon stepped forward and looked me hard in the eyes. He then tweaked my nose, fondled my elbows more than I usually like, and called his fellow priests over into a huddle.

A few minutes later, he emerged from the pack. "Oh, this fellow. I thought we were talking about someone else. He does indeed meet the description." The advisors all nodded again, indicating that they had known I was a prophet all along.

"What is your name, Holy Prophet?" the Holy Archon asked.

"Harry."

"Then you shall be known henceforth as Harry the Prophet, but we should really think of a new name for you, so as not to confuse you with the Hairy Prophet, also known as St. Magnacious the Chimp."

"O Holy Prophet named Harry," King Berin said, "he who will need a new nickname later, what is it that The One wants this righteous army full of believers to do?"

I stepped forward and paused dramatically near the spot the king had been monologuing toward before. "The One has instructed me to tell you to end this war. Give peace a chance."

The crowd gasped, and one particularly large man in the back fainted forward, taking out several other advisors. The generals performed an especially impressive bit of synchronized scowling. I would have clapped if it hadn't been so menacing.

Verix stepped forward with a pleading look on his face. "Harry, surely you are mistaken. Except for the last battle, we have routinely defeated the rebels. With the inspiration of the Holy Paddle and yourself, the first prophet in living memory, surely we will crush the enemy and destroy the last of the Sculander armies in the field."

"You should not address a prophet of The One in such a manner, son," the Holy Archon said. "The proper address is Holiest Speaker or Harry the Prophet, with official nickname to be chosen later."

"It's all right," Verix said. "I knew him before he was famous."

"Oh. Then it is allowed by Holy Law," the Holy Archon said.

I wasn't sure what to do now. I wasn't liking the amount of time and energy that a battle would take, even if the Garandians were likely to get routed. Even in a well-choreographed battle, a lot could go wrong. I might get trampled on accident or become surrounded by ever-zealous fans and get carpal tunnel from all of the autograph signing. On the other hand, if I kept pushing an obviously unpopular order, they were likely to revoke my prophethood. Propheticism? Prophetability? Whatever. You know what I mean.

"The One was very clear that he wants this war to end," I said.

"You heard him," King Berin said with renewed vigor. "We must end this war now!"

The crowd erupted in cheers and applause, and the king sent messengers out immediately. Verix smacked me on the back and completely knocked the wind out of me, which prevented me from speaking further, though I doubted anyone would have heard me over the noise anyway.

By the time I was able to speak again, most of the tent had emptied. The only people present were the king, Verix, Arik, the Trio, and myself. King Berin beamed with enthusiasm and stared reverently at the Holy Paddle.

"That wasn't what I meant," I said.

"You said The One wants the war to end," the king said. "So, we're going to end it with our blades."

"Your Majesty, I hate to interrupt, but my group has completed our mission to deliver the Holy Paddle," Wolf said. "We would like to receive our payment and leave."

The king continued to stare at the paddle. "Why don't you stay through the battle? The Holiest Speaker seems fond of you, and I would like a little extra protection. If you agree, I will pay triple the usual day's fee. Do you accept?"

"Of course!" Cat said. "I've always wanted to see a battle."

Wolf looked like he wanted to hit him, but he must have been too afraid to interrupt a king.

The king finally pulled his gaze from the paddle, not that I could blame him; it was really shiny. "Verix, bring our guests to the command area. The army needs to see our new prophet. Holiest Speaker, if you could prepare something, I'm sure they could use the inspiration."

"I can think of a finger I want everyone to see."

FREE BOOB JOBS AND ACTION FIGURES FOR ALL

King Berin gathered all of his generals and advisors, as well as me and the Trio, on a large platform at the back of the assembled army. Marshal Scritz stared daggers at me. I knew that look; I must have ruined his childhood dream of becoming a prophet. I'd had the same look when they told me that no colleges offered a degree in ninja turtling. The Holy Archon was not present, as this war was technically a conflict of interest for him, being between two groups of followers of The One, though he clearly favored the Garandians.

After he was sure everyone was settled, the king silenced the crowd with a gesture. It must be great to have the power and respect to accomplish that. The last time I had attempted it, the only thing it had accomplished was getting a lot of food thrown at me. The yogurt that rolled down my pants was surprisingly soothing.

King Berin projected with the practiced voice of a master speaker. "It brings me great pride to see my loyal countrymen doing their duty to defend our honor in this war. I know that many of your friends and loyal companions have paid the ultimate price in protecting this land from the ungrateful and cowardly rebels.

The cost has been high, and your hardships have not been forgotten by me or any of my retainers."

He went on, "I know that this army before me has everything it needs in the brave hearts of you men and women to drive the rebels into the grave so that we can all go home and enjoy the peace and prosperity that is the right of every man, woman, and child in the great Garandian Empire."

The king paused then, probably expecting a round of boisterous applause, but he found himself staring into the eyes of a bewildered and somewhat bored crowd. After a few confused looks at his advisors, he continued. "You're probably all unsure of what may happen in the upcoming battle. You may even be convinced that only defeat lies ahead of you, but I have two things that will show you beyond a shadow of a doubt that the Almighty himself believes in victory for your Garandia."

That last part seemed to pique the interest of the crowd. Most of them were now actually looking up instead of at their feet.

"My loyal subjects have uncovered two holy things that were thought lost, the first of which is the very paddle used to slay our Holy Lord by his wife, Jaenia, in her ultimate betrayal. We have in front of us the legendary Padalus Rexiconum!"

The crowd gasped as one. If you've never heard an entire crowd gasp at the same time, it's a thing of wonder After the initial shock had worn off, most of the crowd seemed to regrow their looks of defeat. The king was very confused by this reaction. He had clearly thought this revelation would immediately inspire his soldiers to charge ferociously into the Sculander army and drive it into the sea or to some final resting place. He probably hadn't even expected to need me.

Once his confusion had worn off, the king raised his hand, and again the crowd stared with rapt attention. I really wanted to learn how he did that. Think of the things you could do with a power like that. Actually, the only things I can think of are following the silence with a brief pause, staring seriously into the eyes of the crowd, and saying, "Underwear. That is all." Thoughts like that are probably why I'll never be able to get a crowd to listen to me.

"With the Padalus Rexiconum to inspire us, our army can easily crush the pathetic rebel army before us. But that is not the only thing we have to show our enemy that The One favors us above all others. Just moments ago, the Holy Archon himself verified the discovery of a new holy prophet, and he serves not the rebels—not the Lithians—or even the holy people of Paruxia. He serves the Garandian Empire, your Ga-ran-di-an Empire!"

The crowd seemed to perk up a bit, but no one seemed to be particularly inspired by that, except for a guy in front who was clapping like an idiot. Cat was behind me, so it wasn't him. I squinted real hard, and I swear it was Chris, the same person I see at all my conventions, who is just a bit too eager to meet me. Verix pushed me forward to stand right next to the king.

King Berin whispered, "I think I have them just about ready to charge fearlessly toward the rebels. All you have to do is say, 'The One approves of our battle as righteous and holy' and I'm sure they'll attack immediately."

Then the king turned away from me and addressed the crowd again. "This man next to me is Harry Olson. He has been appointed by The One as his voice to us, his chosen people. And now, let us see what words of wisdom The One has for us. Harry?"

I stuck my hand up exactly as the king had done as a request for silence, even though everyone was already pretty silent. As one, the crowd turned around and shambled toward the camp. In exasperation, the king stepped forward again and stuck his hand up. The entire crowd turned around and stared in perfect attention.

How did he do that? The crowd hadn't even been looking at us.

"Friends, Romans, countrymen, lend me your ears." I waited for a reaction and got the usual look of confusion.

"What's a Roman?" a gap-toothed man with big ears asked.

He had a good point. I needed to restart with something more relevant. "Ask not what your country can do for you; ask what you can do for your country."

"What can our country do for us?" a skinny, bespectacled fellow a few rows back asked.

"I said, ask *not* what your country can do for you. Whatever. Forget it."

Okay, I needed to dumb this down a little more. Something straight to the point. I considered going back to my "end the war and peace" thing, but I figured the war would go on regardless of what I said. I decided to just ask them to attack and get this whole thing over with.

"My fellow Garandians, The One has spoken to me and instructed me to tell you all that if you attack now with devotion in your hearts and fervor in your veins, you will crush the rebels and end this war today, or at least by the end of the week. Maybe a month, tops. And with the Sculander rebels crushed, you can all go home and make babies or do whatever it is you really want to do."

Give me a break. I'm not an expert public speaker. You try coming up with an inspirational speech with no time to prepare. Most politicians have a team of experts to write this stuff for them.

"Did he just say we're fighting babies?" a guy with his helmet on backwards asked.

"No, I think he said they have rabies," a portly woman next to him said.

"Could you repeat that for us?" an Atlian in what looked like sunglasses asked. "There seems to be some confusion."

I don't know who it was who said that it's really easy to

inspire an army of extras in a fantasy/reality show to attack another army of extras, but they were wrong. I probably should have said something about them all becoming famous if they attacked. I really didn't want to repeat the whole thing again, mostly because I had no idea what it was I had just said.

"Look, The One wants you all to attack that army over there." I pointed behind them to the Sculander army that was forming up.

"But we haven't been paid in over a month," the gap-toothed man in the front said. There was a rumbling of agreement.

"My family is starving, and they need money!" a Hulk Hogan look-alike in chain mail said.

"And I have to pay for my breast job," the guy with his helmet on backwards said.

"The prophet Merfin once turned fishes into coins," a guy in an eyepatch said. "Can you do that?" The crowd seemed really enthusiastic about that one.

"Well, no. If I could do that, I wouldn't be here. I'd be on a beach with a bunch of beautiful women, but I hear the Sculanders over there have a lot of really nice stuff. Why don't you all go kill them and take it?"

"What kind of stuff?" the guy with his helmet on backwards asked.

"Big shiny stuff that's worth a lot."

"What about trakons?" Sunglasses asked. "I need money to feed my family."

"Lots of trakons and jewels, but you have to kill them to get it. The One told me so."

"We all don't really like killing people," a skinny, bespectacled fellow in the middle said. An awful lot of the crowd seemed to agree with him.

"But you're in the army. Killing is your job."

"Didn't The One tell the prophet Merfin that killing is wrong?" the bespectacled man asked.

"No. He said drilling is wrong. The One likes it when you kill people, but he's very anti-oil. He's funny like that." It'd be nice if these actors or the writers who had written their lines had actually read my books. The One is a real douche of a god. He'd be the perfect god for soldiers or anyone on a reality show, which I guessed now included me. "So, go get them."

The army, as one, took a step back.

"Come on, guys. The One has told me, his prophet, that the Sculander rebels are wicked and that you should kill them all and take their stuff."

"Can we do it tomorrow?" a big barbarian asked. "We could use a day off. Don't we get vacation days?" There was a murmur of agreement from the crowd.

"You've all been sitting in camp for the last week!" Marshal Scritz exclaimed.

"Most of us aren't feeling very well," a big barbarian said. "It's right in the heart of allergy season."

"Look, I'll give out a signed Dyfantus the Bold action figure to the first person who turns around and charges the enemy," I said.

"Is it the one with the purple saber or the black one?" the Hulk Hogan look-alike asked. "The purple one is very rare." That was true; only forty of them were known to exist.

"The purple one, of course." I'd have to get mine from back home, but I hoped they wouldn't hold me up to that. I could always claim I'd been acting.

The Hulk Hogan lookalike actually appeared to be starting to turn, but by then, a great roar had erupted from the back. It appeared that my motivational techniques were working a lot better farther away. I wondered if it was because they couldn't actually see me back there.

WHEN CRYING IS A GOOD THING

While I was regaling the people near the stage with my witticisms, the battle started without them. The sounds of blades striking flesh and the screams of the pretend dying were all I could hear. Wolf yelled something in my ear, but the only way I could tell was by the movement of his lips.

After a while, he grabbed me and dragged me to the back of the platform, where the king and other non-combatants were being led away. Though he wanted to watch this great victory, the generals had managed to talk the king into leaving. Arik took charge of the king's guard and personally led Berin from the field. The king only agreed to leave if Verix stayed and protected me. He thought my presence would inspire the troops.

Once they were safely out of view, Verix ran to the edge of the platform to take stock of the situation. It was clearly killing him not to be a part of this epic battle. He had, no doubt, lost out on a fantastic chance for greater glory and honor by being assigned to me.

After a few minutes, he ran back. "We're losing! The rebels were the ones to attack us, not the other way around."

"Well, do something," I said. "You're the hero. Why don't you go turn this whole thing around?"

"You're right, Harry," Verix said, "but the king insisted that I stay and protect you."

"You have my permission."

I should have felt bad about this, but I really wanted him and the others to leave so I could escape. Plus, he was a fantastic fighter, and if the Garandians lost this war, I wasn't sure what I'd do with my books after this; the Sculander-Garandian War was the entire basis of my book series, after all.

Being the brave and loyal knight he was, Verix charged head-first into the sea of soldiers.

"We should join him," Cat said. "Think of how famous we'd be if we helped them win."

"Cat, I've been in nineteen major battles," Wolf said, "and trust me, this battle is already over. The Garandian army will be lucky to have enough men to garrison the city after this."

"You should join in, Cat," Jackal said. "Go. We'll be right behind you."

"Thanks, Jackal," Cat said. He charged straight ahead without looking back.

"So, so dumb," Jackal said. "I'm going to miss him. Well, not really, but it was fun messing with him one last time."

Wolf stared seriously into her eyes. "Jackal, you can't just let him die. Sure, he's an idiot, but he's *our* idiot. We're responsible for him."

"Fine, have a conscience. You know we'd be better off with literally anyone else."

"Come on, let's go. We have to get him. You know we do."

"Oh, all right."

They reluctantly charged into the melee after him. Fortunately, Cat was pretty easy to find, thanks to the trail of bodies behind him. Unfortunately, he had charged straight into the rear of the battle, so all of those bodies belonged to Garandians.

As much as I would have liked to see Cat in action, I really didn't want to be involved in that battle, or any battle, for that matter. It was too dangerous and unpredictable, even if it was fake —though it did look pretty real, what with all the blood and the unattached limbs lying around.

This was a pretty anticlimactic way to part with the Fanged Trio, but that's how it is sometimes. As I walked out of camp hoping to find an escape from this travesty, it dawned on me that this was the first time I had been alone in over a week. I felt so free that I strongly considered running around naked in celebration. After much debate, I decided it wouldn't be a good idea to get caught on tape running around naked again.

After about thirty minutes of wandering through the deserted camp, I realized I was not going to find anything useful other than spare weapons or some slightly used food. There were no abandoned vehicles or other methods of transportation in sight.

Judging by the sounds, the battle was dying down, and I figured I should probably get to safety before I got involved in the after-battle festivities—like everyone's favorite party game, "stab the guy who's running away." The city was probably the safest place to be, so I ran as quickly as my out-of-shape legs would take me, between "stop and pant really hard" breaks.

Fortunately, the gate to the city was still open. As I approached, one of the guards stopped me. "Halt! Which army are you from?"

It took a few moments before my mouth would allow me to speak. "The Kiss Army."

The guard looked to his companion. "Did we change the name of our army again?"

"It was called the Army of the Humble Cockroaches last week, wasn't it?"

"No, it was Grass Clippings of the Apocalypse. But what is it this week?"

"Something like Armpit Noises of Doom. Definitely not the Kiss Army."

The guard scratched his forehead. "Was it ever the Kiss Army?"

"Don't think so. It might have been called the Heavy Petting Army last month, though."

I growled. "Look, guys, I was just joking. I've come from the Garandian army."

"I didn't think Granada had an army anymore. Did you, Curtos?"

Curtos shook his head. "Granada doesn't exist anymore. Spain conquered them a while ago."

No, there was no Spain or Granada in this world. These guys were morons, which meant they fit in with everyone else in this story. "I said Ga-ran-di-an. Garandian. You know, the country you're wearing the uniform of."

"Oh. Garandian. My mistake. Then, sorry, we can't let you in." He nodded confidently.

"And why not?"

"Because we were ordered to not let anyone in unless they were in the Garandian army."

I gritted my teeth. "I . . . am . . . in . . . the . . . Garandian army."

"Oh, you're in the Garandian army. Why didn't you say so? What's your business here?"

"I want to get in."

"Oh. Sorry, then, sir. We can't let anyone in."

"You just said you'd let me in if I'm in the Garandian army, and I'm in the Garandian army." I stomped my foot in frustration and didn't look at all like an angry toddler.

"We would, but the gate is closed up tight."

I turned my head slightly to double-check that the gate was open. "The gate is open!"

"Yes, it is, sir. Would you like to go in?"

"Yes!"

"And which army are you a part of?"

After I'd smacked my palm to my face and wept for a few minutes, I decided that arguing with this guard was about as pointless as arguing with a computer. I pointed to the left, and when the guards looked that way, I ran past them.

"Hey! Where do you think you're going? Stop!"

Fortunately, the guards didn't chase me.

"Did you hear which army he was from?" the first guard yelled.

"Oh, yes. The Garandian army. He's safe to let through," the second guard yelled back.

"Good. Why was he running, then?"

When I ran out of breath and stopped, I realized I had no idea where I was. I'd found myself in the middle of a very large public square surrounded by wooden booths. It appeared that I was in the market area. Even though it was the middle of the day, the area was completely deserted. I was very disappointed by the lack of tumbleweeds.

I decided to yell, mostly to see if anyone was around to help me, but also because I really love the sound of a good echo. "Hello? Is anyone there?"

After a few moments of waiting with no response, I decided to walk toward the main keep and see if they'd let me in. I was sure Arik would help me if they'd let me see her. I turned toward the keep and jumped with a start when I found a man standing right behind me. He was short, with plastered-on dark hair and an equally plastered-on smile.

"Are you in need of some assistance, sir?"

"Yes, I need to find a safe place. The Sculander army is probably heading this way."

"You're in luck, my good man." The odd man put his right hand on my shoulder. "Can I call you Harry?"

"Well, that is my name, but I'm not sure how you know that."

"Great, Harry. Harry, do I have a deal for you. You're in luck today. When I say a quick, reliable ride, what comes to mind, Harry?"

I put my hand to my chin to indicate how wise I was. "Well, either a Jaguar or a Mercedes."

"No, you don't want those, though they are pretty nice, Harry. What you really need is a three-legged donkey. Nothing beats the style, comfort, and dependability of a three-legged donkey. Three-legged donkeys have long been the mark of the stylish peasant on the go. With one of my donkeys, you could be the envy of your neighbors and catch the eye of every eligible young lady you pass. Wouldn't you like it if all of the ladies were giving you the wink instead of the local thug?"

"Well, that would be nice."

"Fantastic. For only a hundred and twelve payments of ten trakons, I could put you on the back of a deluxe three-legged donkey today. How does that sound, Harry?"

That didn't sound like very good terms to me. One hundred and twelve payments? For ten trakons, I could get a new broadsword and a nice sheaf, or three pairs of some very stylish pantaloons. "I did hear two-legged donkeys were the best."

"Harry, no offense, but you don't strike me as the kind of man who could afford one of those babies. Two-legged donkeys are reserved for only the wealthiest of nobles."

"But I'm a prophet of The One! The Holy Archon himself named me Harry the Prophet."

"Well, then, that's a different story."

This guy was really, really good. I wondered if I could talk him into selling my merchandise later. I bet he could sell my stuff to people who had never heard of my series. Then again, after this show had aired, everyone would probably have heard of it, just not in a good way.

"Harry . . . err . . . Mr. Prophet, I'll let you have my best two-legged donkey for free, if you keep an advertisement for my dealership on the sides at all times. Sound good? A prophet should ride in style, after all."

"Wow, thanks."

"Splendid. Here you go. Hop on."

I had no idea where the donkey had come from. He had me walking in circles, and there wasn't anything near us the whole time. I was beginning to think this guy was a wizard of some sort, which didn't make sense, since the Atlians and the Old Gods were the only people who used magic in Vyenra. Was he supposed to be the god of donkey selling?

I climbed onto the back of the donkey after several failed attempts, vowing to take lessons on how to properly climb onto the back of a mount when I finally got out of this show. I really was terrible at it, even though my riding skills had become quite decent.

The back of the two-legged donkey was surprisingly comfortable—even more comfortable than my Honda Civic back home. The donkey wasn't air conditioned, however, and it had gotten exceptionally hot and humid. The effort of my numerous attempts to mount had left me dripping with sweat and desperately in need of water. A chili dog would have been really nice, too.

The cries of the fleeing army were getting pretty close. It sounded like they'd entered the city. I assumed the guards at the gate couldn't stop all of them at once with their inane questions, and I really didn't want to get run over, either accidentally or as part of the plot, so I pulled on the reins and put my heels into the beast's sides. I really needed to get moving fast, as it sounded like the army was only a few blocks away. I also wanted to see just how fast this thing could move, as the salesman had described it as the fastest thing on land other than a cheetah or an angry ex-girlfriend. Unfortunately, the donkey just stood there and chewed on a bit of grass growing in the cracks between the cobbles.

"How do you get this thing to move?" I demanded.

There was no response from the salesman. I looked around and he was nowhere to be seen. I had only been looking away for a second. How could he have left so quickly? It was just like a salesman to be everywhere at once when you needed to buy something but disappear when you needed help.

I put my heels into the donkey's sides and pulled on the reins again. The only reaction I got was what looked like exhaust coming out of the donkey's back end. Fortunately, the wind was blowing away from me. I looked around in the unlikely hope of finding an owner's manual, but there didn't appear to be any. It's too bad donkeys don't have glove boxes.

The fleeing army sounded like they were less than a block away. I began to sweat more profusely. Even after a few more tugs on the reins, the donkey still would not move. I contemplated climbing back off and making a run for it, but with my ineptitude in dismounting, I realized that was not an option. I let go of the reins and began to weep.

Evidently, weeping to two-legged donkeys is what turning the key and pressing the accelerator is to a car. The donkey jolted forward at an incredible pace. I was fortunate that I had a deluxe donkey with a seat belt and safety harness, as those were the only things keeping me on its back—well, that, and fear. That fear prevented me from finding out one of my life's biggest questions —just how does a two-legged donkey move? More than likely, they can't—it's special effects and a pulley system that gives them the illusion of movement.

I really wish I had been able to look down then. The ride was surprisingly smooth, even with the wind blowing hard in my face. The salesman really should have given me a helmet. I probably ended up swallowing all of the flying insect species wherever it was we were filming.

The city blurred by. I saw brief glimpses of houses I had passed on my way in, then I saw the docks. Suddenly I was over water, and I had a brief view of the palace back on the island of Garandia. A blur, and then I saw the ruins of a massive, abandoned city. I blinked, and then I was over water again. Then land. The last of my tears must have dried, because the donkey came to a halt in front of a rather nice-looking building in a well-maintained part of town. What town? I wasn't sure. I began to wipe the bug bits off my face, then jumped with a start when a hand touched my thigh.

"Harry? Is that you? How did you get here?"

When my vision finally cleared, I saw Verix standing next to me. "Verix! Where am I?"

"You're in the Chistine District."

"Of Caltisport?"

"Yes, of course. Where else would you be?" Verix rubbed my donkey's coat reverently. "Wow. My family could never afford one of these, and we're nobles."

"Is the battle over? How did you get here?"

"It was a rout. I managed to rally some of our soldiers and kill the enemy's leader, Sterlton Penwhicker, but it wasn't enough. I barely made it out alive, and then I came straight here through the southern gate. We need to get out of town immediately, as I don't think the townspeople will be able to hold out for very long. Some of the rebels managed to get in with our fleeing troops."

"Then we need to get to the docks. Do you know the way?"

Verix nodded and led my donkey forward. I really wanted to look underneath it to see how it was moving, but knew if I did that, I'd fall off. Given my difficulties with mounting, it was a risk I couldn't afford to take. I tried looking for a reflection in a window to see below, but none of the buildings we passed had any windows at street level. I wasn't sure if that had been done to prevent me from seeing how the donkey worked or to save on the cost of windows. As luck would have it, right before we finally got near a large window, a noise caught our attention from behind.

"World, look oooooout!" a deep baritone sang. "How could you ever dooooooubt?" He continued, "The duo escaped lock-oooooout."

"It's Axin and Weeeeeel!" his companion finished in a falsetto. "Here to kill you with zeal."

"Critics described their performance as loud," I said.

"You're terrible," Verix said to me as he let go of my donkey's reins.

"Did someone say 'things too terrible to say out loud?'" the first armored man asked. They both had their visors down, so I couldn't see their faces.

"I surmise they did, my compatriot," the second one said. "That is our cue, is it not?"

Verix moved in front me and drew his sword. "Axin and Weel. How did you two escape from prison? Have you joined the Sculanders?"

The first one, Axin, pulled up his visor to show us a naughty grin. "We didn't need to escape. They let us off for good behavior. Only our master was convicted. Now, give us the scribe."

"This is your idea of good behavior?" I asked.

Weel snorted, his visor amplifying the sound so that it echoed down the narrow street. "Relatively speaking, since we're only going to kill two people—yes, that would qualify as good behavior by comparison. We did once sack three allied towns in a week, just to get our month's numbers up."

Axin lowered his sword and smiled wistfully. "I can still hear the screaming of the innocent. Puts me to sleep every night. Now, since our master is currently unavailable, we must get his revenge by proxy."

Verix's gauntlet squeaked as he gripped his sword harder. "I'll die before I let the likes of you have my friend. Harry, I'll hold them off as long as I can. You get to safety."

Never one to have to be told twice not to stay and get stabbed, I turned my donkey around. It would have been kind of neat to see the sword fight, but then I'd have to listen of more of Weel's terrible butchering of the English (and identical Garandian) language.

As I teared up slightly, my donkey trotted back to the spot where I had found Verix. The sound of the army had gotten a lot closer. They should have still been at least fifteen minutes away, but they sounded much, much closer. If I had to guess, I'd say they were only a few minutes away.

Every gap in between the houses was blocked off, and there were no side streets between me and the sound of the coming mob. I was evidently being forced into confronting Axin and Weel, so I turned back around. Perhaps this was the showrunners' way of making up for all of those terrible rumors they had spread about me and these awful singing knights. They did owe me a scene where I showed off my heroism, and those two would be the perfect targets. I dismounted the donkey to help, but first I would need to find a weapon.

Verix had disarmed Axin completely, but Weel had bashed my friend down to his knees. Verix desperately unleashed a flurry of swings and barely managed to stumble to his feet, which gave Axin time to pick up his sword and hit him from behind. Verix swung wildly, at least giving himself some breathing room, but it didn't look good for him. I desperately wanted to help, but I still couldn't find a weapon.

One of Verix's swings caught Axin on the side of his helmet. Axin staggered and then collapsed to the ground. Seizing the opening, Weel disarmed Verix and knocked him onto his back. I wasn't sure if Axin was unconscious or dead, but he didn't react when I took his sword. With Verix completely at his mercy, Weel pulled off his helmet and panted.

"If the king finds out that you've killed a fellow knight in cold blood," Verix said, "you'll be banished, and all of your family's land will be confiscated. Also, you'll be suspended for three whole jousting tournaments unless you win an appeal."

"Fortunately, you'll be too deceased to notify him of such an occurrence. I shall relish this instant in its entirety for the rest of my existence." Weel slowly massaged his rival's neck with the blade.

Verix's eyes brightened when he caught me sneaking up behind Weel. "Why, exactly, do you hate me so much? Be sure to take as much time as you need. Relish it all you want. You've earned it as a worthy opponent. Start with your childhood. Tell me about your parents."

"Well, it all started in a small baronetcy just outside Trobanton called Gurb. My progenitor had gained his spurs under the previous Duke of Trobanton, Brintan, and my mother was a nurse serving in the last great insurrection in Sculan. I was born during the largest and longest blizzard Garandia had suffered in over two centuries. The precipitation was so thick . . ."

Weel was so absorbed in his story that I was able to get completely behind him. I positioned the blade right behind his neck and made a few slow practice stabs to get the exact motion down.

It truly amazed me how much I'd grown since this journey began. At the beginning, it would have never occurred to me to attack someone so much stronger than I, but here I was, in a dangerous situation, and my second instinct was to attack. Without hesitation, too!

". . . and the horse kissed me. It was completely unexpected. I didn't know what to think. I mean, I wasn't interested in the equine in such a way, but I did enjoy it . . ."

At the last second, I decided to grip the blade two-handed, which, given my less than epic strength, was a sound idea. Unfortunately, it still wasn't enough, as Weel's armor also extended to the back of his neck. The sword bounced off the back of his neck with a loud clang, and it fell from my hands. While I had leveled up in bravery, it had evidently not come with any secondary abilities that would be helpful in the performance of brave deeds.

Weel paused at the sensation and was about to turn when Verix sprang a question on him. "Why did you have to take your singing lessons in secret?"

Weel turned back toward him. "Ahh, excellent query. You see, my father's rival for my mother's affection was a rapping minstrel named Sir Lutes-a-lot, which forever poisoned him from the melodic arts."

After my hands had stopped throbbing, I picked up the sword again and aimed for the gap in his armor near his armpit. This time my aim was true, and the sword pierced halfway through the cloth below. I could almost see skin through the indentation I had put in his undershirt.

Verix rolled his eyes, but, being the patient, disciplined knight he was, continued questioning without pause. "Do you find bullying rewarding, or do you just do it because you're so much of a natural at it?"

"You really do get me, worthy adversary. I find it rewarding *because* I excel at it. My favorite memory is the instance in which I accosted a particularly emaciated turnip collector . . ."

I began sawing the undershirt with the sword. After a few more minutes, I finally had a hole big enough to get a good stab through it, but just as I snapped the blade back, Axin grabbed my shoe. I tripped and fell forward onto Weel. Because of his heavy armor and heavier body, I only managed to bounce off him and slide to the ground. This finally got his attention, and he turned around.

"You! Do you have any idea how much effort we have expended in our quest for your re-apprehension?"

"Four thousand five," I said.

His face screwed up in puzzlement. "Four thousand five what? Hours? Calories? Trakon?"

Before I could answer, Weel dropped to the ground, a blade buried under his armpit. The same armpit I had heroically softened up.

Verix shrugged. "Sorry. I got tired of waiting."

Verix walked over to Axin, who had begun to rise, and punched the back of his head with his gauntlet. He stopped moving, but he appeared to be breathing, barely. I was about to complain that his action wasn't consistent with the character from my book, but I stopped when Verix winced in pain and held his side.

Very clever of the actor to do that. I couldn't help but rush to his side in sympathy. And don't you go saying it was all an act and I shouldn't have believed him. He looked just like the character I had poured my heart into. The guy was like a son to me—a much better-looking, more athletic son who didn't look anything like me—but he was the closest thing I had.

"Don't worry, Verix. You can ride my donkey back."

"What donkey?" He gritted his teeth but managed to stand all the way up.

I really do create some fantastic characters, don't I?

I turned around, and in the spot my donkey had occupied only a moment ago, I found nothing other than a small piece of paper. I knew I should have locked him up. In the movies, this kind of thing never happened. The heroes always left their mounts unattended, and the mounts were always there when they came back. It really didn't make sense. If you left your car unlocked in the real world, there was a good chance it might be stolen.

What do you secure a donkey with, anyway? Do you use a bike lock? Do you take the saddle with you so they have nothing to sit on? Maybe there's something like the Club for horses and donkeys. Curiosity got the better of me, and I picked up the piece of paper off the ground.

Dear Madam or Sir,

Thank you for leaving your Deluxe Two-Legged Donkey unattended. We regret to inform you that your donkey has been stolen. Do not worry; it will be well taken care of. We promise to feed it and give it ample exercise. We will also present it to many eligible female two-legged donkeys.

Don't forget to write this loss off on your taxes! If you need a tax consultant, please leave a note of inquiry on anything of value in the area, and we will be sure to write back.

Sincerely,

The Guild of Spies, Thieves, and Insurance Salesmen, Inc.

If this had been the real world, I'd be pretty angry at this point. Fortunately, I didn't actually own the donkey. Those thieves sure did write a polite letter, though. That softened the blow considerably. Plus, this solved the problem of figuring out how the donkey could stand up. I couldn't look at the thing without getting lost trying to explain how it managed to move.

Verix glanced at the note over my shoulder. "Don't worry. I can make it. The port is only as few blocks away."

Don't you think less of me, reader, for not offering to give him a piggyback ride or offering to carry him. Remember, he was only acting hurt, and not even doing a very believable job of it. Besides, the showrunners hadn't fed me in seven hours, and I was feeling it. If anything, the actor should have carried me.

All pretense of acting grievously wounded completely faded as he sprinted toward the end of the street. I was about to call him on that when the distinct sound of a commotion turned my attention to the opposite end of the street. The invading army was out in full force, and they didn't look like they wanted an autograph. (Or, if they did, they wanted to end the autograph session by killing me to increase the autograph's value.) Not wanting to die or sign autographs, I followed my friend to the port.

RIGHT IN THE POOP DECK

The sound of the stampeding army provided a very effective motivation, and the embarrassment of being outrun by an allegedly wounded man helped even more. We arrived at the port to find the remnants of the Garandian army attempting to board all at once. It was utter chaos as too many men tried to force their way onto hastily fleeing ships. There was little organization, just every man for himself. The lone exception was the far wharf, which was protected by royal guardsmen.

Everyone in the army seemed to know Verix, which helped us get to the far wharf pretty easily. As luck would have it, the first guard we met was Arik.

She sprinted over to check her companion's wound. "Harry! Thank The One that you found him."

"It's not as bad as it looks," Verix said.

She peeled back his breastplate. "Not that bad? So, I guess that means you'll only pass out in ten minutes." She handed him a cloth to hold over the wound.

Verix nodded in thanks. "The enemy army is only a few minutes behind us. Can you spare a sword?"

One of the other soldiers walked forward with a spare sword, but Arik shooed him away and pointed toward the boat. "You and the prophet are going straight on board. Harry needs your protection more than I do, friend. Harry, I am personally assigning him as your guardian, and I want him to look after you from a bed."

"You can't order me!" Verix winced in pain and almost fell over, but I was able to catch him and prop him up.

Arik whispered in my ear to give him an order.

"Verix, I order you to protect me from harm," I said. "The sea is a dangerous place, and I'll need you to save me from sea monsters, the nefarious Old Gods, and myself. Hey!" I said to Arik. "I don't need him to protect me from myself. I'll have you know, I'm quite the capable runner."

I didn't mind that they'd changed the gender of Arik, but it wasn't right for her to make fun of me like that. Just for that, I vowed to make her/him wet herself/himself whenever things got dangerous . . . which would be a lot like me. Aha! I thought. I'd make him/her bad at mounting horses. No, still me. Bad at math? Can't tell the difference between Coke and Pepsi? I'd think of something later.

"You're right," Verix said. "He does need protecting. That was quite brilliant of you, Harry, to illustrate that fact by pretending you disagreed with the last part."

I gave up and dragged him toward the ship. It really wasn't worth arguing with them anymore, and it would keep me from finally ending this, anyway. Besides, their arguments were stupid, and I doubted anyone would agree with them anyway.

A couple of guards attempted to stop us from boarding, but after one look at Verix, they let us pass. The captain assured me that we would be on our way in a few minutes and that he was honored to have a prophet on board. I was told that the king had been very relieved to hear of my safety, though he had locked himself in his cabin to pout—or something similar to pouting that was more regal. The captain let me set Verix down on a crate as one of his men went to clear out a cabin for us.

About thirty seconds after we'd reached the deck, the Sculander army arrived and began an effortless slaughter of almost everyone in the dock area. The already panicked Garandian soldiers were solely focused on flight and put up no resistance whatsoever. The only thing slowing the Sculanders down was the sheer numbers in the area; they could only kill so fast.

As soon as the slaughter began, our captain wisely shoved off. The king was too important to risk another minute waiting for a few more soldiers to get to the ship. Soldiers, even elite ones, could be replaced, but a king could not, the captain stated. I was sure a great many people would argue that this particular king would probably be pretty easy to replace, though I would argue that horribly incompetent kings are just as difficult to find as great kings are.

The Sculander army finally reached the royal guards, but Arik rallied the guards to her, and they made a heroic stand. The Sculander advance ground to a halt there, but throughout the rest of the area, the slaughter continued unabated.

"Get them, my friend," Verix said. "I wish I could be there with you."

"Me, too," I said, too caught up in the scene to say anything else.

Arik's skill and leadership were on full display at the wharf. She was truly awe-inspiring. She and the eight remaining guardsmen were holding off almost the entire Sculander army. The Sculanders couldn't even dent the defenses of those brave warriors, but fatigue or a lucky shot would eventually whittle the guards down one by one.

After a few minutes, the Sculanders had focused solely on the six remaining guards. All other resistance had ceased, and this local battle was the end of the centuries-long Sculander-Garandian War. It was a very sad thing that a brave and honorable person such as Arik would die in vain, but such is the way of war.

The Sculanders backed off, awed by Arik's skill. They had apparently given up on a frontal assault. My last sight of the port as we sailed out of view was of Arik and her guard taunting the cowardice of their foes while three great ballistas were dragged into the port.

I felt a great sadness inside me. It's a terrible thing to see the impending death of one of your favorite creations, even if she wasn't quite how I had written her. I knew that this scene was only fiction, but it still hurt deeply. Verix wept into his hands, and after a while, I began to weep too. With this war over, what would I write about now? After I'd cleared my eyes, I noticed that all of the sailors on deck appeared to have been crying along with us.

"That was an incredibly moving stand," I said to the captain.

"It was, at that, but we're crying because we left our ball back on shore. I just bought it, too. Now, what are we going to do in our free time?"

"We're going to go down to our cabin now, if that's all right."

The captain rubbed back tears. "Uhh, sure. Right this way. You wouldn't happen to have a ball on you, would you?"

"No. Sorry."

"Could we borrow your socks? We could wad them up and use those."

"I'm not wearing any socks." I had burned them after the tribesmen ordeal.

"Have any bouncy balls in your pocket? We'd even settle for one of those."

I glared at him. "No, I don't have any bouncy balls, and I don't think they exist here."

"Darn. There has to be something around here that we could use."

This was ridiculous. A woman had just died, and all this jerk could think about was a ball. "Why don't you behead one of your men and use that?"

"Brilliant! Cartilious has been completely useless since he signed on. We'll use his."

I stared at him, horrified. I'd only been joking. Had this guy been an Aztec in another life?

A man appeared from below and gestured for us to follow.

The captain helped me lift Verix, and we went down the stairs. "Thanks for the idea," he said as we walked. "You're really a great guy. No wonder The One picked you to be a prophet. Well, this is your cabin. If you need anything, I'll do everything I can to get it. I owe you big. The men would have been quite useless without a ball to play with. Oh, and the doctor should be on his way."

I waved the captain off, and he left with an extra skip in his step.

The cabin was very spacious, as far as cabins go. It had a bed, chest of drawers with several changes of clothing, and even a large porthole with frilly curtains. I was about to check to see where the camera was—so it could catch me in the most favorable light—when the doctor tapped me on the shoulder.

Standing behind me was a person wearing a red wig on top of a bronze helmet. Not that that mattered, as the wig clashed horribly with the blond mustache. The newcomer's dress looked like it was about to burst on his muscular frame, but I guessed I shouldn't complain too much, as it did cover his groin.

"Heeello," the doctor said in a high-pitched voice that couldn't possibly belong to a real person. "I hear you are in need of assistance. What seems to be the problem?"

I pointed to Verix. "He's bleeding. Can you go get a real doctor?"

"Good heavens, sir. I'll have you know that I *am* a real doctor. What's wrong? Don't you think a chick can practice medicine?"

I sighed.

The doctor leaned in. "Psssst . . . Harry, it's me, Cat. I'm here in disguise, but don't tell anyone."

"I . . . won't."

"Great! Jackal and Wolf are here, too. Wolf knows a thing or two about fixing boo-boos. He should be in soon."

Luckily, Jackal and Wolf came in before I could have an aneurism. Wolf's hands were full of bandages. Neither of them had on a disguise. Jackal gave me a big hug while Wolf went straight to Verix.

"Wow," I said. "I thought you guys were gone, for sure. How did you get here?"

Cat stepped in between us. "We managed to fight our way through the entire Sculander army."

Jackal shook her head. "He got turned around, and we 'fought' our way out to roughly the same spot where we entered, which I guess was fortunate since he was stabbing Garandians."

"The resistance was furious, but due to my superb skill, the enemy didn't know what had hit them." Cat pretend-slashed the air. I winced from the sound of the back of his dress ripping open.

"Again, because they were on your side and had their backs to you. When the two of us got out of the crowd, Wolf saw you running toward the city, so we followed."

"I fought my way in like a hero. I killed both of the gate guards single-handedly."

Jackal shook her head in disgust. "He stabbed them after they asked him a question. We couldn't find you when we got in."

"We encountered a deadly Sculander knight when we entered."

"Your friend, Arik, was there looking for Verix."

"But after a lengthy, brutal struggle, I defeated him and forced him to tell us where the port was."

"Arik is a she, and *she* disarmed you while she was yawning. Fortunately, she overlooked your attack because we're friends of Harry's and Wolf told her you suffered a head injury in the battle. She escorted us to the harbor."

Cat pointed to the wig. "Where I used my cunning art of disguise to sneak us aboard this ship."

"Arik gave us a pass to get on, and we almost didn't make it aboard in time because you made us stop while you changed into that ridiculous outfit."

Cat puckered his lips and held up a tiny flat container. "The trick was the makeup."

Jackal slapped him and grabbed the container. "Who told you that you could use my makeup?"

I shook my head and looked over at Verix. Wolf had taken the knight's shirt off and had used all of the bandages to cover his torso. Judging by the rising and falling of Verix's chest, he was supposed to be acting like he was sleeping and wasn't supposed to be dead.

"I think he'll be fine," Wolf said.

Jackal had Cat down on the deck and was slapping him repeatedly.

"Should we break them up?" I asked.

"Only if it gets too bad. It's good that she's standing up for herself, and hopefully this will teach him a lesson. Doubtful on the last part, but with her around, he'll probably have to start behaving more. They'll be good for each other. Just don't tell them that."

I smiled. "I won't, but I should be going home soon, anyway."

"That's right. Did you get the Phoine from the king yet?"

My eyes widened in surprise. I'd forgotten about that thing! I knew I was going home soon, but I wasn't sure how they were going to arrange it. "How would one go about seeing the king?"

Wolf looked toward the door. "I don't know."

Because this show was anything but subtle, there was immediately a knock at the door.

A RING, A KING, AND A DING-A-LING

Wolf opened the door and a royal guard walked in. I could tell he was a royal guard by his blindingly shiny armor, and because he was obviously taking me to the king.

The guard saluted. "My apologies for the intrusion, sirs, milady, but the king has requested the presence of the prophet."

"Oh? What's it about?" I deadpanned.

"A royal guard's job is to fetch, not ask why."

"That's a great motto," I said. "You guys should put it on a button or on your shields."

"Ohhhh. What about a t-shirt?"

"You do *not* have t-shirts in Garandia. Come on. Are you guys even trying? Why don't you open your cellphone and Tweet the motto after you post it on Facebook?"

"I don't know what those are, sir, but we do have shirts in Garandia."

"No, you said t-shirts. Of course you have shirts, but you don't have t-shirts. Those wouldn't exist in this time period—well, the time period this is based on. You heard him say t-shirt, didn't you, Wolf?"

"I'm not sure. Does it matter?"

"Yes, it does. Is it too much to ask that you don't bring up period-inappropriate things? No, don't answer that. I know you're just going to answer in character and pretend you don't know what I'm talking about. So, back to the topic at hand. Yes, t-shirts would be greaaaat. You could also do beer cozies and baseball caps."

He clapped his hands. "Oh, yes. I love those things too! I can't wait to tell the other guards. You really are a true prophet—only the Almighty could have inspired such brilliance."

"Yeah, whatever. Just show me to the king, and let's get this whole thing over with."

The guard led me down a level while I continued my ranting. I had completely given up on even attempting to play by the rules. If these actors weren't going to pretend they were in a fantasy world, then neither was I.

He led us to the only door on the lower deck and we entered. This ship appeared to have been built specifically for the king. In the center stood a dais with a throne that was slightly smaller than the one in the palace. The king was sitting there with his head in his hands, staring down at the deck. The servants standing nearby were holding plates of food with flies circling them. Marshal Scritz was standing behind them. Guards flanked all three doorways.

My escort cleared his throat loudly. "Your Majesty, I have brought the prophet, as requested."

I trudged forward without a care in the world. If they were going to ruin my world, I was going to ruin theirs by roughing up this poor imitation of my King Berin. As he was the perfect symbol for this awful show, it was my duty as an author to abuse him.

The king continued his downward stare. "Yes, yes. Thank you, nameless guard. Harry the Prophet, with nickname to be named later, I would like to commend you for your service, though it appears it was all in vain."

I stopped my steady advance, as it sounded like he was about to say something nice about me. As angry as I was, I wanted to hear that before I attacked him. "Oh?"

"We owe you a reward."

"It had better be good," I murmured under my breath.

"As reward for your assistance in rallying the troops, I would like to give you the Phoine of—"

"Lurk!" said a voice from the doorway.

I don't think I need to tell you who said that. I mean, come on; he said "Lurk." How many people in this book have said that? Really? You don't know? Have you been paying attention? Fine, it was the lurker from the circus, but I'm not helping you remember anything else.

The king finally raised his head, paused briefly to examine the awesomeness that is me, then turned toward the newcomer. "Who is this man?"

Marshal Scritz cleared his throat and walked in front of the king. "This man is one of the many agents that I sent to look after this moron, Your Majesty. He may have thwarted Ferelic, Weel, Axin, and Artenarix, but fortunately, there were others. I had the man before you assigned to a fairly popular circus in the north of our island: Jalev's Circus and Gourmet Pancakes."

"And what does this have to do with anything?"

The marshal smirked. "While there, he ran into a certain prophet. As for what my agent found, I'll let him tell you."

"Lurk, lurk." The man cleared his throat. "My apologies. It takes me some time to get out of character. While I was at Jalev's circus, I barely escaped from this bearded fellow and learned quite a bit about him. For instance, did you know that he let Axin and Weel do numerous unspeakable things to him?"

"Of course. Everyone knows about that," the king said. The rest of the room all gave indications that they also knew that.

"How could everyone possibly know that?" I demanded.

"You just have the kind of face that says, 'I like to let singing knights do naughty things to me,'" the marshal replied. "Continue."

I would have corrected him, but I really didn't care at this point. "If that's all you have, then let's get on with my reward."

He pulled out a scroll and began to read off of it. "It is not all I have. After you left the circus, you began to work with the Tickling Bandit."

The crowd gasped. "The bandit?" King Berin said. "He hasn't been seen in over fifty years."

"I'm sure Wolo will get to that, Your Majesty," Marshal Scritz said.

"You're that Wolo?" I said. "From the farm? I didn't know the Lurker and Wolo from the farm were the same person."

"Really? I didn't even change disguises. Wasn't the bright red mustache a dead giveaway?"

I guessed I owed Lois Lane an apology. Apparently, it isn't easy to tell that two people are the same person if you're not looking for it. "Well, you talked differently, but that doesn't really matter, because I wasn't working with the Tickling Bandit anyway. I was chasing her. She took the package we later delivered to you, Your Majesty, and we had to chase her to get it back. Weren't you paying attention at all, Wolo?"

"Well, I was kind of busy cowering, and I may have missed a few things."

"By the way, as one coward to another, that was some great cowering. You should be commended." I tried to shake his hand, but he backed away, obviously intimidated by my rugged good looks.

"Uh, thanks. You were also seen crossing in the middle of the street and not using the crosswalk."

"There aren't any crosswalks in this world!"

"And he erased all of the crosswalks."

"Seriously?" I said.

"He was also working with a monkey outside of a circus or zoo. Were you not?"

I looked down at my groin. "Don't most men?"

"Not that monkey. I mean the actual monkey at the farm."

"Oh, yeah. You mean Mr. Plot Device, or Mr. Monkey, as they call him at the circus."

"Not the famous Mr. Monkey?" the king said. "He's our most brilliant economist."

Scritz nodded. "The Sculandians said they'd end the war in exchange for his services."

"But it's illegal to have a monkey outside of a circus or zoo," Wolo whined.

"It's only a five trakon fine, Wolo," the king said. "Besides, Mr. Monkey has a special exemption."

I wiggled my eyebrows at Wolo, though carefully, so as not to shake any of my sexiness his way. "That's all you have? You didn't even mention . . . Sorry. I don't actually have anything." As is my habit, I had almost blurted out something incriminating, but then remembered—quite unusual for me—that I hadn't actually done anything incriminating.

"I think I saw him litter once."

The king waved him away. "That will be enough."

"Can I have my payment now, Marshal? Spying on him was a lot of work."

"I suppose, but you really should have found something useful. Just look at him. He practically screams that he's about to do something stupid and self-destructive."

I shrugged. "It's true. I really do."

"I don't know why you insist on being paid in jewelry." The marshal removed his ring and handed it over to Wolo. Seeing that he had been defeated by an opponent who was clearly superior in every way imaginable, the marshal stormed out.

Wolo ignored the marshal and smiled at his reward. "Rings fascinate me. I can't stop looking when I see a new one."

He held his hand out to display his new ring, and its neat Norse runes. I would have pointed out the inaccuracy of those runes since I hadn't stolen Norse iconography for my world, but what hadn't been inaccurate so far? When I got a better look at it —which is extra hard to do while you're glaring—I realized what it was. My ring! Dyfantus had taken it from me when I accidentally got his nice shirt all muddy. How could I have forgotten? "Hey, give me that!"

I grabbed Wolo's hand and gave it a good twist, then realized I had the wrong hand and grabbed his other one. Several guards attempted to break us apart, but I would not yield. I guessed, having overcome so much in my journey, I had finally developed some courage. I knocked two guardsmen down, kept a few more at bay by wagging my eyebrows, and still managed to get my ring from Wolo. Victorious, I turned my glare into a cocky wink and raised my arm in triumph. My arm, unused to being raised in that manner, went a little off course and punched King Berin right between the eyes. The king dropped like I do when I'm playing dead.

What a terrible actor. I'd barely tapped him. No matter how much scorn I glared into the back of his head, he wouldn't move.

WRITERS VS. GENERALS – THE TRAVEL EDITION

While the guards were staring at their fallen king, I ran for the door. I am an excellent judge of character, and those characters were clearly less of the "wanting an autograph from the creator of the world that currently employs them" inclination and more of the "do a bit too good of a job acting like they want to stab the creator of the world that currently employs them so that they can impress future employers" inclination. While I knew their weapons were fake, fake weapons still leave big bruises. Plus, there really wasn't anything else to accomplish in that room. I had my ring. My grandpa would be so proud.

I ran through the first door at the top of the stairs and slammed the door behind me. Pushing with all my might, I leaned against it and wiped the sweat from my forehead. "Since you're mercenaries, I'd like to hire you," I said to the people behind me. I hadn't had time to turn around, but I could see at least one shadow. "I can't really tell you what for, but you know me, so I'm sure you'll trust me. I don't really have anything of value on me, but I could pay you by writing you all into my next book. Just think about all the work you'll have when they make all of my books into movies."

"And what exactly did you do?" I could hear one of them—probably Cat—draw his blade. It's good to have friends who are so eager. I might even turn them into their own spin-off series.

"Nothing. It's all a misunderstanding. If you can help me get the Phoine, which the king just promised to me, it won't matter."

"Ahh, yes, of course. The Phoine. Did you commit any other crimes before you met me—us?"

I put my ear to the door. It sounded like the guards had passed. I breathed a sigh of relief. It was a good thing too, as my strength was almost spent. Give me a break! I hadn't eaten a well-balanced, nutritious meal in over a week. I was slightly dehydrated. I was seasick (even though my body hadn't realized it yet). I'd only gotten nine hours of sleep the night before. I was really worried about my cat—so worried that I couldn't even remember its name. I likely had a cold. I was overheated. I was on TV, and no one had offered even once to put makeup on me or fix my hair. The sun was in my eyes (by bouncing off the shiny door handle). I had to go the bathroom. And worst of all, I was a writer without anything to write the story down with.

At least the person behind me was offering me a knife, so I could at least carve a few words into the door. I reached back to take the very kind offer, but the person resisted. I tugged again, and he still wouldn't let go. I turned around to let my friend know that now was not a good time for tug-of-war but was shockingly not greeted by a friendly face.

Marshal Scritz was six inches shorter and roughly six decades older than I. With his thin frame and hunched back, I should have had an easy time getting the knife from him, but he held on like his life depended on it. I was torn between letting him have it, as any struggle might cause a heart attack (in him, not me, you jerks), and not being put on television losing a physical confrontation with an old man. I decided that with all of the crap these people had put me through, I'd let them deal with the lawsuit if anything happened to the actor. Besides, they had put him in this situation, not me. I tugged harder, but he still held on.

"How did you get in here?" I said.

"This is my cabin. Didn't the nameplate give it away, or can you not read?" He rolled his eyes and pushed me backwards. "You really are as stupid as the reports suggested. Do you really think this is all some sort of elaborate play?"

I stumbled but bounced up and grabbed the knife again. "You're only trying to confuse me, like Berin did by falling down when I barely tapped him."

Marshal Scritz rolled his eyes again and stomped on my toes. "Let me guess: you killed him. The one constant thing in all of my reports is that you don't seem to learn anything from your mistakes."

I whimpered in pain and gave up. That thing looked really sharp, and it was probably better to lose a fight to an old man than get stabbed by one. I am a prolific bleeder, after all. "I didn't kill him. I just roughed him up a little, and how could you possibly know that? You left before we did."

"I didn't know it until now," Scritz said. "Finally, I have something on you."

"Like it really matters in this TV show. I can see the cameras poking out of the closet over there."

Marshal Scritz shuffled backwards to get the closet in his line of vision while keeping the knife pointed at me. "Nothing inside but a mop. Probably the mop that scrubbed your brain out."

Inside the closet was Cat. This time, he had changed into a white wig and a skintight brown outfit patterned like the grain of wood.

"Nuh-uh. They clearly scrubbed all of yours out."

Scritz dropped his knife arm down to his side. "Really? That's the best you can do? How is it possible that those intelligent, talented operatives lost to you?"

Cat had put his index finger over his mouth. Like I really needed to be told not to tell the guy with a knife to turn around. Scritz was standing with his side pointed toward the closet, so I had to get him to turn around.

"OK. Then the cameras are in one of the corners. They can get pretty small these days."

We turned toward each corner of the room as one. With the bright lighting from the numerous lamps placed around the room, it was pretty easy to see, especially with how barren the room was; it contained only a bed and a desk.

I didn't have to see the camera to know this was a TV show. I had seen—OK, almost seen out of the corner of my eye—several cameras during my journey. They couldn't all have been my imagination. Sure, I hadn't actually touched them, but I'd never touched the moon, either, and it was plenty real (though I'm still crushed that it's not made out of cheese). I mean, this place was too ridiculous to be real. No one could possibly follow a religion whose savior had been spanked to death. I cleverly looked at the corner farthest away from the closet last.

"Fine, then. You have one of those tiny spy cameras on you."

"I don't know what a camera is, exactly, but where would I hide it in this robe?"

Cat tackled him from behind. "In the closet! That's where he's hidden."

I patted Cat on the back. "Great job, Cat. I think you could have delivered a better line, but overall, great job."

Cat picked Scritz up off the floor and shook him. "Why don't you give him the knife back, and I'll try again? Maybe something about me hitting him in the back? Say, buddy, could you maybe scream in surprise when I tackle you this time?"

Scritz bounced around like a rag doll but didn't make a sound.

"I think he's out, Cat."

"I hate when they interrupt a much-needed do-over by losing

consciousness. At least he wasn't inconsiderate enough to die on me. I hate it even more when they do that."

Saying "interrupt" predictably summoned an interruption. There was a knock at the door. "Open up! We know you're in there."

"No one here but a few little girls. Tee-hee," Cat said automatically. His little girl voice was surprisingly convincing.

"Well, did you see a fat guy?" the guard said through the door.

"They went that way," Cat said. I was beginning to think they were somehow projecting an actual little girl's voice from somewhere.

"Thanks. We'll go get them now."

I heard the sound of boots marching quickly away and gave Cat a questioning look. As usual, he was oblivious.

Fortunately, his voice returned to normal. "Say, why do you think this guy is still after you? His friends were after the package, but you don't have it anymore."

"Nothing here makes sense. This whole plot is terribly written. I'm actually glad he's out so I don't have to listen to him."

Cat grabbed a glass of water from nearby and tossed it on Scritz. I should have known they'd make me listen to their cockamamie plot. Scritz predictably woke right up.

I sighed. "Why do you want to kill me? And please make it fast—short sentences and bullet points only."

"You killed my brother and ruined my family business."

I hoped that would be enough, but Cat stared at me until I spoke.

"Who is your brother, and what business?"

Scritz cleared his throat, hopefully to deliver his last line. "He died due to injuries sustained in a slap fight with you, after which you celebrated by contaminating one of our prize muck shipments. When the tainted shipment got put in with the rest, it ruined the entire batch. Because of that, our creditors foreclosed on all of our holdings."

"OK. Thanks." I looked at the door, hoping the guards would return so I could finish this show and go home.

After a few minutes, Cat cleared his throat. "So, how about that weather?"

Scritz somehow managed to shrug while still in Cat's powerful grip. "Well, we can't really see it from here, but it's been surprisingly nice lately, though I hear there are some storms blowing in from the south."

"Speaking of blowing—"

"Cat," I said, "do not finish that sentence."

"Really?" Scritz said. "He's got me curious. I'd like to hear the rest. It's not like we have anything else to do."

"You don't get a vote. You're a prisoner. Besides, you don't know him very well, and you have no idea what sort of filth is likely to come out of his mouth."

Cat held Marshal Scritz up in front of me like he was a ventriloquist's dummy. Scritz said, "Fartius Maximus, or Cat, as he is now known, was born on Fernagust 23, 2470 to Weyma and Tamin in the village of North in the south of Garandia. His father was a soldier who was away most of his life, and his mother raised him. His mother taught him all about the importance of standing up for yourself, the value of physical fitness, and origami. His favorite color is down, his favorite direction is blue, and he loves politics."

Cat said, "It's true. I love reading about who's going to win the next election for king in our absolute monarchy. Will it be Berin, or will it be Berin?" He put his hands over Scritz's eyes and whispered to me. "My money is on Joe from Accounting."

He took his hands off of Scritz's eyes. "Sorry," Cat said. "You can continue."

"Fartius is known for his juvenile, often offensive sense of humor, his equally offensive odor, and his skill in offense. In second grade, he got a B on his report card in—"

I put my hands over Scritz's eyes, and he stopped talking. "OK. I get it. You know him pretty well."

There was a bang on the door again. "Excuse me, little girl, but 'that way' doesn't really help when we can't see which way you're pointing. Could you be more specific? The guy we're chasing is very dangerous. He just killed the king."

"A king?" Cat said. "Which one?"

"I'm not sure. Hey, guys, which king was it?"

Cat whispered to Scritz, "For your sake, they'd better be talking about another king. I am a loyal Garandian, and I will not be a part of any king slaying—unless it was by accident or you happened to be naked. Hypothetically."

There was another knock at the door. "I've consulted with my colleagues, and they say it was King Berin."

"I heard he went up on deck," I said in my best little girl voice. It wasn't nearly as impressive as Cat's, but it still fooled them.

"Thanks again," the guard said through the door.

"Wait," another guard said. "There are no children on board. This is a warship."

"We know you're in there, prophet. Please, open the door."

As I looked around fruitlessly for somewhere to hide, Cat opened the door to the hall. The closet! Why hadn't I thought of the closet?

The guard standing at the door gave me an impassive stare. "I think you know why we're here, prophet."

"Why did you open the door, Cat?"

Cat shrugged. "They said 'please.' I can't resist politeness."

The three guardsmen marched into the room in line and stopped in front of us. When they turned, their mouths dropped open in horror.

"Marshal Scritz!" the one in the middle said. "What have you done to him?"

I looked behind me to find that Marshal Scritz was sprawled on the floor with a knife in his heart. I wasn't sure how they'd managed to get so much blood on him without making any noise.

"What?" Cat said. "You said he killed the king, and I figured it was my patriotic duty to return the favor."

"The prophet killed the king, you idiot," the guard said. "Seize them!"

His two fellow guards grabbed us and tied us up at the wrists. Surprisingly, Cat didn't struggle. I didn't either, because I figured it was pointless and that it was the best way to get this thing over with. I already had my execution speech planned out. Hint: it would involve a lot of cursing and male nudity. Another hint: you're going to want to fast-forward past that part if you watch it on TV.

"Wait," Cat said. "Which prophet?"

"Cat, there's only one other person in here," I said.

Cat wrinkled his eyebrows. "Well, clearly I'm the idiot he's referring to, so it's not me. That would mean—it was Scritz! When did he get named as a prophet? I thought Harry was the only one."

I KNEW IT ALL ALONG

They took us up to the main deck and presented us to a thin guard with his arms crossed. Because of the deference the other guards gave him and the big plume on his helmet, I assumed he was in charge. He had the visor of his helmet down, so I couldn't tell who he was. The sky was starting to get cloudy and a little dark, which I took as a bad sign.

Another group of guardsmen had escorted Wolf, Jackal, and Verix a few feet away. Jackal waved at me excitedly, and Wolf sighed in relief when he saw Cat. With the way Verix swayed, putting his armor back on must have taken nearly everything he'd had left. I was relieved when he finally leaned on the mast for support. The crew of the ship seemed to be making every effort to find things to do away from us in the edges of the stern and bow.

Mr. Visor gave us a long stare. I wasn't sure if the pause was meant to add to the length of the show or because he thought it made things more dramatic. "So, prophet, you kill our king, and then try to run away? On a ship? Where did you think you'd go?"

Cat raised his hand, and the man nodded in response. "Harry didn't kill the king, Marshal Scritz did. Don't worry, Wolf. I did my patriotic duty like you taught me and killed the squirmy bastard. I was judge, jury, and exequatur."

"You're a legal document authorizing you as a representative of a foreign state?" Mr. Visor asked.

Cat shook his fist. "Nuh-uh! You're a foreigner! I'm one hundred ten percent Garandian."

Wolf patted Cat on the back. "That was a really fantastic thing for you to do, Cat. I'm sure you'll be rewarded greatly for your service."

Cat lowered his fist. "Ha, you said 'service.'"

During the exchange, one of my escorts shook his head toward his leader, and Mr. Visor responded with a subtle nod of confirmation. I assumed that meant he knew I was the one who had killed the king but was allowing the ruse with the Trio to continue. I was already suspicious of him because he wasn't showing his face, but now I knew he was up to something. Whatever it was, I hoped he got it over with soon.

"With the death of the king," Mr. Visor said, "Garandia finds herself in need of a replacement. Fortunately, we have the perfect person on board. The only person who has the ear of The One. King Berin himself confided in me that this person should replace him instead of his idiot son. His Majesty believed his death had been commanded by The One so that his chosen prophet could succeed him."

Cat stepped forward and shook his hand. "I accept."

Wolf dragged him back. "He means Harry, idiot."

"How was I supposed to know that? I mean, I have the one ear in my pocket, like he said, and Scritz was a prophet, too. I heard that if you kill a prophet, you inherit his powers."

Jackal edged away from him. "If you kill a prophet, the only thing you inherit is The One's wrath."

"Is that why I'm suddenly blind and can't remember where I parked my horse?" Cat said. Then Wolf pulled Cat's hand off his eyes. "I'm cured! And I just remembered I don't have a horse anymore. He left me when I refused his vacation request."

Mr. Visor removed his helmet. He had a rather nicely trimmed black beard that formed a sharp point at the end, and he appeared young for such a position until I squinted and noticed the slight wrinkles on his face. "As Berin has commanded, I name you king. All hail King Harrold!"

Everyone on deck applauded very respectfully, as is appropriate for a position of such dignity, with the exception of Verix, who was probably miffed that he hadn't been consulted by the other royal guards. Cat and Wolf both patted me on the back.

Having been in a similar situation several times, I wanted to get clarification before I got too excited. "King of what? King Fart? King of the Nerds? King of Guys Named Harry?"

"Well," the visorless Mr. Visor said, "we were thinking of making you king of Garandia. King Fart rules Paruxia, we don't have the authority to make you King of the Nerds, and I think you have to win a tournament for the last one."

I dropped to my knees and wept. While I had created a previous Garandian king called Ary Holson who was named Best-Looking Person in Garandia in early drafts of my third book, my editor had made me take him out. I'd tried telling her he wasn't me. I mean, sure, he did match my description superficially, but I wasn't left-handed and I didn't wear an eyepatch. If the writers were going to make me king, I would forgive them for everything. OK, most of the bad things they had done to my world. (There were an awful lot, after all.)

"That's fantastic, Harry!" Jackal said.

"Yeah, and as king, you can finally pay us," Wolf said.

"I want to be your personal guard," Cat said. "Sir Cat has a nice ring to it."

Mr. Visorless clapped his hands. The way he did it reminded me of someone, but I couldn't place who. "What a splendid idea!"

he said. "The royal guard has a lot of openings, and it would be good for our new king to have people he trusts protecting him." He pointed at two guards and instructed them, "Take them down below to get them fitted for armor."

The Trio triumphantly followed them below. It was good to see my friends in such a great mood. My spirits were at an all-time high, but for some reason Verix still had a sour look on his face.

"Now, there are just a few things we need to get squared away before we introduce you to your new subjects back home," Mr. Visorless said.

"Have we met before?" I asked.

He turned toward the other guards and laughed.

I figured I must have seen the actor in something else, and I shouldn't bring it up. Of course, now that I finally had something that could ruin this show, I didn't want to. "OK. My mistake. Do you need to fit me for new robes? Is the statue guy on board? I was thinking of one twenty feet tall. You know, nothing too ostentatious."

He turned and rolled his watery blue eyes. Those eyes—where had I seen him before? "No, he's back at the castle. Your castle."

The guards laughed raucously. One of them even rolled on the deck. It was good that my new employees were such a fun bunch. I wondered what they'd look like if I covered their armor with tuxedoes. It would cut down on the blinding glare. I'd get my new captain a really nice one too, the exact opposite of the crinkled thing my writing nemesis Billiam wore. God, why did I have to think of him at my time of triumph?

Verix, on the other hand, looked like someone important had died. He was my favorite character and was supposed to be my friend. How dare he? Why couldn't he enjoy my triumph like my other friends?

I decided to give my first royal decree and raised my hand

dramatically. "Sir Verix, I command you to smile. If you can dance a little jig too, that would be lovely. We shall call it the Royal Happy Dance."

Verix's eyelids drooped. "I am sorry, Holiest Speaker, but it is my duty as a loyal knight of Garandia to protect the legal right of Prince Ambric as next in line to the throne. I cannot allow this scheme to continue. Sir Maillib, I place you under arrest for treason." He winced as he took a step away from the mast and drew his blade. The other guards followed suit.

"Ohhhhh, Sir Maillib," I said. "You're the guy who gave me a ride when I first got here."

I looked around and was surprised that everyone was giving me a dirty look. You'd think my new subjects would be happy that their new king had remembered something difficult, but I decided to cut them some slack just this once, as this was a rather tense situation.

Sir Maillib gave me a half-smile and signaled the others to lower their weapons. My loyal guards complied. Verix lowered his blade an inch or two, but still looked ready to pounce.

A lone tear trickled down Maillib's face. I hadn't seen his face when he gave me a ride earlier, yet he still looked awfully familiar. Was he related to someone I knew? Maybe I'd known him decades ago, and age had changed him considerably.

"Verix," Sir Maillib said, "your skill is well-known, but don't think for a second that you can outfight the six of us. Are you seriously going against the word of the man whom you have loyally followed for your entire life and that of our deity, as well?"

The rest of the guards spread out in front of Sir Maillib.

Verix bit his lip. "Who else did King Berin tell this to?"

"He only released the one faint whisper before he passed. No one but I was close enough to hear it." The corners of Maillib's lips spread into a smile. The guards in front of him couldn't see it, but Verix and I could. Verix didn't hesitate to charge forward.

Given how things had ended with Arik, Verix was one of my few main characters left alive. As this show would likely be heavily linked to my books by the public—no matter how hard I tried to distance them from it—I would have a very difficult time explaining how he had died in the show but was alive and well in my books. It would be so much easier if he lived.

However, if he won, I wouldn't get to be king, and after how awful I was likely to look with everything else that had happened, I really needed something to raise me in the eyes of the public.

While I was coming up with that brilliant bit of analysis, Verix downed the first guard before he even had time to react. The guard did a fantastic job of acting like he had been actually stabbed. When Verix's sword slashed just under his helmet, it slid out with just the right amount of resistance. Blood wetted the decks in a steady stream, just like real blood and not in a geyser, like in a Tarantino movie.

They really had picked the perfect actor for Verix. He just had that way about him—the way he delivered his lines, the way he moved, the way he stabbed people—that perfectly matched how I had envisioned the character. As much as I wanted to look good in this show, I couldn't betray him. He was like a son to me—a son who was roughly the same age as I, didn't look anything like me, and charged into danger instead of away from it. I exhaled, picked up the blade of the fallen guard, and moved forward to try to help. But I probably didn't need to. Verix disarmed the next closest guard and pushed him into the one behind him, causing both to tumble overboard.

Barely realizing what I was doing, I got caught up in the excitement and engaged the nearest guard. He lunged forward with his blade, but I, being the lighter and quicker one, easily dodged his blow. (Shut up! I was lighter because he had all of that heavy armor on, while I was wearing only a thin though very stylish tunic and slightly wet pantaloons.) The guard's lunge unbalanced him, leaving him open to an easy finish. Clearly, the showrunners were finally keeping to their agreement to make me look heroic and had instructed the actor to do just this thing. I made sure to stand at the right angle for where I imagined the camera to be and "stabbed" him by sliding my sword parallel to his body. The actor dutifully clamped his arm down on my blade, and his momentum took it from my grip.

Perfect! "Just because I'm not going to be king doesn't mean I can't feel like one inside!" I said.

Blood squirted out, and the actor tumbled to the deck. I was about to roar in victory when I noticed the blood coming from the wrong side. I stared at the fallen actor in utter bewilderment. They couldn't get anything right, could they? I'm not proud of this, as he was only doing his job and was probably not the one responsible, but I kicked the fallen actor in the side. To his credit, he didn't react in any way. The body rolled, and my sword clattered out onto the deck. As the body rolled completely over, I realized why the blood was on the wrong side; there was a massive hole under the opposite armpit. The special effects and makeup people had really done a good job, but why had they put it on the wrong side?

Focus, Harry. The viewers at home likely wouldn't even notice that—unless they'd also read this book. They would, however, notice me standing there staring at a corpse while someone else fended off two people. Some genius on the internet would probably say it was because I had some weird corpse fetish, too.

Verix turned away from me, with blood dripping from his blade, just in time to parry a blow from the last nameless guardsman. Blood had begun to dribble out of Verix's breastplate, and his blows were much slower. In spite of that, he was still able to keep his opponent at bay. Maillib attempted to use Verix's distraction to get in behind him, but fortunately, my character was protected by his creator! . . . No, not his actual father. Come on, people. While the writing had been pretty terrible on this show, even they wouldn't introduce a new character out of nowhere like that. Isn't it obvious who saved him? No, it wasn't The One. It was me, Harrold Delano Fitzgerald Milhouse Olson! I took my mighty blade from the deck and tripped the sneaky bastard from behind. The sound of metal clanging on the deck was incredibly satisfying. Would someone with a corpse fetish do that? No, really, I'm asking. Oh, right: you can't answer me because this is a book. Sorry, I'm tired.

I knelt down and put my hand in front of my mouth so the cameras couldn't see my lips move. "Hey, Maillib. I'm going to put my sword under your arm, and I want you to grab it between your arm and side to make it look like I stabbed you."

Maillib rolled over to speak to me. "Ahh, so I can sneak up on Verix when he lets his guard down. You will make the perfect king for me to work with."

"No, I know this is all a show and that you're an actor. I want to make it look good without hurting you."

Maillib was aghast. "Marshal Scritz was right. You are an idiot. This is real." He pointed at the nearby guardsmen, displaying the very realistic cut in the gap between his gorget and helmet.

I shrugged. "So what? You have a really good special effects guy."

He pointed at the other dead guard. "See for yourself."

I kept my sword pointed at him but did as he said so I could get this over with and go home. The more they dragged this out

. . .

The smell got to me before I could finish checking the wound. The man had most definitely crapped his pants, and trust me, I know what crap smells like from—well, let's not get into that. Let's just say I know the smell of poop very well. The wound looked very lifelike, but as I said before, it could have been from good special effects and makeup. I studied the man for several minutes, and his chest never rose.

I forgot all about Maillib and knelt down to study the alleged dead man. There was no pulse. The blood dribbling out looked very real. As someone who uses fake blood a lot to get out of confrontations, I know real blood when I see it and taste it. Still, the man had not moved. I shook him a few times, and the only thing that accomplished was getting blood all over my hands. I turned around in my crouch and wiped my hands off on the nearest thing. Unfortunately, it was another corpse. Were they multiplying?

"Now do you believe me?" Maillib said.

"But the cameras," I said weakly. "I saw one in the crow's nest."

"You mean that?" Maillib pointed at one of the nearby crewmen. The crew had stayed as far back from the fight as they could, either too afraid to participate or not sure what side to take. The crewman in question meekly held up a metal object and finally rolled it our way on Maillib's signal.

I picked it up and looked through the thing in the hope that when I looked back, Maillib would be gone. The good news was, zoomed in, his forehead looked like a butt. The bad news was, the object was only a simple spyglass. There was the possibility that they could have hidden a camera somewhere else or tossed it overboard, but my gut told me they hadn't.

Thankfully, I found a ship in the distance to distract me from my swirl of thoughts. I almost missed it against the darkened sky.

A bolt of lightning struck the distant ship, causing its sails and mast to erupt in flames. It appeared that my terrible luck could be passed on just by my looking at something. The poor person climbing the sails was engulfed in flames and dove into the sea. While it didn't appear the ship would sink, the fact that the ship was now without any sails in a vicious storm didn't speak well for its survival. I was glad for the distraction, less glad when I realized it wasn't an actor diving into the sea.

I dropped the spyglass and stomped on it. The thin tube broke easily, its parts scattering across the deck. As I stared at the bits of glass and metal, my illusion of this all being a fiction shattered as well.

This meant an entire country full of real people thought I was a coward. I mean, I was, but I didn't want to be famous for that. I had so much more going for me, like my writing ability and my skill at throwing swords at bushes. Had I killed real people? No wonder Marshal Scritz hated me so much. I'd go through all of that too, if someone had killed a member of my family. And Arik was probably really dead, too! My character! And Verix would be next.

I cleared my head and looked at the scene in front of me. Maillib raised himself up on one knee but tumbled back to the deck. Evidently, he had twisted or broken his ankle. I stood between him and the other combatants.

Verix and the other guard had evidently had quite the contest. Both of their shields lay on the deck, battered to uselessness. The guard's helmet had come off at some point, and his long blond hair swayed back and forth as he lunged forward and then dodged Verix's counterattack. Their skill seemed evenly matched, but with the slowing of Verix's blows and the pain written on his face, I knew how this would end. As Verix went in for another counterattack, the guard sidestepped him and then elbowed my favorite character straight into the railing. Verix's sword flew over the side and landed in the water with a splash.

"Any last words?" the guardsman growled.

"Harry," Verix said.

The guardsman's shoulders dropped. "Really? I mean, I know my hair is pretty awesome, but surely you can do better. Since you were such a worthy opponent, I'll give you one more try. Any last words?"

I was right behind him now. I gripped the sword firmly in my hand. My hands were sweaty, so I decided to be extra-cautious and hold it with both hands. This was much too important a time to risk losing a sword. Verix was completely helpless, pinned against the side of the ship. He was a real person, too—but that meant my target was also a real person. Could I kill a real person?

Yes, I could. I was troubled that that hadn't been a harder decision for me to make. OK, no, I wasn't. However, I was troubled that I wasn't troubled.

If this guard killed Verix, that would mean I'd get to be king, and not in a TV show, in a real fantasy world. An awesome fantasy world with magic, cool characters, physics-defying donkeys, and people who turned into deadly, adorable puppies. I could live with the last two, especially since I'd be rich. The wealth and the lavish lifestyle that went with it would all be mine. Not to mention all the respect I'd get. And don't you go saying they wouldn't respect me because of all of the cowardly things I'd done or the vicious, untrue rumor about Axin, Weel, and me. As king, they would have to respect me, or else I would use my kingly powers to make them. I would throw a parade, too. Kings can have all the parades they want. No one would ever make fun of my outfits. All the cookies and candy I could ever want. It would all be mine, and all I had to do was not do anything— which happened to be my specialty.

But Verix was my character. I couldn't let him die. Or was he my character? He was real. I could see him right there in front of me in the flesh, and blood . . . that was dribbling down his side.

Time to be the hero, Harry. You have to do the right thing. This has all the makings of your destiny. You were meant to be the hero. All you have to do is stab the nameless jerk in front of you . . . Although he probably did have a name. He was a real person, not "Guard Number Five" in a TV show, unless his parents had named him Guard Number Five. This world did have a guy named Mopansin Trantinviavax III, after all.

No, I had to do the right thing. There likely wouldn't be any parades for what I was about to do, but . . .

Parades. And beautiful women. And wealth beyond my wildest dreams. (OK, not really, since I had dreamed up a place just like this, but you get my meaning.)

My knuckles whitened as I gripped the sword to do what I had to do. Which was . . .

Visions of power and wealth flashed before my eyes. The crown was magnificent. Just the right combination of size and shininess.

No! I had to save him. I had to . . .

A blade jutted out of Verix's midsection, right below his breastplate. I checked my hand, and the sword wasn't mine. His face lolled to the side, saving me from the accusation that I knew would be in his eyes. I had taken too long to decide.

At least I still got to be king—but that was going to be one sad parade.

I REALLY KNEW IT ALL ALONG

I stared in horror at my fallen friend for quite some time. The seas were beginning to get rather rough. The waves splashed over the edge of our ship, right on top of Verix's noble corpse. He was definitely not an actor pretending to be dead. There was no way anyone alive could fail to react to that much water splashing on their face. My first thought was how disrespectful it was for the showrunners to do that to him during such a dramatic moment, but then I remembered there was no such person or people running this thing. No, this was being done by Mother Nature, or rather, one of the Old Gods, probably Jammy the Gassy, the lord of the sea.

I decided that my first act as king would be to hold a state funeral for Verix and Arik. They'd earned it. I'd even make them national heroes, and I could write books to extol their virtues. I could rewrite my books and find a whole new audience! I would be the king who wrote, King Harry the Writer. The Author? King Harry the Scholarly. King Harry the Scholarly Author Who Writes and Is Awesome.

"Guard Number Five, get someone to write this down. I wish to proclaim my second royal decree."

"Who the hell is he talking to?" the guard said.

I would have to instruct him to not kill anyone in the future until I gave him my official approval. I waved my hand elaborately in the direction of his voice. "You, o slayer of heroes. Your boss has informed me that I am to be your king, so do as I say, or we will have you shoveling dung in a fortnight, and not the nice dung, either. Oh, no, we will have you shovel the really smelly dung from when we get drunk and feed the horses chili and burritos. Also, get a second scribe so that we may give the cook the recipe for burritos, as we wish to have that for dinner tonight."

"Can I kill him now, Maillib? Please?"

The sound of him drawing his sword shook my eyes from Verix. How dare he! He didn't even have a name—unless it was Dyfantus, whom he happened to look a lot like. He had taken the time to clean off all of the blood, just like Dyfantus would have, and had managed to keep his tabard immaculate throughout the struggle. For some reason, this guy didn't seem to like me much either, even though everyone else I had met had loved me instantly—not counting the ones who had a good reason to kill me.

Mole on the left side of his chin . . . "Dyfantus! I thought you were in prison."

Maillib limped forward, leaning against Dyfantus for support. "Marshal Scritz managed to get him out. Our plan was to have Dyfantus slay the king, but, as fortune would have it, you did that for us," Maillib said in a strangely low voice. With the crashing of the waves, I could barely hear him.

Feeling this was a good time to get some practice for all of the speeches I would have to make to my subjects, I spoke much louder so that the crewmen farther away could hear too. "That's right, because I, your future king, slew my predecessor. I did what even the deadly Dyfantus could not do."

Dyfantus looked ready to pounce on me, but his friend held

him back. To make the scene more dramatic, the sky erupted into lightning and its annoying friend, thunder. Just a few flashes at first, but then, all at once, the sky exploded in blinding light, bringing to mind a badly managed fireworks display. Fortunately, the rain was still in the distance. It would be a very ill omen to be crowned in the rain. I think. I made a mental note to talk to the omen guy.

Maillib continued in his low voice, "Listen, Harry, you seem like a nice guy, so I'll play this straight. After we double-crossed Scritz and got him out of the way, my plan was to make you a puppet king. I and my friend here have quite a few enemies, but since you are an outsider, and the people do love a religious figure, no one would likely object to you. However, now that I've gotten the chance to observe you in person, it's become apparent that the reports of your unpredictable, self-destructive behavior were not exaggerated. If anything, they downplayed it."

"What do you mean, self-destructive?" I boomed. I was really getting the hang of projecting to a crowd. "If I was self-destructive, how did I safely deliver the Padalus Rexiconum past such dangerous opponents as Artenarix the Clever and Ferelic the Even Cleverer, and then get named a holy prophet of The One? Sure, I accidentally killed the king, but if I hadn't done that, you wouldn't have been able to name me as his replacement."

"Well, for one," he whispered, "it's pretty self-destructive to be broadcasting that you did that to an entire crew of people. Before now, the only people who knew you killed Berin were the guardsmen in the room, all of whom are now dead, a few syco-phantic courtiers and attendants who accidentally fell overboard, and Marshal Scritz."

"I killed Marshal Scritz—" Before I could add the question mark to that sentence, Dyfantus hit me in the gut with the pommel of his sword.

"Perfect," Maillib whispered. "I actually talked your deadly, slow-witted friend into that closet. I figured without his glasses, Scritz wouldn't be able to see him. It was just your own ridiculously terrible luck that put you in the room. Since you are such a loyal Garandian and, in spite of our differences, are a pretty nice guy, I'll give you the reward the late King Berin promised you, the Phoine of Destiny."

He handed me an ornate wooden object shaped like a horn, about the size of my forearm. In spite of how close its name was to "phone," the Phoine did not look like it would be picking up any signals anytime soon (even if they somehow had cellphone towers, which wasn't out of the realm of possibility). It was encircled by three dials at about the middle. The first dial indicated date, the second showed location, and the third weight. I quickly set the thing to my cabin (though I was tempted by the option for Fort Knox), the date I had disappeared, and I'm not telling you what I put for weight. Right where you'd breathe into a horn, there was a button that said "Go."

"Perfect," I said. "I guess it's only natural that you let me leave this show in the most clichéd way possible."

I looked up to say goodbye before I pressed the button, but Maillib and Dyfantus were too busy arguing to hear me. Given the way he kept pointing his sword toward me and saying, "I'm going to kill that fat moron," I got the impression that Dyfantus hadn't forgiven me for messing up his shirt or peeing on him earlier. I waved goodbye to Maillib and pressed the button—just in the nick of time, too, as one of the sailors threw a shoe directly at my head.

A bright light blinded me.

"Owww!" When my vision returned, I was still aboard the ship and probably had a shoe print on my forehead. Judging by the number of people still rubbing their eyes, everyone else had seen the light too. With other objects more dangerous than shoes headed toward me, I frantically checked the dials to make sure they were set correctly. They were, so I pressed the button rapidly over and over.

No lights this time. Also, no change of scenery. This time, I got hit in the shin with a peg leg and some false teeth. Thunder crackled behind me, leading me to believe that the blinding light had been a bolt of lightning. The darkened sky was no longer in the distance. I was reminded of the ship I had seen aflame, but couldn't see anything in that direction other than rain and an occasional stroke of lightning.

"Why hasn't the director yelled, 'Cut!' yet?" I asked.

"Stop throwing things at the prophet," Maillib said.

"Yeah. I want the only thing he feels to be my blade as it slices the fat from his belly," Dyfantus growled.

"No, friend. I have other ideas for him. Trust me on this. My plans have worked so far, haven't they?"

Dyfantus gritted his teeth and didn't say another word. After what seemed like an eternity, he nodded slowly.

"Go below and make sure the Trio stay there."

"Of course," I said. "It was just too easy to expect this would finally be over."

Lightning illuminated the sky behind Maillib. I'd call it ominous, but awesome words like that shouldn't be used near characters with stupid names. Dyfantus shook his blade one last time and then grumbled his way down the steps.

The captain of the ship stumbled forward. "My lord, unless that idea is for the prophet to pray to The One for our salvation, it likely won't matter. Permission for my men to go back to work and try to sail us out of this."

Maillib nodded hastily. Then a bald sailor ran up and whispered in his captain's ear.

"Sir," the captain said. "My man has an idea, but he wants immunity for any crimes he might commit."

Maillib's face was white as he stared into the distance. "If I live, you can have your immunity. Now, be quick about it. We don't have much time."

I gave the sailor a dirty look. "If you're asking him to get your shoe back, you're too late." I tossed his shoe overboard.

"We could sacrifice someone to the Old God of the sea, Jammy the Gassy," the sailor said. "In the old days, if you sacrificed to Jammy, he would call off a storm."

"Blasphemer!" another crewman said. "You can't let him do that, Captain. We'll all go to . . . that place we go to when we die if we've been bad. What's it called?"

"I believe it's called No-No Land," I whimpered. I hadn't actually named their version of hell in my books, but humor usually helps me cope. The pit of my stomach informed me I'd have to do better.

Maillib finally turned away from me. "What does this sacrifice entail? Please tell me it's an animal that we have on board."

"Well, animals do work sometimes, but Jammy gives extra consideration for sacrificing a person, especially a virgin."

"Sir," the sailor who had objected earlier said. "You can't sacrifice a person. That's definitely going to get us all sent to No-No Land when we die."

Maillib sighed. "Well, do we have any virgins on board?"

Everyone shook their heads except for two sailors in the back who vigorously finished their naughty fun time to escape their fate.

"There has to be someone," the captain said.

Suddenly, all eyes turned to me. "Oh, come on," I said. "I've been with plenty of women."

I took the lack of any further argument as agreement, but evidently, I was wrong. With a nod from Maillib, a few of the crewman advanced on me. Right before I covered my eyes, a crewwoman in the back spoke. "But what about Axin and Weel? I heard he did some pretty naughty stuff with them."

"No, no," Maillib said. "He was quite adamant that that never occurred."

Two crewmen grabbed me. I tried to struggle, but they were huge. I considered throwing the Phoine at them, but decided to keep it as a souvenir and tucked it into my pocket. The thing stuck out half a foot, but they didn't seem to notice.

"What do we need to do?" Maillib said. "Is there any particular ritual involved, or can we just cut his throat and be done with it?"

"It has to be with flames, because Jammy is also the god of fire," one of the sailors said. "He lives in the sky, so the smoke is the only way to get his attention. Prophets are extra-flammable, too. It's why they always end up getting burned at the stake."

"Oh, that's brilliant," I said. "Fire on a ship. It looks like you'll have to find another way."

It turns out that smugness doesn't help one get out of an execution. In a remarkably short time, they had me tied to a post and surrounded by kindling, which was an odd thing to have in such a quantity on a ship. They really did an excellent job tying me to the post; I couldn't escape, yet was still surprisingly comfortable.

"Could you say good things about us to The One when you see him, prophet?" the captain said.

"Yes, I'll tell him you were really nice murderers."

"Now, now. There's no need to get snippy with me. We really are sorry about this." He gave the signal, and his men lit the kindling.

At least the smoke smelled nice. I detected a hint of mesquite. Is it wrong to think about barbequed food while you're the one actually being barbequed?

Maillib's eyes fixed on the Phoine. "Hmm. It still doesn't work, then. I was hoping you might be able to recharge it."

"With my holy powers?" I said.

"No, it feeds on cowardice. It hasn't worked since the last great coward had a heart attack when he misheard 'gruel' as 'duel.' What? Did you think something that lets you run away would be fed by bravery?" He laughed, and the rest of the crew soon followed.

"So, that's how we're going to play this. I'm not a coward anymore. The tape will clearly show that." I threw the Phoine at him, but it clattered limply to the deck a few inches away, missing him by a good three feet. Undeterred, I gave him my best defiant face, lessened somewhat by the tears rolling down my cheeks. The tears were from the smoke, not because my body was agreeing with him. "In spite of your attempts to show me how real this is, it's now obvious that this is all a show. That's the only possible way I would have failed to save my favorite character. The people running this obviously contrived to distract me so they could kill him dramatically."

He mixed in a hint of "perturbed." "You're back to that now, are you? What kind of idiot would have a play in the middle of the ocean? Where would the audience sit? You really didn't learn anything, did you?"

"Whatever," I said. "The rain is about to get here, and your whole plan to burn me alive will fail miserably. It looks like I'll have the pleasure of seeing you die with me. We can discuss where you failed at the after-party."

It turned out that explaining why the villain's plan will fail before it actually fails is a really bad idea. Maillib frantically called the crewmen over, and they soon had the fire burning at full blast. My watery eyes were now the least of my worries. I was definitely going to sue after I got out of there.

As I started to lapse into unconsciousness, my vision began to blur. Everyone stretched out, and they all looked kind of fat. The thought almost made me laugh, but it came out as more of a wheeze. As my gaze dropped, Maillib's shiny armor darkened to black. It sort of looked like the wrinkled suit my rival, Billiam, always wore. The two of them would have gotten along perfectly. They just . . . you know, if you trimmed Maillib's beard into a goatee and changed his eyes to black . . .

"Billiam! I should have known. Only you could turn my wonderful books into this mockery."

Maillib stomped on the Phoine. "Billiam . . ."

He said more, but I couldn't hear him. Not that it mattered, as I was sure it was some stupid thing to explain how he didn't know who that was. I tried to give him one last defiant smile, but my whole body was numb. As my head lolled without the energy to rise, my ring appeared to glow, but it might have been my imagination. Your mind can play tricks on you when you're starting to lapse into unconsciousness. Trust me, I'm an expert on the subject. Whatever the case, I had clearly gotten the better of them.

HAT AND I PLAY SOME POKER

I awoke with a start. Was I dead? Was this heaven? Hell? Jail? The after-party? I wiped the thick sweat off my face and looked around at my surroundings. Walls made of wood. Not much in the way of decorations. Desk with a computer on it. A familiar computer. My computer! I had to be either back home or in heaven. Probably not in hell, unless there was no power. That was how I'd picture hell, being in my favorite place with no electricity to power anything.

I stood up to check my computer. The screen flipped on. Not hell, then. All of my familiar programs were there, and the outline for my next book was open. I really hadn't gotten very far. Did its being there remove the possibility of this being heaven? Would God make you work there?

The answer to my questions came through the door. Hat's face erupted in a broad grin, and he almost dropped his tray. "Sir! You're awake!"

"Hat, am I glad to see you." Uncharacteristically, I hugged him hard.

"I was so worried when they found you on the shore, sir. Where have you been for the last ten days?"

"I was there, Hat. In Vyenra! And no, it wasn't real, or I wouldn't have—it was definitely a TV parody of it. At least, I hope they intended it to be a parody. Can you believe that?"

Hat set the tray down and jumped up and down. "Wowie! You were really in Vyenra? That's amazing. What did it look like?" Hat can be a bit too into my world sometimes. That's part of what makes him such a good assistant and part of what makes him a bit annoying.

"It wasn't really there because there is no there to go to, Hat. It was a terrible fantasy show based on my world where they got everything wrong."

Hat scratched his head. "They found you a mile away, and I haven't heard about anyone filming anything nearby. You'd think that would be all over the news. No one ever films out here."

"Focus, Hat. I'm the brains of this outfit, so if I say it happened, it happened." I stood up and began to pace. "I must have signed over the TV rights to my show when I signed my first contract. You were right; I really should have read the fine print. Anyway, whoever has the rights to my show kidnapped me and forced me to do a reality show based in my world. And not a good reality show like . . . Oh, that's right. There aren't any good reality shows. But even compared to other reality shows, it was terrible. I'll be traumatized for life."

"Sorry, sir. It can't be that bad. You're just overreacting again, like you did when they got your name wrong on the third book. You thought your career was over then too, but that mistake got you a lot of free press and it ended up being your best seller."

"No, you don't understand. Those idiot writers made Hammurabi a foul-mouthed gambler and Berin a terrible king! They even killed Berin off, through no fault of my own."

"That sounds awful." He put his hand on his chin. "Hmm . . . what if we wrote your side of the story? If we can get a book out faster than they can get the show on the air, it'll lessen the blow to your reputation."

"That's what I was thinking. You're a genius." I patted him on the back.

"Why do you only call me that when I agree with you?"

"Let's get started now. I need to get this out before I forget."

"Are you sure it wasn't a dream?"

I laughed. "With all the TV I've watched, don't you think that was the first thing I checked? I pinched myself several times and was injured on numerous occasions. I was even knocked unconscious. If it was a dream, any one of those things would have woken me up in the real world. Plus, I remember everything that happened during the journey, and you never remember everything from a dream. There's no way it was a dream."

"Well, then, let's get started. We need to do this for your fans." He sat down and grabbed a pad of paper. "It'll be faster if I do it this time. We can clean it up later."

We worked tirelessly over the next few days, pausing only to eat, go to the bathroom, and sleep, often simultaneously to save time. While I had done a few marathon writing sessions in the past, I had never done so many in a row, but I had to get this all out fast before I forgot anything.

Hat was every bit as eager to get this done as I was. He was fascinated by my descriptions of the televised version of Vyenra. He really didn't seem to care that it was all fake. I honestly think he would have worked on this book until he passed out and then started working again when he regained consciousness.

My publisher even agreed to fast-track it after I threatened to self-publish. I'm a pretty big deal, so they really didn't have much of a choice.

". . . And then the guards escorted me on deck after Cat killed Marshal Scritz, and some guy named Maillib named me king. The end."

Hat finished scrawling the last word and looked up. "That's an amazing story, sir. It's a shame it ends so abruptly. I really want to know what happened when you became king. I'll bet Hammurabi came back from exile and fixed everything. He always comes through. Why don't you elaborate more on what happened on deck? Who was this Maillib, and how could he make you king? Was Verix all right? His wound sounded pretty bad."

"Hat, stop asking so many questions. I'm sure the actor who played Verix was fine. They put the crown on my head, and the combination of my awesomeness being given such an awesome job was too much, so the show ended. They must have drugged my food at some point, because the next thing I knew, I was back here. Remember, nothing that happened on this journey was real."

He scratched his head. "But Hammurabi and Marshal Scritz said it was real."

I sighed. "Of course they did. That's what the actors were told to say."

"They would have said that if you were really there, too."

"Yeah, but what about all of the cameras I saw?"

Hat flipped the pages of his notes and pointed at a passage. "You told me to put 'I thought I saw a camera' every time you mentioned one, sir. Did you ever actually touch one?"

I gave him my "I pay your salary, so I'm right" look.

"Of course, sir." He winked at me.

"No wink. It's not real. How many times do I have to tell you?"

"Sorry, sir. It's a nervous condition." He winked at me again.

"Are you winking to indicate that your nervous condition isn't real? And does that mean your first wink was in fact valid, thus indicating that you do, in fact, still believe Vyenra is actually real?"

"You've lost me, sir." He winked again.

"I'd strangle you, but I would never have gotten this done without you."

"I appreciate you not strangling me, sir."

"You're welcome. Now, if you'd please leave, I'd like to write a few things down—some very personal notes about how I felt on my journey, you know, like my therapist told me to do. Nothing you need to worry about or see."

"Of course, sir. It's good that you're keeping a journal." He whistled as he left the room and shut the door behind him.

That therapist was a quack. There was no way I was going to write down what my obviously flawed memory was telling me had happened. The whole journey had been building me to be the hero. I must have done the right thing in the end. The character of Verix had to have lived through it. I was only remembering things wrong. It was clearly a TV show, and the trip back to my cabin must have damaged my memory. There must have been something in my food.

It was getting late, so I rolled into bed. Unfortunately, something in the pit of my stomach refused to let me sleep. After three hours of restlessness and trying every tummy medicine in the cabinets, I was still no closer to blissful dreams. With nothing better to do, I decided to write down what had happened with Maillib and Verix.

I typed with a speed I had never accomplished before. With each new word, the pain in my stomach lessened. My shrink was still a quack, but she must have inadvertently gotten something right. With the last keystroke, all the pain in my stomach ceased.

I fought off the call of dreamland long enough to name the file "Naked Grandma Pictures" and then put a password on it that even Hat wouldn't guess—not that he or anyone else would ever click a file with that name, but it's better to be extra safe. I then rolled myself into bed and was immediately greeted by scenes of dinosaurs that shoot sharks that shoot exploding fists.

I woke up the next day and shouted for Hat to make me his famous pancakes stuffed with bacon with a side of chocolate-covered bacon. He tried to tell me he'd made some hours ago, but I insisted he make some fresh.

While I was waiting, I gave the draft a quick read. It was surprisingly clean. I attributed that to Hat's unusual amount of help. He didn't normally help me on first drafts, but I had a tight deadline for this book and I needed to get it out as fast as possible before I forgot anything. I handed it over to Hat while I ate.

"After we type it up and do a bit of spelling and grammar checking, we might even be able to send this out, sir. I guess it's a lot easier to write when you've actually experienced the story."

I dipped my chocolate-covered bacon in the syrup, also made of chocolate. "I don't know, Hat. This doesn't really show me in a very favorable light."

"You were named a holy prophet and a king. What's not to like?"

"Err, yeah, but some of the stuff I did at the beginning was kind of embarrassing."

He gave me a patronizing smile. "Well, you still got to meet all of your major characters."

"That usually didn't go very well. Weren't you paying atten-tion? I'm more concerned with the number of times I was cowering in a ball or running away from danger."

He nodded slowly. "And when you urinated in public."

"I forgot about that one. At least I was covered in mud, so no nudity."

"You do get slapped a lot, too."

"Do you see my point?"

"Yes, but this book is very honest. That has to count for something." He smiled guilelessly. I wished I still had his innocence, but the show had taken that from me.

"When you write your own book, you can be as honest as you want, but this is my book. I don't want to look like a urinating coward. We'll have to edit out all of the stuff that makes me look bad. It'll be a bonus if it makes me look good."

"I can't let you lie to your fans, sir." Hat was getting a little too close to me.

"Calm down, Hat. These are my books, and I can do what I want with them."

"You owe them the truth." Hat was standing only a few inches from my face. He had to get on his tippy-toes to do it. I'd never seen him get like this before. He was always the obedient assistant. Sure, he'd occasionally disagree with me and we'd discuss the issue, but if I pulled rank on him, he'd always back down. His eyes told me he wasn't going to back down from this one.

"Fine, Hat. I won't change anything." I didn't want to get into a fight with my assistant. I'd seen him fight before, and while he was short and skinny, he was feisty, especially when it involved anything about my world. He'd once taken out three *Star Wars* fans who were making fun of my books and made them cry. They really should have worn cups.

Hat started to back away. "Thank you, sir! I knew you were an honest person. Those critics didn't know what they were talking about."

I grabbed the draft and went upstairs to begin my least favorite part of the writing process: editing. I really wanted to make myself look braver, but the look on Hat's face told me he would never allow that. He almost looked like he would assault me, and this was the man who considered me a god—not a major god, mind you; a minor god, like the god of hall monitors or toilet bowl cleaners.

I couldn't believe that I, the author, was letting my assistant dictate what would go into my book. However, it would take me a long time to break in another assistant, and I really needed one if I wanted to get this thing out fast.

After a few days of editing and seeing just how many stupid and cowardly things I had done, I decided to change a few minor things that Hat probably wouldn't notice. I cowered fourteen percent less, didn't pee myself in public, stabbed people on purpose, and even released a few profound prophecies. Before I hit print, I quickly added a talking parrot and gave myself a cool hat.

I was sure this book would finally make me a star, or at least as much of a star as you can be when you write books. It would be great to have a summer home and a few servants instead of barely scraping by with only one cabin, three cars, and a house.

"Hat, come in here. It's your favorite time! You get to be the first person to read my new book."

Hat beamed the kind of smile I only display when I receive my first advance check. "As always, sir, it is an honor to work for you. I really appreciate that you didn't change anything. It means a lot to me and all of your fans."

"I did have to change a few minor things just for flow. You know, to make it more consistent. Nothing that changes the story as a whole."

"I trust your judgment, sir. You are the professional." Hat hungrily tore into the printout. I knew he'd read non-stop until he finished, so I took a nice long break to give him space.

"I'm going into town to catch a movie or four."

"Fine, sir," Hat said without even bothering to look up.

I smiled the smile of a proud father who'd just stared at his newborn child for the first time. I doubt Hat even heard me leave.

When I came back late that evening, Hat was standing at the door waiting for me. I had come back a little earlier than I'd planned due to a slight tummy ache. I shouldn't have gotten a third extra-large popcorn with double butter, but I was trying to make up for lost time after more than a week of terrible food. My next book would introduce Vyenra to pizza and fried chicken.

"What is it, Hat?" I asked.

He had an enigmatic look, neither showing anger nor happiness. He usually had a big smile on his face because he got to work with me, the perfect boss, every day. "You changed some things, sir."

I shrugged half-heartedly. "Nothing major."

"Jackal was not in love with you when you dictated it to me."

"I think you're remembering it wrong, Hat."

"Maybe my memory is a little off on that, but I know you didn't have a talking parrot."

"It was something I remembered when I was editing. I forgot about it the first time."

"Ahh. Well, I'd better get back to reading. So far, I've found a few inconsistencies that you'll need to clean up, but they're mostly minor."

I nodded and headed upstairs. I hoped I hadn't polished off all of the antacids. "I'll read them all when you finish. It's late, and I'd like to get some sleep."

"Good night, sir. I'll show you what I found in the morning."

"Night, Hat."

I got out of those uncomfortable clothes with the even more uncomfortable belt and into some soft pajamas. Fortunately, this time I managed to overcome my stomach issues and fell right to sleep. Unfortunately, my dreams were not filled with cartoon characters or beautiful women who know kung fu; they seemed to involve lots of old men telling me to repent while refusing to tell me what for. After I woke for about the tenth time, I decided to re-read the thing that had allowed me to get some restful sleep the night before in the hope that it would work again. If it did, I'd change the names and put it online as a new sleep aid. I'd either get rich or be murdered by the powerful sleep aid cabal. If you hear that I've choked to death on a tiny pill, please take this to the police.

The computer screen hurt my sleep-deprived eyes, so I printed out a copy and began to read.

I woke up fantastically refreshed twelve hours later. Part of me felt a little guilty that Hat had probably worked throughout the night, but that was his job. I was the boss, so I got to sleep.

I walked down the steps and, as I neared the bottom, was greeted by a disheveled yet heavily caffeinated assistant. He had a manic look in his eyes. I don't know how he'd managed to read for more than four hours at a time. My eyes hurt when I do that.

I let out a big yawn—probably not the best thing to do in front of someone who hadn't slept in a day and a half—but it was involuntary. "Have you finished already?"

"Yes. I have."

"And what did you think?"

He always told me the current book was the best one yet. I guessed that was more of a tradition at this point. Still, it's nice to hear great things about something you've put so much effort into.

"You changed a lot."

I shrugged. "Nothing too major. Just enough to make it a better story while keeping it as close to the truth as possible, like you asked."

"All the women in the story fall in love with you."

"Not all, only the attractive ones."

"You had the Garandians proclaim you the second coming of The One."

I gave him a beatific grin. "They called me The Two."

He grimaced. "You defeated Dyfantus, Verix, and Arik all at the same time in a duel."

"It was one of the requirements to prove I was The Two."

"I guess I could live with you making yourself look unbelievably good since you kept the stuff about the world mostly intact, but then I read these new parts."

"What new parts?" Even my yawn sounded confused.

"The new ending you finished last night. You were making that weird noise you do when you fall asleep on top of a book or an Impressionist painting, so I went into your room to roll you over and I found the new ending underneath you."

I half-choked on my next yawn and marched to the bottom step. "Who told you to go into my room?"

Oddly, Hat didn't back down. "You did. You told me if I ever heard that noise again to 'immediately come in before I choke to death and leave an embarrassing corpse. And, if you do find a corpse, burn all of my lobster porn and change me into my formal Spider-Man Underoos and matching loincloth.'"

"Oh, that's why I was tucked in so nice. Wait—so you didn't fall asleep when you read it? I'm asking because my financial future could depend on it, and not because I think the writing was bad. It was some of my best work, but you weren't supposed to see it."

"Fall asleep? No, I couldn't stop even to go to the bathroom. We'll need a new couch, by the way. How could you lie to me and tell me it was all a TV show? I love your books more than anything. How could you not tell me after all of these years that Vyenra is real?"

Hat gave me a glare so forceful that I stumbled off the stairs. I regained my footing, but it was really hard with his nearly poisonous coffee breath floating around.

"Hat, calm down. I don't know how it really exists. I made it all up. Maybe it was when I rubbed that lamp three times."

"It was a picture in a magazine, and the kid you made your wishes to was dressed as Papa Smurf. Even if you somehow didn't know it was real, how could you lie to me about the ending? How could you do that to Verix? You said you modeled him after you."

"I think you need to read it again. I didn't do anything to Verix."

"You're in denial!"

"I deny your denial." I was afraid I'd get a sunburn from Hat's glare. "Hat, calm down. I'm the one in charge here, and what I say goes. We'll keep the ending the way I wrote it the first time."

"We will not! You killed him." He poked me in my favorite nipple.

I pushed his finger away. "Sir. Don't you mean 'sir'?"

"No, I will not call you that until you put the real ending in. Your fans deserve the truth. Vyenra is real, and her true story must be told!"

"It's my book, not yours. I can and will do with it what I want. The law is on my side."

"Not according to the changes in your will. It's only if you're alive and conscious."

"How do you know that? Only my lawyer knows that."

Hat very rudely didn't answer me. Instead, he grabbed a fireplace poker and hit me on the head, which I suppose was the answer to the other question running through my mind: Was this scene in the cabin all a dream?

I fell to my knees and attempted to raise my arms, but they wouldn't move. This wasn't real, I tried to say. But it had to be, because it hurt so much. How could he do this to me? How did he know about my will? Why did I have to wear my Care Bears footie pajamas to bed on this of all nights?

"You like to talk in your sleep, Harry. That's how I know. Don't worry, soap operas taught me how to knock someone into a coma without killing them. Once you wake up, you'll see how much better the true version is. I'm sorry, but I have to do this for all of your fans."

I felt the impact in my heart before the last blow hit.

The End

Did Harry live? Will Hat ever call him "sir" again? Is Maillib really Billiam? Did Wolf finally get Cat to wear pants?

You might find the answers in **Book 2:** *Why I Didn't Save Anyone.* **Now available on Amazon here!**

Want to hear when the next book is released? Sign up for my exclusive *New Release Mailing List* at:
www.matthewhelbig.com/mailing-list

www.ingramcontent.com/pod-product-compliance
Lightning Source LLC
Chambersburg PA
CBHW060954120726
47910CB00002B/631